I KNOW WHO YOU REMIND ME OF

I KNOW WHO YOU REMIND ME OF

stories

Naomi K. Lewis

ENFIELD & WIZENTY

Enfield & Wizenty
(an imprint of Great Plains Publications)
345-955 Portage Avenue
Winnipeg, MB R3G 0P9
www.greatplains.mb.ca

Great Plains Publications gratefully acknowledges the financial support provided for its publishing program by the Government of Canada through the Canada Book Fund; the Canada Council for the Arts; the Province of Manitoba through the Book Publishing Tax Credit and the Book Publisher Marketing Assistance Program; and the Manitoba Arts Council.

Design & Typography by Relish New Brand Experience Inc.
Printed in Canada by Friesens

First Edition

Library and Archives Canada Cataloguing in Publication

Lewis, Naomi K., 1976-

    I know who you remind me of / Naomi K. Lewis.

Short stories.

Issued also in electronic formats.

ISBN 978-1-926531-51-9

    I. Title.

PS8623.E967I12 2012   C813'.6   C2012-903577-7

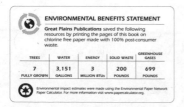

For Jason

stories

WARP

The man behind the cash had stringy brown hair, furry arms and, on the index finger of his right hand, a metal finger cuff with a long claw at the end, which he tapped against the desk, not moving another cell in his body. The rock T-shirt store had been Karen's idea. Her first idea had been the beach, but she, Malachai and Michaela were the only people out there, struggling against the wind and holding up their arms when sand blew into their eyes. When Mal's bangs had flattened against his forehead as he shrugged up into his sweatshirt and kicked at the sand, Karen wanted to hold his hand, but then he smiled to himself in that way that looked like a snarl, showing his pointed eyetooth that overlapped his incisor, and seemed untouchable.

"The ocean smells like ass." Micha's voice was close but barely audible over the water crashing against itself. She usually backcombed her bangs slightly and pinned them to the side with a barrette, but she hadn't bothered today, and her hair was blowing into a nest around her face. Gulls squawked in frustration as they swooped low, poised to risk their lives. Each wave rose high and foamy before throwing itself down against the shore and then flattening out against the sand as it was drawn back to drown in the next assault. "It smells like the fish store in the market, times fifty."

"It's freezing," Mal yelled so Karen could hear him. Like she didn't know. She only had her purple Guatemalan jacket.

"Screw this," said Micha. "I'm going back."

Karen tried not to think her brother and sister were brats; they were just mourning the scene that should have been, the lost dream of hair stiff with sea salt and *It's a Small World After All*. This was not that Florida.

"Actually, it wasn't a hurricane," Mal had said an hour earlier, over their fish-and-chip lunch. His face was stark white and would stay that way, because this wasn't the kind of Florida that sent you home with a tan. "A tropical depression."

"Tropical storm," Dad said, rubbing his blond mustache with a tissue-thin napkin. He was health-nut brown, but not from Florida; he ran ten kilometres every morning before work, even in winter. Mom was pallid as Mal, her hair dyed dark brown and straightened. Mom, who avoided chemicals, washing the laundry in vinegar instead of detergent, even socks — Mom, who didn't shave her legs and didn't want Karen to shave hers, either — had brought her new hairdryer on vacation so she could keep blowing the hair pin-straight using a technique she'd mastered with a giant expensive brush.

"No," said Mal. "A tropical depression isn't as bad. That's what the lady cleaning our room said. A storm is worse, a hurricane is the worst."

The maid had described the rain that battered the small town, shook the walls and flooded the basements; she said things would settle down soon. That's when Karen wondered if her mother had always suspected she'd stop loving Dad. A twenty-eight-year-old cousin recently said, after Karen spilled her guts, "You won't always love Gavin." Impossible to picture, but, following a logical line into the future, probably true.

Micha added, "She said we're in the wake. That's the part after." Her cheeks were pink with chronic good health and disgust.

"The Mexican woman?" said Dad. "You were chatting it up with the Mexican hurricane expert cleaning our room? Well, I'm glad to hear her effing analysis. Why don't you make some normal friends for once?"

Micha drove her fork into the batter of her fish like it was Dad's cheek.

Mom said, "Karen, will you find something fun for you and the kids to do while your father and I talk?"

"We don't like to be called that," Mal whispered.

Micha pulled her fork out of her fish and stabbed it back in.

When they reached the boardwalk, where it was less windy but still windy enough, Micha patted Mal on the head. Like that of all his skateboarder friends, his hair was cut short at the sides and left long on top so his dark bangs hung into his eyes. The same almost-black hair was shiny and cut into a bob on Micha. "Do you like it at the pet hotel, Burton?" she said.

"Meeoww nooo!" Mal's lip curled up to show the razor-sharp eyetooth again. "It's a crap factory."

"Sounds like Florida. Sorry you had to travel in the Pet Voyageur." Micha spoke back toward the ocean, as though her voice might reach the real Burton home in Ontario.

They stood on the boardwalk, waiting, and Karen had to think of something else for them to do. If not for the twins, she would have gone straight back to the hotel and to bed, to think about sex with Gavin. But all of them waiting in the gold-carpeted hotel room for their parents to come back, for who knows how long, was unbearable to contemplate. The room smelled damp and salty and carpety, and required bunks to cram the three of them in; Mom and Dad had the single beds on the other side of the bathroom. Only they'd never slept after driving in from the airport the night before; they talked, voices lowering and raising. They weren't outright fighting anymore.

The hotel was on the beach, though the windows faced the other way, toward a street with a bunch of vinyl-sided stores, clean and shiny from all the rain, including the rock T-shirt dive and the diner where Mom and Dad had bought them lunch and Mom had put them in the bad books right away by asking the middle-aged, nicotine-stain-haired waitress if they could all have salad instead of potatoes.

"I'll have chips with my fish, please," said Dad. "And so will my children." In real life, he was the one who'd gotten Mom into healthy food, and they all knew he was only trying to be an asshole. Still, lunch tasted awesome; the fish was fresh, and the chips were thick wedges straight from the deep fryer. Eating slowly, and looking out the window, Karen ate most of hers, while everyone else just picked. Instead of listening to her family, she waited to see a person, any person, out on the street. A man rode by, slowly, on a motorcycle, and glanced in the window, smiled at Karen. She smiled back, grateful. He reminded her of Gavin, the boulder-like build, the broad back. She liked that in a man, she'd decided. Liked a man thoroughly anchored by gravity, who made her feel anchored, too, when his body pinned hers to the bed.

The T-shirt store had those chimes that ring automatically when the door opens, so the claw guy watched the three of them enter. With the sudden lack of gloomy sunlight and harrying wind, the room was dark and eerily quiet. "His soul blew away with the hurricane," Micha whispered, as they approached the back of the room.

Karen moved extra-large Metallica T-shirt after Metallica T-shirt down the endless rack. Gavin always wore band T-shirts, but not Metallica. He was always friends with bands whose shirts he wore, bands only a select few had heard of. His shirts smelled a certain way, lemony and dry. Just his detergent, Karen knew now, but when she'd met him, during her work-study term at the TV station, and before she'd actually seduced him, she had supposed that smell emanated from within his pores, and she'd longed to push her face into the warmth at the crook of his neck, for the source. At the TV station, people always called Gavin by his first and last names, and mentioned him behind his back without really saying anything, in a tone mocking and admiring at once. One day, she'd walked past him in an empty hallway, and thought, *Gavin Onion*, and caught a whiff of cottony citrus and that other smell that was just Gavin, and then he looked at her straight in the face and said hi, and that was it; she tried to fight it, but after that, whenever she saw a phone, she wanted to dial his number, and whenever she thought about sex, which was pretty much all the time, she thought about him.

"Can you get these for us?" said Micha. She and Mal had found extra-small shirts somewhere, Alice Cooper and Beastie Boys, and held them in front of their chests.

"Do you even know who Alice Cooper is?" Karen asked her sister. "Where's your allowance?" The door chimes rang again, and a biker walked in, helmet under his arm. The guy who'd driven past the diner.

Micha repeated Karen's questions in the high-pitched nasal voice she reserved for mocking, adding, "You're the one with the job, popcorn queen."

Karen wondered, not for the first time, if her sister was a bully in her school life. "No." She headed for the sweatshirt rack. "You can't have them."

"Karen." Mal followed her. "I know who the Beastie Boys are. I listen to them all the time."

"Sorry."

"Boss, boss, boss!" Micha tossed her T-shirt over the rack. "Why'd you bring us to this stupid store then? If we can't get anything?"

The claw guy was staring at them, but the biker just shuffled through second-hand tapes, in his own world. No point mentioning the allowance again. As soon as Micha said she was leaving, Mal was beside her, ready to defend her wish or die trying.

"Can we *please* have the key," said Micha.

"Fine." Karen handed it over. She watched from the doorway as they crossed the street, Micha marching in a decisive straight line, Mal swaggering a step behind, and entered the hotel side by side. They were not so much alike as complementary, their primary loyalty always to each other. Her mother was the same with aunt Verna, and Karen also had twin great-uncles. Ran in the family. Dropping two eggs at once. She sometimes wondered if she'd inherited that tendency, and if by shedding two ova each month, she might use up her supply twice as quickly as the average woman. She was also doubly afraid of pregnancy. Always put the condom on Gavin herself; she did it in a sexy dominating way, but really she just needed to know it was done right, with no air in the tip, so it wouldn't explode in a starburst of consequences. Funny that Gavin had a twin, too, who was reportedly nothing like him personality-wise and had moved out West. Identical, though, so not hereditary.

Though she'd eaten so much at lunch, Karen was hungry again, and bought a bag of cheese-flavoured corn chips. The man couldn't pick up coins with the claw hand, so he had to twist awkwardly, reaching over with his other hand to get her change from the cash register. She pretended to look at T-shirts again, her back to the cashier and the biker as she fit a whole triangular chip over her tongue, flooding every taste bud with MSG. Her parents had never met Gavin, but if either of them did, and could get over the him-corrupting-their-seventeen-year-old-daughter part, they would be able to relate at least to his veganism — like Karen's parents, Gavin luxuriated in gastronomical restraint. She'd grown up eating beet chips with yogurt-seaweed dip, and putting flaxseed oil in her breakfast smoothies. One thing her mother and her father and Gavin would definitely agree on was revulsion at the sight of Karen reaching into an aluminum bag of food-like product and then licking the orange chemical powder from her stained fingers.

"Alice in Chains?"

The blond biker. Not so much like Gavin, really, close up, besides the bigness. He hunched a little in the shoulders, and had wider hips, a heavier way of standing. Plus, he smelled of leather jacket. Karen thought of Gavin's brother, who was somewhere in Western Canada looking like the person Karen loved but being someone else. The biker said, "I saw them play in Tampa last year. You a fan?"

"Not that much, really."

"I've seen you around. I'm Harlan." He touched his pale beard. Her mother said men with beards were usually hiding something, something beyond just their facial skin.

"I've only been here since last night," Karen said.

"Well, I guess I saw you this morning, then." He waited for her to say something, so she offered him a chip, and he reached into the bag for a fistful. "Where'd your family go?"

Karen rubbed rock-T fabric between her fingers, the way her mother always did to test cotton for quality. "My little brother and sister are mad at me because I wouldn't buy them shirts."

"They're twins, right? How old?"

"Yeah. They're twelve. And my parents are out having this *talk*. I mean, they've got serious things to discuss, if you know what I mean. It's just a big, I don't know. Disaster."

"Why wouldn't you?"

"Pardon?"

"Get them the shirts?"

"Well. I don't have a lot of money." She had exactly four dollars and 93 cents in her bank account.

"I hear that." He wandered over to a bin full of posters and flipped through them for a while. Then he said, "I live uptown. With Jane. My girlfriend. Do you have a boyfriend?"

"No," Karen said, because Gavin wasn't her boyfriend.

"Just as well. You should just be fooling around, having fun."

She shuffled a few more shirts down the rack. How badly she wanted to be back in bed, thinking about Gavin.

"Hey." Harlan turned as though he'd just thought of something, and she jumped a little. "I don't know if this would really be your, whatever. Scene. I mean, it's kind of whatever. But I was just thinking, you need cash, and I need someone around your size for this photo shoot I'm doing. The Christmas shoot. I'd pay a hundred bucks. It'd take like an hour."

"What — now? What kind of photo shoot?"

"Now, sure. Whenever. It's, I mean." He leaned closer. "Sexy pictures. But classy. No sex, nothing like that. But me and my girlfriend know this guy who deals in pictures of beautiful girls."

"Oh." Beautiful? *You're perfect*, Gavin always said. *You're the hottest girl in the world.*

"You've got a great look," Harlan said. "That whole freckles thing. The long hair. Name?"

Karen thought of the sexiest person she knew. Actually, she didn't really know her, just knew who she was. "Berry." Same high school, a grade ahead, curly dark bob, mesh shirts, long body like a wire.

"Great," Harlan said.

Karen crumpled the empty chip bag in her hand, and the orange stuff wedged under her thumbnail. Really pretty disgusting.

"Perfect," he said. "We wouldn't even need to change it. How old are you?"

"Seven —"

"Say eighteen."

"Eighteen. How old are you?"

"Twenty-four." What was it with twenty-four-year-olds? "Damn," he nodded seriously, as though making an objective observation. "You are cute." *You were made for fucking*, was what Gavin said.

Harlan had an extra helmet in his backpack, and it was heavy in Karen's hand. She set it on top of her head, cautiously, and Harlan pushed until it eased down. She felt like an astronaut.

"You should really have a leather jacket," he said. "But at least you've got on jeans and those skinhead boots."

She climbed on the bike behind him, and he told her where to rest her feet.

"Hold on to me," he yelled, over the revving engine. It sounded like her grandfather's old motorboat at the cottage, and smelled like it, too. Gasoline. She put her hands on his sides, and he said, "You're going to want to hold on tight." She moved her hands slightly forward. He accelerated, and her body shifted backwards. She grabbed him around the waist, barely saving herself from flying off. After turning a corner onto a steeply uphill street, he quickly gave her a thumbs up. The engine vibrated her helmet, a shell of noise. Gavin wouldn't believe it when she told him. That she'd done something so daring, just sleazy enough to make him want her even more. Or — the thought occurred to her too late — would he think it was cheesy, the motorcycle part, cheesy enough to ruin the sexiness?

The wind pushed hard against Karen's forehead, and seemed to come from the side as well, whipping frigidly through her jacket. She leaned her head forward to ease the strain on her neck, and saw Harlan's hands tight on the grips. The wind lifted his jacket in the shoulders, and blond tufts stood like little animals on the black leather at the back of his neck, below his helmet. He was solid, wasn't going anywhere. Karen, on the other hand — had anyone ever been blown from the back of a motorcycle? She imagined her parents having to tell about it, how she died. Maybe they'd have to stay together after that. She leaned into Harlan and hugged.

He lived a ten-minute drive from the hotel, it turned out, all uphill, in a dirty white stucco building with pink trim. They took the stairs to the fifth floor, walked down a wide concrete hallway. Through his apartment door, aromas of cigarettes, disinfectant and air freshener preceded the small foyer.

Harlan called, "Janie, look what I found. A little Christmas elf."

A stick figure emerged. Her long hair was brown with the consistency of bleached, and her tank top displayed a small, leathery cleavage. Jane leapt at Karen, grabbed her hands, and gazed up at her face in delight. Karen thought maybe she'd been confused with someone else, but Harlan said her fake name, and Jane repeated it, shaking her head like it was the best news she'd ever heard.

"Looks like the girl from the Aerosmith videos."

"I know," said Harlan.

Karen followed Jane into a tiny kitchen, where they drank red Kool-Aid at a meticulously clean yellow Formica table, and Karen explained her family was from Canada.

"Why'd you folks come here?" said Jane. "Didn't you hear about the storm?"

"My little brother and sister wanted to go to Orlando, but my parents said this would be better. Smaller. Beaches to ourselves. Anyway, I heard it was just a depression."

"Depression? I'll tell you something, honey. That was a goddamn storm. You ever seen rain like that, Harl?"

"Well, yeah." Harlan was across the hall in what Karen saw was the bedroom, taking expensive-looking photography equipment out of drawers. Attaching a massive camera to a tripod and checking rolls of film.

"Anyhow," said Jane. "We thought there wouldn't be any tourists this year. You all staying over Christmas?"

"Yeah," Karen said. "We're staying for a week. But we don't really celebrate Christmas."

"How come?"

"We're not religious."

"Religious?"

"Hey," called Harlan. "Janie, can you find the Santa getup? Come on."

The outfit was velvety, red and white, a short red dress, almost a shirt, with white trim. With it, Jane gave Karen a wide white belt, red thigh-high stockings and a red Santa hat. Red g-string underwear. Karen changed in the bathroom, then put her hair in a ponytail and washed her face with Noxzema, like Jane said. Dad would not have been impressed; he said Santa Claus was a blatant symbol of misappropriated imagery in the employ of consumer capitalism.

"What do you think, Harl?" Jane said. "For makeup?"

He considered Karen.

"Fresh-faced look, right?"

"Oh, yeah," he said. "Just red lips. That bright red? Christmas red. And some," he moved his fingers in circles beside his cheeks, "some blusher."

Sitting on the toilet seat, Karen rubbed at her mouth in case of chip remnants, then closed her eyes and let her lips go limp so Jane could go to work with her fake-leather bag of brand-new makeup brushes.

"Used to do this at the mall," Jane said.

"What do you do now?"

Karen opened the eye Jane wasn't working on to see the other woman's intent face, little wrinkles extending her frown, close up. "Me and Harl got a good thing going."

"What do you —"

"Also, too," said Jane. "Just a second." She left the bathroom and reappeared seconds later with a long strip of coarse, woven green and blue fabric, which she held out for long enough that Karen reached for it. Jane yanked it back. "I make these belts," she said, "and sell them on the beach. That's what I like doing. Crafts. Use a solid colour for the weft, add these other ones on the warp, the part you actually weave through, see?"

"Yeah. Where will these pictures end up again?"

"Oh. Nowhere big. This computer thing, not magazines or anything. Harl knows way more about it than me."

"I have to be back at the hotel by four."

"Not a worry. Anyway." Jane smoothed Karen's non-existent eyebrows with a brush. "I do straw weaving."

"Straw…"

"With drinking straws? Like weaving the yarn through them. You rig up this loom, right, with straws, and fa-la-la la la. Anyway, that's how I make the belts. They're ten bucks apiece. You could wear it with jeans or a dress or whatever."

"Okay."

"Okay, take out your ponytail. Perfect. Shake it around, like — yeah. Fucking hot. Harl!"

He stepped into the room, praised Jane's work, nodded at her significantly.

"Oh, okay," said Jane. "Listen, honey. I gotta ask. How's your pussy?"

"What do you mean?"

"I mean, one, are you on the rag, and two, how much of a bush you got? Let's see?"

Past Jane and Harlan, Karen could almost see the front door.

"You knew you'd have to show your stuff anyway, right?" he said.

"That's not exactly what I…" Her clothes were folded neatly on the shelf behind Harlan. He saw her look. "Um, no," she said. "I don't have my period, and I wax a bunch down there. And cut the rest off."

"Let's see," said Jane.

"Might as well give us a peek before the camera's on." Harlan's tone reminded Karen of her mother's when she struggled to nurture in the face of idiocy. "We can't do this if you got hair sticking out every place."

"When do I get paid?"

He took five twenties out of his wallet, but Jane said, "Make it ninety bucks. She wants one of my belts." He replaced one of the twenties with a ten and put the money in Karen's jeans pocket.

Bracing herself with her hands on the toilet tank, Karen secured one foot on the sink. They were like doctors, she told herself. They were professionals. Jane lifted the skirt. "Nice." She pulled the underwear to one side before Karen had a chance to react.

"Oh yeah," said Harlan. "Perfect. Wait. She missed a couple of hairs."

Jane picked up an electric razor from the sink and said to keep still. She shaved in a few places, then said to turn around, pull down the panties and bend over. Harlan held Karen's cheeks apart and Jane shaved whatever hairs were between them. "That's going to itch growing back," she said. When Gavin shaved Karen down there, he'd put the trimmer on the second setting, so she'd have a bit left.

Jane said, "Here." A pair of black high heels, a size too big.

"Season's greetings," said Harlan. "Heh heh."

They spent an hour on the shoot. Jane positioned Karen, and Harlan moved around with the tripod, getting all the angles. Sometimes Karen had to bend over; sometimes she lay on the bed. For a few shots, they had her take off the dress and hold a wrapped gift with a big bow on it, in such a way that her arms pushed her breasts up. Harlan had Jane pluck a hair from one of Karen's nipples. For most of the shoot, the Santa hat and the thong underwear sat unused on the dresser, and at one point, Harlan told Karen to lick her lips, but then he saw her pierced tongue.

"Ew," said Jane. "What is *that*?" And Harlan said to just keep it inside her mouth.

Halfway through, they took a break and each had a glass of Kool-Aid, and Jane told a story Karen didn't listen to, about one of her friends getting drunk and falling off a boat.

"Listen," Harlan said. "You're doing a good job. But try to look happier, okay? Like, smile, right? Okay, let's do this."

Karen was tired, kneeling on the bed, when Harlan opened a drawer and held up a huge dildo, textured with bulbous, intersecting veins. He said, "There's another hundred in this for you." He held it firmly just above the foam balls.

"Just gotta stick it in," said Jane. "Two hundred for up the ass, too."

"No," said Karen. "I have to go."

"We have tons of lube," Jane said.

Karen pressed her palms into the comforter to hide that she was shaking. "Seriously. It's after three, and I have to check on my little brother and sister."

Harlan stood behind the tripod, pointing the dildo in her direction, so she could see the lifelike hole in its tip. Jane sat on the bed beside her. They didn't move. Not even their faces. They just stared, like snakes about to strike.

Harlan took a deep breath. "Right. You should get dressed, then. Thanks, Berry."

After locking herself in their bathroom, Karen washed her face again with the Noxzema and put her clothes on. No way she'd tell Gavin about this, now. She would never tell anyone. Ever. She braced herself to open the door cool and unafraid.

Harlan sat slumped in an armchair, licking beer from the hairs around his mouth. He said, "Some people get it, some people don't."

Jane drove her back to the beach in a tiny, dirty white car, and stopped near the boardwalk where Karen had walked with Mal and Micha a few hours earlier.

"You cool?" said Jane.

"Oh, yeah." Wind battered the car's windows, and waves careened and crashed, assaulting the air with their dead-fish stench.

"Harl's a great guy. He's just a teddy bear. Just disappointed, because his guy really wanted those penetration shots. But that's not everyone's bag, right? I get you. We've been together almost two years, now. I think we got a pretty good thing going, with his business idea. First it was all me in the pictures, and I still do some, but you gotta have some variety, right? Not everybody would understand. But nobody gets hurt, and it's got an artistic side to it, too."

"Right."

"Darnit!" Jane slapped the steering wheel. "You forgot to pick a belt."

"Oh. That's okay."

"No way, you already paid for it and all." Jane told Karen to get out of the car, and she did the same, then opened the trunk to reveal a huge box of her straw-woven belts, in a variety of colours. Karen picked a yellow one near the top of the pile, shot through with grey and blue.

"I like that one, too," said Jane. "Good work today, Honey. Give me a hug."

Jane draped her skeletal arms around Karen's shoulders to hang there limply, like a stretched-out sweater.

Walking down to the water, Karen let the wind throw her hair around, tie it in knots, slap it stingingly against her eyelids. She picked at the familiar loose threads inside her jacket pockets. It had happened, but that was that. She tried to think of possible consequences. It wasn't like she could get a disease. They hadn't molested or robbed her. Didn't know her real name or where she was staying. And in a few days, she'd leave this town, state and country and never come back. She'd done something gross and dangerous, but now it was over.

Nothing bad had happened to her.

"I'm fine," she said, into the wind.

She knotted the belt around her hips and vomited half into the water, where the tide would wash it away, and felt better, though the ocean drenched her boots and the cuffs of her jean. A few steps further, she washed her mouth out with seawater, which tasted unbelievably bad, but maybe better than vomit, and splashed her face, stinging her eyes. In stories about sailors, the men always longed for and treasured fresh water; now she understood. She patted her back pocket for the ninety bucks, and considered tossing the cash into the ocean. Or maybe she'd buy a gift for Mal and Micha, the T-shirts they wanted, to redeem herself. Going with Harlan was probably the stupidest thing she'd ever done. Though there would be no consequences. The stupidest, worst thing she'd ever done. A gull hovered over the thrashing water, hesitating. Dove at the foam and disappeared.

Fiddling in her mouth with the slippery metal, Karen managed to unscrew one end of her tongue ring and pull the thing out. She'd been warned never to remove it, or she wouldn't be able to get it back in, but there it was, in her hand, and then there it was in the ocean, sinking. The thing bothered her all the time, and gave her a lisp. Plus, it wasn't really her. Was really Gavin, had been his idea. Hardly anything was really her; she'd even started dressing like that Aerosmith video girl, Alicia Silverstone, because everyone said they looked alike, and she'd bought tapes Gavin played while they lay in bed together, assuming that if he liked them, they must be good. The truth was, without him telling her, she would never have even guessed that Green Day was okay to like, but Aerosmith wasn't, and she still didn't understand why. Before Gavin told her otherwise, she'd been sure Aerosmith's songs were actually better, more complex, and more enjoyable to listen to, turned up loud.

"Shit," she yelled. No one would hear her; her words just disappeared into the wind. "Fuck," she wailed, drawing out the word, and then hollered it again. Why did Gavin have to be so nice to her, staring hard, like he'd never forget her? Why did he have to sleep with his forehead pressed between her shoulder blades? And why did she never believe him when he reminded her he didn't love her, was biding his time, waiting for someone real?

She ran for the hotel, slipping in the sand, then slowed to a fast walk, tucking her hair into a loose bun and pulling up her hood. She took the ancient, slow elevator and had almost caught her breath by the time she walked into the hotel room. Mal was watching TV and Micha was drawing, and they were wearing the Beastie Boys and Alice Cooper shirts. Karen squatted behind her sister and leaned into her hair.

"What's this?" Micha tugged.

"It's a belt."

Micha leaned away and turned to see it. "Can I try it on?"

"Sure." Karen untied the belt, and Micha took it. "I'm sorry we fought, M and M."

"S'okay," said Mal. He had his shoes on, on the couch.

"You know," Karen said, "Dad's not really a jerk. It's not us he's mad at."

"He doesn't like the Mexican maid," said Mal. "He's racist."

"No. He's just looking for anything to be upset about. He's just —"

Micha was colouring with pencil crayons — an ocean scene with massive waves. A small figure was disappearing into the water.

"Is that me?" said Karen.

"Not anymore. Now it's Brian O'Connor, Mom's *friend*."

What did Micha know about Brian? Mal didn't look away from the TV.

"Are you crying?" said Micha. "Karen's crying!"

Micha and Mal surrounded her with their arms and pressed in from both sides, while Karen said, "Sorry," and pressed the heels of her hands under her eyes. Mal asked if she wanted to wear his new shirt, and she said sure. The cotton already smelled like him, and she changed behind the bathroom door, breathing hard so she wouldn't cry again.

"Put something on," Karen told Mal. "You're shivering." His chest was practically blue, it was so pale.

"But what's wrong?"

Wrapping the purple jacket around his shoulders, Karen said, "Nothing. I don't know. I was just really lonely."

Mal's eyes filled with tears. "So were we," said Micha.

"I'm lonely for Burton," Mal whispered.

"And Mom and Dad still aren't back."

So they sat on the sofa, side by side, Mal with Karen's jacket buttoned up to the neck, Karen in the Beastie Boys T-shirt, and Micha in the Alice Cooper with Jane's belt knotted tightly, too high around the waist, and they waited. Through the window, they watched the waitress who'd served them lunch lumber to her car. Her cigarette went out in the wind, and she tried three times before it lit. The soulless T-shirt salesman ate a banana outside his store and tossed the skin on the ground, and seagulls landed on buildings' roofs and flew away.

Mal said, "I wish on Christmas we could have grocery-store rotisserie chicken and coleslaw. And a cake. Like that time Aunt Verna took us —"

"Those are factory farmed," said Micha.

"— even though we don't celebrate it."

Their parents came around the corner and down the street from the left. Dad had removed his black windbreaker and tied it around his waist, but Mom's light-blue was zipped up to the neck. She walked three paces ahead, then stopped, hands on her hips, and looked up. A seagull sat on the roof of the T-shirt store, pinning an empty foil chip-bag with one foot and pulling at it so it caught the light. Mom's hair was curling at the ends from the humidity, and pretty. She squinted and moved her pale hand over her eyes. Dad walked on, toward the hotel, without her.

NIX AND SIX

The widower stalks me through the night.
I see his eyes in the dark...
Look at me — no! Look away!
His body's curved a bit like polished wood.
I want to drag his venomous limbs
across my strings
like a bow on an axe (guitar).
His eyes are so blue.

I pushed my binder over to Serena and gazed at Mr. Casey. "How would you graph this line?" he said, meeting my eyes. I nodded appreciatively, but made no attempt to answer. He took in the empty tabletop in front of me — no binder, graph paper covered in drawings — and rolled his eyes, then tried someone else. Serena had read my poem and was gripping her multi-coloured pen, head bent over the page, crispy beige hair behind her ear. She wrote all her poems in a rainbow of colours; that was her thing. My pens were all black. I wanted to dye my hair black, too, but my dad said that was the final straw, and if I did, he wouldn't help me get my guitar and amp.

"Slope of the line," Mr. Casey said, again. "Y-axis. X-axis. X equals this and Y equals what."

Math apparently wasn't my forte, which was too bad, because I'd wanted to be a physicist, like Jeff Goldblum in *The Fly*. Only four months into high school, and that dream was slipping away down one of Mr. Casey's slopes. Lately, all I wanted was to listen to metal ballads when I was sad, and industrial music, which sounded exactly like the inside of my brain when I was mad, and write poems about the boy who sat across from me in music class with his cello. He was fifteen — a year older than me, and was tall, i.e., not a boy at all. A man. A man with long, lanky limbs, plaid golf pants and gleaming saddle shoes (worn, I assumed, ironically). A lock of chocolatey hair fell over his forehead when he leaned to see his music stand, and he tossed it back, revealing crayon-blue eyes. Aristotle Cone. I couldn't write down his name, or even his nickname, Stot, without dying, so in my poetry the widower was a metaphor for him, because he was like a black widow spider, where the female eats her mate, only in his case, he was the one consuming me. The night was a metaphor for my waysided dreams. Once I got the guitar, I'd set the words to music.

Serena pushed my binder back to me. She'd written four words in green, and signed them in blue, all in the middle of a clean page.

The pee is vile.
—Six

After the bell rang, I headed for the music room, bracing myself for shared air with Stot. Serena walked beside me, because she had a class in the same direction. "The pee is vile," she said. Her mouth was narrow, so when she smiled, she showed fewer teeth than the average person. December now, and I'd met her at the beginning of the year, but we weren't really friends outside of math. I had friends like that in most of my classes, even another poem-writer, better than Serena, in science, and a bad-attitude ally in phys-ed. My real friend, Freida, had moved with her parents to some third world country in Africa the year before, since her father's vocation was all about combating poverty in such places, using economics and water supplies.

"Nix!" Serena called down the crowded hallway, in her extra-high voice. Her best friend, Nichola Akbari, was fixing her hair in a mirror stuck to her open locker door, about ten people away. Nichola was the kind of girl where you know who she is, but she has no idea she's ever met you before, even though you're in the same English class and worked in a group together mapping the town where *To Kill a Mockingbird* takes place. She wore these loose jeans that would have fallen down except for her belt, and a tight white shirt, basically the same thing Serena wore most days, only Serena favoured pastels.

Nichola didn't respond until we grew nearer. Then she said, "Six," in a throaty, sarcastic voice. I stopped when Serena did, but Nichola didn't look at me. I would have bet my Coke can collection she didn't know about the poems Serena and I wrote, and that, put on the spot, Serena would have denied any involvement. I wished I'd kept walking, but now I was standing there, and would have seemed like even more of a freak if I just left again.

"Nix!" Serena said. Nichola had invented her own nickname, and it had stuck. Boys passing her in the hall called her that, and I'd seen a wide array of girls handing her notes in class with NIX written across them. Our English teacher even let her sign her work that way. Serena was trying her best with Six, but it wasn't really working out. Nichola was the only person I'd ever heard call her that.

"Guess who called me last night?" The pitch of Serena's voice was affected by excitement as well as volume.

"Yeah? *Yeah?*"

"Jizmack!"

"Well, duh."

"What?" I said. "I thought you liked a guy called Henry?"

"Shh." Serena looked around desperately, as though the hallway were crawling with spies. "Same person," she whispered. "That's what everybody calls him. His friends. Oh my God," she told Nichola. "He called, and he was like, are you coming to Midnight on Friday?"

"Cute," said Nichola, pronouncing it, "kee-ot."

"*Kee-ot*!" Serena agreed. "And he goes, Are you and Nix going to dance?"

"And you were like, Duh?"

"Yeah. Your hair looks *so nice*." Serena gazed at Nichola's shiny black ponytail like its beauty hurt her, then touched her own stiff, bleach-damaged locks. Her mouth distorted into a frown.

"Yeah, yours doesn't look way better than last month or anything." In her locker, Nichola had taped a series of black and white photographs of herself posed in front of a graffiti-covered wall and posed like a rapper.

"You always look so perfect," Serena said.

"Right," said Nichola. "*I'm* the one."

"Jizmack was probably only calling me because he really likes you." Serena looked just about ready to stab herself.

"I'm the one he likes. Yeah, that must be it."

"I have to go." I touched Serena's arm. "Bye. I have music class. Bye."

"Bye, Tess," Serena said, giving me a quick smile before turning back to Nichola and bouncing around like a little girl in front of a caged tiger. I forgot about both of them the next second.

In music class, Stot was wearing a V-neck sweater, navy and white, like a sailor, with grey pants and those saddle shoes. His presence had a profound physiological effect on me that did not make sense to the rational mind, which is why I could only capture it via poetry. I always tried not to glance his way, but one time I couldn't resist, and I looked at him, and he looked back. The worst moment of my life thus far.

No music test that day, thank god. Instead, we all played *Funeral March of a Marionette* over and over. I knew I sounded good — I always did when everyone played together and no one could hear me. But then when I had to play it in class by myself, I'd feel Stot's blue eyes burning into the side of my face, and my hands would shake like I had a nerve disease, and all that came out of the violin was screeching. As a result of my abysmal music tests, I was one in only three of my classmates not required to play at the Christmas assembly, and I was pretty worried about my report card, too. My dad wanted me to excel at violin to prove I was serious about music, before he helped me buy my guitar.

But at least I didn't have Serena's problems. On Monday morning, I walked over to her and Nichola in the cafeteria line, for breakfast, and said, "Hey," and then immediately regretted it. Serena's face was contorted with her horrible frown as Nichola told her, "Yes, that's it. I'm the one everyone watches." Her tone was so sarcastic, it was a parody of sarcasm. "I'm the one they want to hang out with. I'm the one. That's it! That's what it is. You're not the one Henry was watching all night. Nope. Nope!"

"Oh yeah," said Serena, her voice reaching for glass-shattering heights. "I'm the one. I'M THE ONE! He didn't follow you outside for a smoke. Not at all." She gasped for breath.

"Yeah, that's right. You're so right. I'm the one."

"No, no," said Serena. "I was the one outside smoking with Jizmack for forty-five minutes. I forgot. It was me."

"I'm the one," Nix said.

"Oh my God," said Serena.

The back of my neck prickled, and the breakfast line swayed, and someone cried, "No budding!" Long-legged purple plaid pants swaggered past us, and I looked up, up at the swaying rebel chocolate-brown lock. Stot tossed the hair out of his eyes, and it fell back. All the blood in my body pounded into my face.

"Spider!" hissed Serena, as Stot swaggered his way to the front and extended his index finger from a frayed cuff, indicating the breakfast pastries.

"Back of the line," said the lunch lady.

"What?" said Stot. The first word I'd ever heard him speak. I'd imagined his voice low and hypnotic like the cello, and not so nasal, but I didn't mind.

"No budding," said the lunch lady.

Stot's shoulders were hunched with the weight of an invisible backpack, and it looked like the weight of the world. I'd already noticed that his black and white shoes, normally viewed on either side of his cello and placed now squarely in a puddle of chocolate milk, were beginning to lose their shine in the toes. He tossed the hair back and showed the lunch lady his tortured blue eyes, but she just waved him toward the door with her hand, unmoved.

"I want a fucking muffin," said Stot.

When female spiders eat their mates, it's not like they have to chase them down — the male spider actually offers himself, sometimes placing his belly under her venomous teeth. As the whole breakfast line rippled with shock, and Serena and Nichola harmonized their choking sounds, Serena soprano, Nichola tenor, I understood exactly how the male spider felt.

"Blueberry," said Stot.

The woman, her fading brassy hair barely contained by her hairnet, stepped back, then glanced at the muffins as though they might provide some reasonable explanation. Before she had a chance to pull herself together, her black-haired red-lipsticked colleague intervened, turning from the potato bin. "Get out!" she told Stot. "Out, young man. Banned!"

"Muffin," said Stot.

"I know who you are, Smarty. You've got an attitude." Stot mumbled something, and she said, "Move. Out. Rude!"

"Oh yeah," said Nichola, as Stot long-limbed it out the other end of the food corridor, not walking fast enough to reveal any discomfort or alarm. "Hi, I'm so cool."

"Look at me," said Serena.

"My name's Muffin Man."

"I'm the one who needs an effing muffin, right now."

"You used to *like* him, didn't you?" Nix said to me.

I managed to shrug. "At the beginning of the year, kind of," I whispered.

I want a fucking muffin, I wrote that afternoon, as Mr. Casey sloped lines and more lines.

Oh, tiny blueberry explosions
contained by vanilla cake!
From a mix or lunch lady made?
The sky is a cataract on the
venomous eye of an arachnid
with its legs stuck in a bowl of batter.

I didn't show my poem to Serena, who was staring off into space, her face twitching in and out of bafflement and misery. Instead, I drew a spider web in the middle of my graph paper — graph paper is ideal for drawing spider webs — with dewdrops sparkling in it like little drops of poison, and in the middle, I drew a girl, ensnared. I was a very visual person as well as having vocabulary and music skills, and could make people look real, even their hands. I gave her long hair and a flowing dress, and lace-up boots, and a cross on a chain around her neck, but not in a religious way. Before I had a chance to draw the spider, though, with its gangly legs and floppy hair and venom-dripping fangs, the bell rang.

That was last period, and after, Serena clung to me like a life preserver, dragging me along while, still buzzing bad vibes about the Henry/Jizmack debacle, and in need of some cheering up, she and Nix went shoplifting at the mall. That is, Serena bought some maxi pads while Nichola filled her pockets with lipstick and hair elastics to dole out later as we sat in the food court drinking pop from big cardboard cups, all side by side, because Serena said we needed to watch the escalator in case Henry came down it. I wasn't sure if she had any reason to expect him, and when I asked, she just made noises like I didn't understand anything. Nix and Six divided up the loot. I knew how thieves affected prices and ruined things for everyone. When I was a kid, I used to sneak around my father's hardware store, waiting to catch some guy slip a bunch of screws in his pocket. Then I'd point him out to Dad. No one ever expected a little girl to be a store detective, but that's what I was. Anyway, I took a dark red lipstick because Nix was about to throw it out if I didn't.

We waited, and every few minutes, one of them pointed out a guy they knew, gliding down from the bus level. Sometimes Serena or Nichola said, "Kee-ot," and the other said, "Not!" which meant she disagreed, or "Oh no, not at all," which meant the kee-otness was too obvious to have warranted mention. My legs were too hot in my long johns and jeans, and my feet were sweltering in my boots and wool socks. As usual, I imagined how I'd tell Freida about it if I could phone her that night, and how she'd shriek with laughter and then say, "Oh, that's awful," and than laugh again, as I told her about us sitting there, stalking some guy seemingly named after his ability to produce large quantities of semen. I began composing a letter in my head. We'd promised to write each other every week, but so far it was more like once a month.

"You know *Henry*?" said Serena, after a while.

"Duh," said Nichola.

"You know?" Serena jabbed me with her elbow.

"I know what you've told me about him." I was too bored, and groggy from mall air, to pretend to care, but Serena didn't seem to notice. She put her hand to her mouth, and then to her heart. She paused, closing her eyes.

"I love him. I love Henry Walker."

Nichola made a sound in her throat, a drawn out, "Ugh."

"Last time we were at his house, I was like, Guess how I feel. And he's like, How? And I say," — Serena looked earnestly into my eyes, I guess as she had Henry's — "It starts with an L, ends with an E, and it's more than like." She covered her mouth, stifling a squeal.

"You were at his house?" She was right; I really didn't understand anything. I would have sooner eaten a worm than gone to Stot Cone's house. What I was really afraid of, though, watching that escalator, was that Stot would come down it instead of Henry, so I guess I was just as insane as Serena, in my own way.

"Ugh," said Nichola.

"What?" said Serena. "Nicky? *What*?"

"Just be cool," said Nichola. "Serena, just. Just try be cool about things."

"Oh. My. God. You are so, so the one."

"Whatever," Nichola sighed.

"You are so cool."

"Let's go practise," said Nichola, and to my relief, they both started putting on their coats and scarves.

I tried to say bye at my bus stop, but Serena insisted I go with them to Nichola's house, and Nichola said, "Yeah, come on." I guess I was kind of curious, since what were the chances of me seeing the inside of Nichola Akbari's house, so I walked with them. Serena hung back with me, letting Nichola take the lead. "The pee is vile," she whispered conspiratorially as we crossed Rideau Street at Dalhousie. I pretended not to hear her. "Spider!" she squealed.

Nichola looked around, her ponytail bouncing against the collar of her coat.

"Oh nothing," Serena sang. "Just thought I saw a spider on that tree."

"It's too cold for spiders," said Nichola.

"Oh, right. Thanks for the news flash, Sherlock." I avoided meeting Serena's eyes, but I could still see her grinning at me. Nichola didn't look back at us again, just hunched up into her coat and let us follow.

Her house was on a residential street right downtown, an old, blue, clean duplex with a walkway cleared of the small snowfall of the day before. The porch was spotless, too, and someone had even hacked at the ice under the mailbox, but given up. Inside, it smelled like a restaurant, and we hung our coats in the vestibule. Everything was wooden and polished.

"Mummy," said Nichola. A woman with black hair and black-rimmed green eyes like Nichola's appeared, holding a wooden spoon as a fairytale princess holds a wand. I could tell right away she wasn't the type to change into track pants when she got home from work, like my dad did. Even on days she didn't go out, she probably wore wool pants and a ribbed, form-fitting sweater, and gold jewellery and matching glasses with gold-flecked frames, which hung from a chain around her neck.

"Pretty Mummy!" Nichola said.

They kissed each other's cheeks and hugged, and Nichola's mother said, "Silly kitten," like the kind of woman who's used to laughing off a lot of compliments.

Serena waited for an in. "Hi, Bets." Her voice was still high, but softer than usual, revering.

"Hello, Serena! And hello...."

"I'm Tess," I said.

"A friend from school," said Nichola.

"Betsabeh Akbari." She moved her spoon to her left hand and offered her right one, which I shook, despite my urge to kiss it, like an admirer in an old-fashioned movie.

"Will you girls be staying for dinner?"

Serena nodded, but only I noticed, and Nichola said, "Serena can't." Though her smile faded for a moment, Serena kept her face neutral.

"My father's expecting me, too." Actually my dad would have been relieved if he thought I was making friends instead of "moping in that room with the door shut." My dad was all about tools and sports and inviting a bunch of jackasses over to play cards, and had trouble seeing the value of solitude. Anyway, no way was I subjecting myself to a dinner alone with Nichola and Nichola Senior.

After a few more exclamations of love with her mother, Nichola led Serena and me upstairs. The walls of her huge room were plastered with posters of rappers, the dresser and desk were covered in schoolbooks and notes with NIX written on them, and the floor was scattered with clothes. I sat on the bed with Serena while Nichola cleared up the clothes, dumping them in a hamper.

"Check this out!" Serena grabbed an envelope from the bed and pulled out a wad of photos. "Midnight." The first few pictures were too dark to make out much, just a disco ball and a bunch of light, but then someone thought to turn on the flash, and there were Nix and Six dancing side by side in a puff of dry ice, their arms raised in unison.

"Okay, okay, wait." Serena scattered the photos on the bed, and found what she was looking for. "That's him!" I took the picture of Henry and examined it closely. He was wearing a ball cap and a huge sweatshirt, and I don't think I'd ever seen someone with less facial expression.

"And." Serena handed me a picture of her and Henry side by side, arms crossed, her smiling frantically, and his face blank as a wall. "Kee-ot?" said Serena.

Luckily I never had to answer, because Nichola lunged to press play on her stereo. She leapt, and landed in the middle of the room, on the clean spot, hands out, palms forward. Eyes serious, lips slightly parted. "Not!" rapped Serena, over the song's real words blasting on the stereo. "Elaborate oh Miss N! You're the one yeah the one who's kissin'…." Her voice was squeaky and deadly serious, and I could tell I wasn't supposed to laugh.

Clasping her hands at waist level, Nichola thrust her hips in time to the music. She spun and hunched, and jerked her arms across her body. Her eyes remained serious, focused on the wall behind my head, but her lips parted in the kind of smile my dad and I always made fun of on synchronized swimmers. Sometimes she raised her eyebrows in a sexy way, or pursed her lips. Beside me, Serena frowned with concentration, bopping to the beat. Nichola thrust her arms out straight at her sides, crucifixion style, and they rippled, fingertip to fingertip. She turned and moonwalked across the floor, laughing, as though that part were a bit of a joke.

Serena mumbled along with the song, the real words now, through clenched teeth, along with the music. She got up to wander the room, a weird vacant look on her face, running her fingers over surfaces, putting her hand on her hip and looking over her shoulder. Then, with the beginning of a new verse, she leapt to attention right beside Nichola, back straight as a board, then started throwing her body around, her arms pumping the same well-practised moves as her friend's, but more flailing than fluid. A few bars in, she remembered to display her few-toothed smile next to Nichola's shiny white wide one.

Don't get me wrong — it was way better than I could have done, had I chosen to try. Sometimes their moves related to the lyrics; when the car's top was down or whatever so the white-boy rapper's stripey hair could blow, Nichola and Serena made wavy motions over their heads, and when he drove around leering at beach girls in bikinis, Nichola and Serena turned face to face, leered at each other, and made hourglass shapes in the air with their hands. Serena met my eyes from time to time, so I smiled a bit, not sure how to react, and waited for the song to end. Man, I missed Freida right then, the stuff we talked about, her jokes, everything, like how we were into Henry Rollins and Depeche Mode at the same time, and also that one Madonna song kind of as a joke but kind of not — not a lot of people would have understood that. I guess it was selfish to envy a poverty-stricken

African nation Freida's company, but just then I felt like I'd never meet a sane person again. Nichola sprang for the stereo, and pressed stop just as the next song started.

"Try to come in right on seven, okay, Six?"

"I did," said Serena.

"On seven, that's when you go from" — Nichola stood relaxed, looking off and up to one side, as though just hanging out — "*One two-three four-five-six*, to" — her body went stiff, the synchronized swimmer smile appeared, and one arm shot up, bent at the elbow — "*seven*."

"Yeah, Nix. I *know*."

"If you want to be a dance girl, you have to practise at home."

"Right. I never practise at home. You're so perceptive. I'm so glad you're so in charge."

"Yeah, I'm the one who's so in charge." She didn't even bother with sarcastic tone this time.

"No, wait," said Six, "Am I in backwards land? Am *I* the one who goes to dance lessons four times a week while *you're* practising alone in your room? Am *I* the one with jazz, ballet *and* modern dance classes, practically every day? Maybe *you're* the one with no stereo, just a clock-radio tape deck, and a mother who works nights so you're not allowed to make noise, and by the way dancing makes noise, and a bedroom too small for dancing in properly."

Nichola didn't even try to retort. She just said, "Six," and her face looked like a normal person's, full of guilt and confusion. She fiddled with some tapes and CDs on her dresser. "I bet Tess is having an awesome time," she muttered, finding her usual tone. "You're so happy you came over, right, Tess? Wow, you must think we're awesome." She stuck a tape in her stereo, turned it on, and turned "3AM Eternal," by KLF, up as loud as it could go.

Serena leaned over and yelled in my ear, puncturing my eardrum, "You should come to Midnight! On Saturday!"

Nichola, dancing by herself in the middle of the room, glanced at me. "Yeah," she said.

"I don't have anything to wear...."

"You can borrow something of mine." Serena showed all the teeth she could manage in her excitement.

"I don't know how to dance."

"Oh, come on. You don't have to! Come, come," she seized my arm, and Nichola concentrated on her moves, swishing her elbows away from her body.

"Okay," I said.

That night, I tried to write a letter to Freida, but I only got as far as decorating the envelope with this sentence that was kind of this special thing between us — *I know who you remind me of* — in curly black letters. It was a thing no one else would really understand. We'd be hanging out doing homework and listening to music, and I'd say, "I know who you remind me of." Or maybe we'd be walking and she'd put her hand on my arm and stop me and say it. "I know who you remind me of." We'd laugh, or we'd get all shivery and sad in that way that feels good, or if we said it in the right surprised voice at the right time, we might even cry, not with sobbing, but just when your eyes ache and get red. Anyway, on that envelope the phrase made me feel like Freida was someone I used to know well and was already turning into someone who'd irretrievably changed, and I didn't have the heart to actually start writing, so I went to sleep.

I was hoping he would hear "underage dance bar" and say no way, but my completely misguided dad couldn't have been more thrilled. He drove me to Serena's after dinner on Saturday, blasting Earth, Wind & Fire on the car stereo; he'd been listening to them full time since he broke up with this Nancy character a week before.

"You can't put all your eggs in one basket in this life," he said, referring to Nancy and Freida at the same time. He didn't even seem to notice Serena's address was a crappy-looking apartment building, the kind university students live in.

By the time I buzzed up to the apartment, Dad had driven away. Serena and Nichola came to the door together, in a haze of perfume and hair product. They were wearing the shortest skirts I'd ever seen, white for Serena and red for Nichola, and matching black tops. I had no makeup except for the lipstick Nichola stole, and was in my black jeans and a sweater.

"Are you guys smoking?" I said.

"Uh, no." Serena gestured toward the couch, featuring a woman in a sweat suit, a cigarette in her mouth and an ashtray in her lap. "My mom."

"Oh," I said all happily, like maybe I'd asked because the smoke smelled good instead of disgusting.

"This is Tess," said Serena.

Her mom nodded and raised a hand in greeting. I felt shy and stupid, and by the time I got over it, I was in Serena's room, which really was too small to dance in; we all had to sit on the perfectly made bed to fit in there. Three separate shelves held tapes, CDs and magazines, lined up and even. Some dance music I'd never heard before was playing from the tape player on a clock radio, and Nichola was bopping in place to it, drinking out of a glass bottle that said *peach schnapps* on it. Serena started going through her dresser and closet, pulling out stuff for me to try on, and when Nichola passed her the bottle, she just took a tiny sip before handing it to me. I sniffed it before I drank. Fiery liquid peaches tingled down my throat, like some kind of magic elixir.

Serena made me try on three different hideous dresses, and I changed behind her closet door, so they wouldn't see my unshaved legs. When I took off each outfit, Serena folded it carefully and put it away.

"How about this?" she passed me a pair of white fishnet tights and a dark purplish dress made of a wooly fabric. "I never wear that," she said. "I think it was my cousin's or something." Her hand appeared around the door again just as I was getting into the tights, passing me the peach schnapps bottle.

"This stuff is so good," I said.

"I know," said Nichola.

"If you like drinking poison," said Serena.

"Oh, sorry, princess," Nichola said. "You and your *coolers*."

"What about your mom?" I couldn't imagine drinking with my dad right there. In fact, I'd never really drunk before, except for the glass of beer Freida's dad let me have at dinner once.

Nichola kind of snorted at that, and Serena said, "She could care less."

"That's why we get ready here," said Nichola. "Whoa. You look *so* cute."

"Really?"

"Ahh!" said Serena. "Kee-ot!"

"Totally," said Nichola.

"These colours aren't so much my thing...."

"Tess!" said Serena. "Kee-ot!"

"Kee-ot," said Nichola.

"Do I look slutty?"

"You look *hot*."

Nichola said, "You couldn't be a slut even if you tried."

Harsh.

Probably more because of what Nichola said, I let Serena have at me with the eye shadow and mascara and everything. I even let Nichola do things to my hair while I held the booze bottle for her. Since my glasses weren't on, I had no idea what was going on, and when they were done, I put my face right up to the mirror to see. My hair was all puffed up, and my eyes had about ten different colours swirling around them. So hilarious I almost blew my mouthful of peach schnapps through my nose.

"Oh great," said Serena. "Perfect."

I lay back on Serena's bed and turned face to face with a pink teddy bear with *Sweetheart* written across its chest.

The next thing you know, Serena's shaking my arm, telling me it's time to go out, and she sounds pretty aggravated. I guess I was asleep. Then I'm in the car and Serena's dad, who looks exactly like Serena, right down to the long beige hair, is driving, and Nichola keeps whispering, "Act normal," in my ear, which is odd, because I'm not saying a word, and she's the one with solid-blue eyelids.

Here's what I remember of Club Midnight. Flashing lights, a lot of them purple, bass pumping loud enough to shake your insides, and little round tables, one of which Serena and Nichola left me at, with some guy called Joey, who looked old, like eighteen, maybe, and was solid, but not fat. He had facial hair. He said a few words to me every now and then, and I nodded, though I couldn't hear what he said. He smelled strongly of cologne and cigarettes, though maybe it was just the air. Hard to tell, since those smells filled up the whole place. Eventually he left me by myself.

I don't know how long I sat there, resisting the urge to put my head down and sleep, before I reached into my bag for my glasses, which Serena had insisted I shouldn't wear. About half my drunkenness disappeared when I put them on. All of a sudden I could see Nix and Six dancing in a circle with some guys in loose jeans, dress shirts and baseball caps, one of whom had a hang-dog expression, and kept his eyes on the floor, and was Henry. I took a long drink of the water in front of me and walked over to Serena.

"Hey!" she said. I shuffled around and watched how they danced, their faces so serious, but gave up and leaned against the elbow-height wall that contained the dance floor like a skating rink. Sometimes one of the dancers would step into the middle of the circle and do some complicated movements. When it was Henry, he kept a cigarette in his mouth while he shuffled around, then posed for a few seconds like a statue, on one foot, then on his back, then right on his head. Everyone in the circle said, "Go Jizmack, go Jizmack." Nichola stepped into the circle, too, and started doing poses behind him, bending around and moving her arms like a robot. "Go Nix," said the circle, as she bent backwards, and Henry bent right over her so their bellies almost touched. Their faces were so close together I was afraid the ash would fall off his cigarette into her eye. Luckily, Serena saved the day by butt-checking Henry and then wedging herself between him and Nichola, where she held her arms over her head and stuck out her lips, and thrust her hips around while Nichola backed off.

"Go Six," I said, and a few voices joined me. "Go Six."

Henry sank to the floor, squatting on one foot with the other foot resting on his thigh, still with the cigarette in his mouth. He put one hand on the floor and tried to propel himself into some kind of handstand, while Serena did some moves from the white rapper routine.

"Go Jizmack," chanted Nichola.

The next song was a slow jam, and the circle dissolved. Serena put her arms around Henry's shoulders and said something in his ear. When she tried to be sexy, she leaned her head really far to one side.

"C'mon," that Joey guy grabbed my arm. "Want to dance?"

The song was all, *We belong together* and stuff, and Joey started whispering the lyrics in my ear, pulling me close and rubbing his hands up and down my back. Serena was doing a similar move on Henry's arms and trying to catch his eye, while he just stared at the floor, holding a fistful of her shirt, right in the middle of her back. Joey whispered along with the music, breathing heavy in my ear. His voice sent little tingles up and down my spine, where he moved his hands all around and around. Henry pulled Serena close, and she pressed her face into his neck. He nodded at Nichola over Serena's shoulder, raising his eyebrows a millimetre. Nichola pursed her lips. I closed my eyes.

I felt like Jennifer Grey in *Dirty Dancing*, my hands on Joey's arms, his hands moving lower and lower on my back, as though I'd done this a million times before, when in reality I'd hidden in the library throughout every junior high dance, and had never touched a boy before. By the time Joey and the song were telling me we'd come to the end to the road but still he couldn't let go, he was holding the fabric over my butt in both his hands and kind of rubbing it around, grinding his hips into mine. I might as well be honest: I was fully grinding my hips back into his, especially when one of his hands moved right under the dress onto my upper thigh. I smelled his hair, and I think I might have licked his neck. And then I looked over Joey's shoulder and it was like, reality check. Nichola peering over some guy's shoulder, her eyes all huge and mortified. In fact, pretty much everyone was staring at me, as far as I could tell. I backed up a bit and tried to wriggle away from Joey's hands. I could only pray he hadn't actually pulled up my skirt to expose my fishnet-covered Smurfette underpants to everyone dancing around us. The song ended.

"Well, thanks," he said.

I managed to find my coat and bag before heading outside, to sit on the front steps, gulping the beautiful, clean, cold air. My head cleared more and more, and as my brain kicked in, the embarrassment mounted. I put my head on my knees and closed my eyes, and didn't even look up when people walked past me, or stood two feet away, smoking. I didn't even look up when voices asked if I was okay. I must have sat there for an hour, at least.

This was the ironic thing about Club Midnight. You'd think the party would be jumping at the hour of twelve, but that's actually when the place closed. All these cologne-monsters came filing out, and I turned and peeked inside; they'd turned the lights on, so the place looked like any old room with some tables thrown into it, which I guess it was. A bunch of kids crossed the street and stood at the bus stop, and the rest started piling into cars with parents driving them, pulled up at the curb.

"Tess." Serena sat beside me, looking about as happy as I felt. "Henry's driving us home. Come on."

Henry and Nichola were already walking away, and I could see Serena wanted to chase them and kick them to death, but instead she said, "Are you okay?" I lied and said I was. After all, only my dignity had been pulverized, and my problems were still nothing compared with Serena's. By the time we caught up with Henry and Nichola, they were in his car, side by side in the front, so Serena had to sit with me in the back. Henry turned up the stereo so the bass shook the whole car, and every now and then he or Nichola said something only the two of them could hear, and she laughed. He pulled up at Serena's building first, and she didn't even look at anyone, let alone say bye. Then he turned down the music for a second to ask where I lived. Which was fifteen minutes away, and Nichola's place only five, but he drove me first. I didn't say bye either. Really no point trying to yell over the music.

I had my own door down to the basement, so I didn't have to worry about waking Dad. It turned out I also didn't have to worry about waking him because he wasn't asleep; Nancy's shoes were in the hallway, and I could hear the two of them talking in the kitchen. So much for moving on and not putting his eggs in one basket, and all that stuff he said about Nancy working in an office and not knowing how to put up a tent. How was I supposed to make good decisions with that kind of example? At least he'd turned off his dad-style rhythm and blues. In my room, right on my bed was a Coke can, with a sticky note on the top. *The latest*, it said. *Dad*. The new Christmas edition, all silver and white. I hadn't realized it was even out yet, though I'd made room on the ledge where I displayed my collection. I hadn't actually drunk pop since my grade two teacher had put these teeth in a glass with some Coke, and after a week they were full of holes; I just liked having every can. I put on my pajamas and washed off my makeup in the little basement bathroom, and then I sat in bed for some time, looking at the festive winter scene populated entirely by rosy-cheeked innocents, and feeling like a frog bitten by one of those gut-sucking beetles.

For the next couple of weeks, I was just studying for exams, and basically pulling my head out of my ass to avoid actually failing my first term of high school. Even in Mr. Casey's class, I did math instead of writing poetry. So it wasn't until the last day of school before the holidays, three days before Christmas, that I really talked to Serena again. Actually, oddly enough, it was Nichola I spoke with first. She stopped me in the hall near my locker, and tugged me over into a corner.

"I feel really bad about Serena," she told me. "I mean, about Henry, and about. Everything. The assembly." The Christmas assembly was that afternoon, but before I could ask why she felt bad about it, Nichola said, "Especially about Henry."

"What, does he — does he like you, or?"

"Well, yeah," said Nichola. "He's always dancing with me at Midnight, or coming outside with me for a smoke, and he's like, it's *you* I like, it's been you the whole time."

"Really?"

"Yeah, he's like, you're so perfect, you're so hot."

"Well..." I struggled for something relevant to say. "Do you like him, too?"

"I don't know. I mean, I regret fooling around with him." Eyes wide, Nichola leaned closer. "I do regret those times. I feel bad. It's just, Serena acts so weird. Like Henry came to the park with us the other weekend? And she wore this jacket exactly like the one I have, the black one." Nichola showed me with her hands how tight the jacket was, gripping her waist. "And she's so skinny, and not in a good way. And then she starts acting all weird, kind of squealing, running around like a kid, and then she goes, look at me, look at me, and *slides down this hill on her ass.*"

"Oh, no." Even I knew that was bad.

"Yeah, on a centimetre of snow, and she's laughing, like hysterical, and Henry's like, she is so weird. I mean, he's like seventeen. And she acts like that in front of him."

"Oh, no."

"Yeah, so she's covered in snow and muck and dead leaves, and meanwhile he says, Nix, *you* look so good in that jacket."

"Oh," I said. "Oh… no."

"I feel so bad," said Nichola. "She's just so annoying sometimes, so embarrassing, immature…." I nodded, without meaning to, and immediately wished I could take it back. Encouraged, Nichola went on, "It's the way she acts. People are like, why do you always hang around with that Serena Wright? And it's like, I've known her since grade five. It's just. I don't know. Hey — have you heard from *Joey*?"

"Who? No…."

"Who? Yeah, right. Did he get your number?"

"Nix!" A girl with a red ponytail just as shiny as Nichola's black one, and jeans just as in danger of falling down, stepped between us, facing Nichola. "Three AM!"

"Thanks for listening," Nichola mouthed to me, then whispered, "He's not a great kisser, just to warn you," before giving her full attention to the redhead, which left me to stand awkwardly until I realized I'd been dismissed.

At the assembly, I tried to sit alone up in the balcony, but somehow Serena found me, and sat beside me. The first thing that happened was a pep talk from the principal, all, great first term and keep reaching for the stars, but don't do drugs. Then the talent section began, with the choir singing a few carols, and then the orchestra, including ninety percent of my music class, played *Funeral March of a Marionette*, and I silently vowed to sign out a violin and practise every day throughout the Christmas holidays and that I'd show them, Aristotle Cone or no Aristotle Cone. He, of course, was in the orchestra, in a white shirt and black dress pants, spidery limbs wrapped around his cello. Watching him from above like that, I was safe. He still had the power to slay, but he couldn't get at me — like an animal at the zoo. And he couldn't see me, no matter how much I stared. Strange to think I'd had raunchy sex dreams about that Joey guy, but my dreams about Stot had mostly involved him walking down school hallways and me running away, much like in real life. For the first time, he barely affected my heart rate. His extra-long bowing arm sawed away, his elbow a definite safety hazard, and his wrist jutted out of a sleeve that was too short. His mouth hung open, too. I imagined what Stot and I would look like as marionettes, our cloth limbs flailing at the ends of strings, yarn for our hair and x's for our eyes; I pictured us marching, marching, pallbearers at either end of the coffin containing my love for him.

When that ended, and everyone was just about dying of boredom, this kid goes to the mike and looks all excitedly at the closed curtains over the stage, like waiting for a cue, and then says, "And now the Three-AM dancers, featuring Nichola Akbari and Tricia Clement, otherwise known as... Nix and Trix!"

The sound of fake gunfire explodes through the sound system, and the curtain opens to flashing lights and pounding bass, and Nichola and that redheaded girl gyrating in perfect synchronicity. I couldn't even look at Serena, who kept making little choking sounds and sitting up straighter, and placing her hair behind her shoulders. I'll be honest: it was harsh. Tricia clearly took dance lessons and had a bedroom big enough to practise in, and her smile didn't even look fake; it looked like she was having fun, and wanted everyone else to have fun, too. Trix was even a better nickname than Six was, if you had to pick one. Luckily they didn't play the whole song. After a couple of minutes, purple light drenched the stage, and Nix and Trix stood at opposite sides of the stage, cart wheeled past each other, and then landed in the splits, with their arms sticking up.

"Happy holidays!" said the MC, back at the mike.

Naomi K. Lewis

"That's fine," said Serena, already standing, her backpack over her shoulders. "She is just so… She is so totally.…"

My style was to stay seated until everyone else had left, so I didn't have to press my body against anyone to get out the door, but the curtains hadn't even closed as Serena joined the crush of kids leaving the auditorium. Nichola did some impromptu breakdancing, and the music even came back on, but quieter than before.

"Go Nix," said Trix. Though most people were just anxious to get out of there, a few voices joined in: "Go Nix." The purple light came back on, flashing, Nichola and Tricia strobe strobe strobing like grape-juice drenched rock stars.

"Get off the stage," someone hollered.

It's easy enough to say a thing like that, but no one paid any attention of course, and if you really want to be honest about it, Serena was right. Nix was, completely, the one.

SEESAW

There is justice in the world, and I am on the business end of it. This justice business has me encased in plaster, limbs hanging from pulleys, hands and feet tingling, continuously pricked by a thousand relentless pins.

But maybe justice is the wrong word, because I was born bad and you can't change who you are, and how just is that?

I met him at a conference three, four months back. An oil executive of all things. Peter Guile explained his company didn't drill holes in the ground, just scooped up sand. It seemed so innocent at first. He confessed over drinks that he found it difficult, the commitment. He said his fiancée was disappointed things weren't the same as they had been in the beginning, six months prior. She had seemed independent at first, but then became more and more needy.

"I know exactly what you mean," I said, because I did know, and I wanted him to touch me, because I am not a good person, and never was.

"Actually," he said, like he was breaking bad news, "you and she have the same first name."

The gin and tonics had put me in a dream-like state, and everything was hazy, the hotel bar lit with tiny table lamps. I leaned my elbows on the table; his eyes were on my arms, bare, spaghetti straps.

"My father's dying of a botched leg-lengthening procedure that's infected his bone marrow," I said. "They broke his femurs and inserted steel rods." I told Peter about my father so he'd find me tragic and unusual, and therefore more alluring. That's the kind of person I am.

It worked: his fingertips found my upper arm. "I'm sorry," he said. "I can't help it."

I open my eyes, and there she is, sitting by the window of my hospital room, with a headful of golden hair sucking in the sunlight and spitting it back out. Sarah Watson. I recognize her right away, though the last time I saw her was in a high school bathroom more than half a country, half a lifetime ago. She had emerged from the stall behind me and met my eyes in the mirror. One of my eyes was circled with thick black liner, the other still naked. Watson's then mouse-brown bangs were short and uneven, parted in the middle to reveal a triangle of naked forehead. She washed her hands in silence and left me to my vanity. Now she is older, tidier, minus the polka-dotted turtlenecks and cords. Sexy square glasses instead of wire-frame ones. Her skin shimmers.

"Watson?" I say.

Must be the morphine. Sarah Watson is not in my Calgary hospital room. Sarah Watson was elementary school, high school, not now, not adulthood. She lives back east, if she still exists at all.

But she says, "Yes, Benedict," and moves her hand from knee to hair, leaving a glowing trail of diamond-sparkle. She says, "Peter is my fiancé."

"No. No."

"Yes, indeed."

She doesn't seem surprised I've oozed back into her life fifteen years later. Maybe she's had time to get used to the idea. And after all, I've been a parasite since she met me, when we were ten.

I hear myself say, "I'm sorry." The morphine makes regret difficult, but now I am sorry, and now I know I've never been truly sorry before; the sensation is wholly unfamiliar. The shock of it is a painful tickle under my sternum. Agonizing laughter.

"You can just stop."

At her command, the tickle and the laughter vanish.

I need to urinate. Soon a nurse will come to deflate my bladder, divine relief. Watson sits, legs crossed, in what looks to be a kitten-soft cashmere dress with knee-high wedge-heeled boots. The enormous diamond on her finger keeps shooting sparks. Of course. Bought by Peter Guile. But I know the truth: Watson is in disguise. She had a bowl cut until the age of fifteen. Her father is a marijuana farmer and her mother is an anorexic, and they were divorced in 1986, the same year as my own parents split up, a year before Watson and I met. Watson cried at camera-film commercials and that episode of *Family Ties* where Steven listens to the *Old Yeller* record. I close my eyes.

"Watson?" I say. "Does Kodak still have those commercials with the old people and the photo albums?" At one time she gulped with sobs just at the mere mention of those old people holding hands, flipping the pages. The phone rings. The woman's voice: *Dad? There's someone here who misses you...* and then the happy little girl, voice sing-song with love. Or was that for long distance?

"Watson?"

But Watson's gone. The sunlight is gone. My sister Tara is in the chair, and my bladder is empty.

"Pain," I say. It's searing, but my head is clear.

"First, Dad. Then, you."

"How can you even compare..."

Naomi K. Lewis

There's no point arguing. Tara wins by default. She was the only one who visited our father in the hospital the year before, while I and the rest of our sisters, half and whole, and Bruce, waited stubbornly, gleefully for him to die.

"Mom always said seesaws were dangerous," Tara says.

True. Mom warned us about gobstoppers, too. But how could I have known she was right about some things, when she had been so miserably wrong about others? Our father, she'd claimed, in her defense, had been charming and kind when she met him, and he wore a moustache like Magnum PI's.

Someone is washing me with warm, soapy water, and I'm thinking, Sarah Watson. Ten-year-old Watson breaking down during an educational video about racism, just as the white girl and the black girl realize they can't skip rope without the Chinese girl. Then it turns out the Chinese girl is the best skipper they've ever seen. Watson, sobbing too hard to walk straight, is escorted from the room by a teaching assistant. At recess, she's still outside, under a maple tree, crying her eyes fluorescent green.

"I live according to a strict set of principles," I told Watson, joining her under the maple. She swallowed hard, forcing the sobs down to plug their source.

I explained I wanted to be a nun. I did. I wanted to live in a quiet, tidy room. The constant company of God seemed preferable to that of Tara, Kara, Caroline, and Bruce. Little Jackie, and perhaps my mother, I would miss.

"Kindness," I said. "That's the most important thing. Forgiveness, and, uh, charity…"

Watson's crying allured me. Not to cry seemed a constant effort for her, undone by the slightest nudge. Also, she was an only child, and lived alone with her mother in a house with stain-free furniture.

At lunchtime, we'd walk three blocks to play hide and seek at the Museum of Nature and Man. I picture twelve-year-old Watson crouched under the belly of a recreated Tyrannosaurus Rex skeleton, betrayal pummeling her like the death throes of an old yellow dog. Fourteen-year-old Watson bloody-nosed, gaping at me through a volleyball net in disbelief. Grown up Watson walking into a hospital room to see the other woman — the woman her fiancé has maimed in a seesaw accident — and seeing me.

If I could hold a pen:

Dear Watson,
I'm sorry I left you in the museum. I didn't want to be friends anymore. I wanted Sarah N, instead. I'm sorry I broke your glasses with that volleyball. I'm sorry about Peter. I didn't know he was yours. You're not still planning to marry him, are you? He said your needs stifle him, that he proposed in the heat of the moment, an almost paternal feeling. He said, "My desire tends to wane." What are you doing out West, anyway?

But this is the thing: why should I be sorry? She's supposed to back in Eastern Standard Time. What is she doing here in Mountain? And I'm the one with the broken pelvis and fractured tailbone and not even a real lay to remember her cowboy of a fiancé by. Also, what was she doing so close to that volleyball net, and why weren't her hands up? And though I should not have left that museum with Newman, and smoked and laughed all the way back to school, Watson's crying had become ridiculous. Theatrical, frankly. After the washing-machine murder of my gerbil (probably by Caroline), Watson had keened while grief packed itself silently into my bones. Iceman wasn't her gerbil to cry about. And what is she doing engaged to a man like that, anyway?

The thing about all this is, I thought the world had already balanced things out, absolving me of the museum incident and maybe even the volleyball, too. Justice: in the last year of high school, Sarah Newman dropped out of school, then ransacked my father's house with her drug dealer boyfriend, stealing my stepmother's tiara collection, the location of which I had revealed in the wee hours of a sleepover. And before that, the World Religions class, the first time Watson and I had been in the same course all through high school, since she was usually segregated with the other "gifted" students. I wondered if she noticed my presence, if she found me enviable because I had grown amazingly spherical breasts, or if she thought the black eyeliner was edgy, or if she thought I was trying too hard.

Mr. Paul did not call on me often, since I was certified ungifted, but then he asked some question about the Buddha and the folds in his path, looked right at me, and said, "Sarah Benedict," in a sarcastic tone that meant he already knew I didn't have the answer. I did know. I did know. Seconds passed, his face growing more and more sarcastic. Of course, it didn't make sense to eat a gobstopper in class anyway, because the whole point is to repeatedly take it out of your mouth; otherwise, as the flavour gradually transforms, you're forced to guess, tormented, about its colour. Mr. Paul just stood there, his eyebrows up, his mouth scrunched. I knew the answer: three. No: eight. Desire is suffering. But my gob was stopped.

I braced my jaw and bit.

The crunch must have been louder inside my head than out, but everyone heard it. They gasped as I leaned over to spill blood, half a tooth, and a huge gory half-red, half-pinkish yellow candy — with only the faintest thud — onto the desk. I should have cried; at least then I would have seemed human.

"Go to the nurse's office, Sarah B," said Mr. Paul.

As I walked to the door, leaving all my books behind, I heard him cry, "Flee, flee!" and the gifted people laughed, and I caught Watson's wide, triumphant eyes.

I sleep and wake and eat and sleep and then Watson is back by the window, this time in jeans and a leather jacket.

She says, "I want to know what happened between you and Peter."

"What are you doing here?"

"I want to know."

"I mean, here. What are you doing here?"

"I'm marrying Peter." Watson stands up and comes over to the bed, to look down at my trussed-up limbs.

"I'm sorry about the museum," I say. "And the volleyball was an accident."

"Listen," says Watson. "We were children, and I don't care. Tell me what happened."

"Where were you hiding?"

She touches my bare toe tip, sending a shock up my leg and into my belly.

"When you find yourself in times of trouble," she says.

In the sixth grade, when we weren't playing hide and seek in the Museum of Nature and Man, the two of us listened to Beatles songs at lunchtime, in her kitchen. The ones we both loved made her cry until her eyes changed from sea to glow-stick green. We talked about our fathers, hers living on his grow-op outside town, and mine with a new hair transplant and a new wife, his third, whom he'd picked up while stopped in his Ferrari at the Tim Hortons drive-through, where she worked. She passed him his double-double, and it was love.

"The museum," I say. "I left you there on purpose. The volleyball, though, was an accident. I couldn't have known his fiancée was you. I don't think you should marry him."

"He says nothing happened." She looms over me. "Is that true?"

Nothing happened. Something: Peter Guile's fingertips against my upper arm; his emails, day after day. Something: Peter on the phone, telling me he's outside in his car, waiting to take me to lunch. Something: Peter on the seesaw in his suit, tie flying up, tie falling down, my bare legs lifting, toes pointing, inviting (*"you don't need any leg-lengthening surgery, that's for sure"*); my short skirt up over him, down below him. Peter leaping backwards and me crashing down just like my mother warned — *no no no* — to earth. My bones splintering against the splintering board under my haunches. I tipped backwards, and the wooden board swung up and then down again to bounce off my pelvis. No pain, just a tingling in my hands, a short-circuit tingling through my fingers, every nerve in my body misfiring. I kept my eyes closed and curled into my mind, waited for the verdict.

"Oh my God," said Peter. "There was a bee."

A bee? A bee? It was bad. It was bad, bad. Death. Wheelchair. My breath came fast as punches. He was phoning an ambulance.

"He has a phobia of bees," Watson says. Her diamond moves, fingers reaching out to touch mine. "How long will you be in here?"

"Six weeks, then physio."

"Will you be all right?"

"More or less, eventually." Or so they say. "You don't need Peter. You're gifted."

Watson sucks in her bottom lip and wrinkles her forehead vertically, just like she did as a kid, but she doesn't cry. She comes back the next day and leaves a bouquet of daisies in a vase.

I'll never know where she was hiding that day.

We'd exhausted the dinosaurs during previous lunch hours, and knew all the good spots under their bellies and behind their giant plaster limbs. Maybe she was in the insect section, though there weren't a lot of good places to hide there, only glass cases. And I'm fairly sure she was afraid of the tarantulas. Maybe she'd crossed over from Nature to Man and, as I slunk out the huge wooden front doors and back to school in a euphoria of guilt and freedom, to French class and the irresistible pull of loud-laughing cigarette-smoking Sarah N, Watson was crouched in a tepee, or behind a pile of furs. I'll never know. I'll never know how long she stayed hidden, more and more pleased she'd found such an effective hiding place, before she had the first inkling of doubt. The growing suspicion that she was hidden but not sought, and finally the moment of true dismay. She showed up late, weeping, and a protective circle formed around her. The girls moved their heads in turn, to look at me in horror.

But maybe my punishment was for something else, all along. My father begged for mercy from his deathbed, and I refused to see him. Unlike me, he had the use of his hands, and sent letters to everyone he'd wronged — all three ex-wives, all nine children. He must have been lying in a hospital just like I am, now. Immobilized, bored, repentant. And I phoned my sister Kara to laugh. The two of us read his identical letters aloud, and described, hilariously, his wrinkle-free, fake-tanned face, face to face with mortality. But he didn't actually die, as it turned out. The infection cleared, his bones healed, and the procedure was a success. He came to see me the other day; he's three inches taller now, with arms too short for his body.

Naomi K. Lewis

FLEX

NOEL 1

Tuesday

I was not at all grateful for the summer job, which was so low on the hierarchy I had no contract and no computer on my desk. My cubicle was nothing more than a closet for my backpack and sweatshirt (I'd stopped dressing like an official after my first day, when I learned the true nature of my work; I learned by accident that a high-school student had turned down the job before it was offered to me).

On the last Tuesday of July, it was five-thirty alarm clock, quick shower, piece of toast (all done quietly for the sake of my sleeping roommate), and I was biking over the High Level Bridge on my rust-bucket one-speed Canadian Tire bike, trying to avoid other cyclists and pedestrians and to keep my eyes open. Surreal how many people biked and drove around at that hour. By six thirty I was locking the rickety piece of shit to a flimsy tree on 116 Street, hoping someone would steal it; in his driveway, Arnaud was already in his car, waiting for me, travel mug in hand, sporty briefcase on the back seat. At seven, we were up north past the suburbs and entering the government office on the military base.

"You feeling all right, bro?" Arnaud let the heavy door of our squat building swing back in my face. He was dressed as usual in a button-down shirt and khaki slacks, like all the other engineers. "Your eyes are all bloodshot."

"It's kind of early...."

"Trust me." Arnaud was referring to the alleged fact that we were working the system. "If my plan works," he said, "by the end of this week, your mind will be literally blown."

I was his slave as far as time was concerned only because he happened to be Monique's brother, and I was profoundly ungrateful to him for securing me the job, and then, when I noted the lack of bus route that far north, the bike. Never crossed his mind to drive ten minutes out of his way and pick me up, or that his working of the flex hour system would do contractless-me little good. Officially, I was a temporary worker. A temp. A big zero. When I pointed this out, he said, "Stick with me and I'll bring you into the system. You get your week off, and this week, it's like no other week." Although he and Monique were twins, she had almost completely prairified, and he had a much stronger accent. In fact, for two people who'd spent their fetal days naked and squished together, they had amazingly little in common. Nothing, really, besides the giant grey-blue eyes — and in its natural state, Monique's hair was probably the same light brown as her brother's.

That Tuesday (dare I call it fateful), I was in a relatively good mood; there was light at the end of the paper cuts. I'd spent the summer that far emptying a several-hallways-long bookshelf into garbage bags; I went home every day covered in dust. Slightly more complicated than it sounds: I'd emptied every binder into a garbage bag and lain the binder back on the shelf so the paper could be recycled and the binder used again. Almost a month of eight-hour days, and I was almost free. There were one or two other flex-hour aficionados in at seven, but I had two hours of relative silence before the government engineers and city planners and the military goons all drifted in. What this office was for, as far as I could tell, was planning and designing army buildings. A federal government operation out west.

Jeanette arrived at 9:02. I watched her wrench the door open and walk down the middle of the hallway toward me. She was wearing light coloured pants that stopped just below her knees, and a tight blouse.

"Exciting enough for you?" she said.

"Almost done."

"Right on." She bumped my hip with hers as she walked by. "I feel like today's the day," she whispered.

What Jeanette's job was, I didn't know. She was tanned the colour of organic honey, and had long brown-sugar hair in a ponytail and the boobs of a swimsuit model. Whenever I passed her cubicle on the way to the washroom, she had her legs tucked up and her sandals kicked thoughtlessly to one side.

Fateful. That Tuesday was fateful, the outermost slope of a vortex, really, because, first of all, I finished the binders after lunch, and expected something grand to happen, like being laid off or given a desk with a computer on it. Instead, my supervisor, the elusive and mustachioed Roger, pointed me up a windowless side staircase.

"The whole storage attic needs cleaning out," he said. "Jeanette's already up there. She'll tell you what to do. You know Jeanette?"

He put his hand on my back and gave me a little shove.

The cramped storage attic, also windowless, was darker than the stairs and lit with one feeble fluorescent light. I took it in: wall-to-wall-to-wall-to-wall shelves. Shelves and shelves and shelves and shelves of binders. A neat pile of boxes, packed tight with garbage bags, awaited me. In one corner was a desk, and at the desk sat Jeanette, legs untucked and feet flat on the floor so she could lean back. She had her shirt pulled up to just under the boobs, and was peeling thin strips of skin from her flat, reddish brown belly. "Hey, Noel." She looked right at me, but didn't pull the shirt down, just picked the edge of another strip and tugged slowly. She got a pretty big chunk. "Burned," she said. "I was sunbathing on a metal roof."

"I think I'm supposed to throw out all this stuff." I pointed at the binders. Someone had already emptied half a shelf in the corner across from Jeanette, and then, no doubt, had found something better to do, leaving a stack of empty binders and one full garbage bag.

"I know, right," said Jeanette. "Giver."

"What?"

"Give 'er." She pulled her blouse back over her body. The shirt was tight and white, with little pink flowers.

I took the first full binder off the shelf, a dark green, popped it open and gave 'er into the garbage bag. "One thousand binders of paper on the wall," I sang, "One thousand binders of paper. Take one down, empty it out...."

Jeanette, I saw, was going through the contents of office-supply boxes, putting pens and paperclips and paper in piles and marking them on a list. I got through about ten more binders before I sang another verse. "Nine hundred and ninety binders of paper on the wall, nine hundred and ninety binders of paper...."

"Shit balls," said Jeanette. "You keep singing that, you gonna get what's coming to you."

"What's coming to me?"

"Wouldn't you like to know."

Meanwhile, Monique's summer was going just great. She was taking symbolic logic and existentialism so she could take fewer courses during the year and still finish her philosophy degree on time, and she had a job at a comic book and CD store. She claimed her parents looked down on her because her twin brother was already an engineer with an income, but I was the one they'd pressured into dumping binders for a living, not her.

Arnaud and I left work at three and got to his place at three-thirty. He rented an apartment in an old mansion; he'd never invited me inside. Monique was getting off work by four, so I biked down Jasper Ave. to D-Side, found a feeble tree and wrestled a bit with my bike lock, then gave up and left the piece of crap untethered. Inside the store, there were no customers. Monique stood in the middle of the floor and her boss stood in front of the cash. Both faced the door squarely, feet apart, eyes full of panic. Monique had told me business was bad. So bad, she'd confided, Jeff wasn't even paying himself anymore. He was afraid the store would go under. Monique's face was stark white in contrast with her turquoise hair. Her feet were bare, and her toenails were sparkly blue. Jeff's fingernails were the same colour.

"Ready to go?" I said.

Monique's eyes opened wide, and she shook herself like she'd forgotten where she was. "Just a minute." She disappeared into the back room.

"What's going on, Jeff?" I said.

Despite his mountainous build, he clasped his hands like a grandmother and leaned away from me as if I were a known and dangerous criminal. "Actually, man," he said, "I go by Field, now."

"Field? Like, a meadow?"

"More like an energy field...." He blinked hard. A black scarf decorated with yellow skulls was fluffed up and tucked around his neck, despite the heat. "This situation is a toxic shock to my system," he said. "I feel like the universe is trying to spit me out right now, and I deserve it."

"I'm sure it's not. You don't. I mean, it's just like this sometimes, right?"

He nodded slowly. "It's really amazing that you'd say that."

Monique reappeared with her black motorcycle boots on. "I need to go with Noel now."

Jeff held his breath for a few seconds before he said, "I totally agree."

"Listen," said Monique, as we stepped onto the sidewalk. "Oh, Noel. I —"

"Do you start to feel insane, just being around that guy? I do. I've had this crazy feeling all day today, actually, like something important's happening just beyond my line of vision."

"Listen."

"You know that feeling, when you put your keys down, and then you go to pick them up, and they're *gone*, and you're like, am I losing it, or what? And then you can't find them *anywhere*?"

"I'm trying to —"

"Wait a second. What the fuck! My bike. My bike is gone." I ran to the tree and shook it, as if the piece of junk might fall from the pathetic branches. "This is the day I'm having," I yelled.

We'd walked the four blocks to 109 Street and turned toward the High Level Bridge.

"What's so funny?" She glared at me.

"Field Onion. The dude named himself Field Onion. Field Onion!"

"The point is," said Monique, "he's taking his name back. Embracing it."

"Anything else he's been embracing lately, that I should know about?"

"What, you're ready to stop talking about the ten-dollar bike, now?" Monique stopped, and I sensed she was about to do this thing where she ran down the sidewalk as fast she could, forcing me to chase her down and catch her. I put my arms around her.

"Did you let Jeff Onion paint your toenails?"

"You already know the answer to that question, Noel."

"What do you like about that guy?"

"Oh, come on." She tried to pull away, but I held on, my arms around her back pinning her against me, face to face.

"No, I mean. You like him, right? You like his company. But what do you like *about* him? I'm just curious."

"Well, he's —"

"Smart? Interesting?"

"Hold on, okay. If you interrupt before I even —"

"Okay, yeah. Yeah?"

"Some people, you can say exactly why you like them. Like make a list of attractive traits. Positive influences they have over your life, let's say."

"Right."

"Smart, for instance." She touched my forehead just for a second, pushing my hair back. "Cute. Smart. Good in bed. Creative."

"Okay...." I pulled back. "And Jeff?"

Monique sighed. "Can you just let go of me, please? I feel weird. Other people. There's just something about them."

"Something about Jeff Onion..."

"Something — aesthetically pleasing? Like, remember when Professor Meyer talked about music? How it just goes into you and transforms you, unmediated by reason?"

Monique and I had met in that philosophy of art class, almost a year before. Remembering her hand on my thigh in the dim slideshow light made my crotch and my tear ducts throb in unison.

"It's like — like eating an oyster," said Monique. "Can you describe what's good about it?"

"I've never eaten an oyster."

"No, you can't. But, mmm, it's delicious."

I tightened my fists. "We're vegetarian."

"Yeah, but I wasn't always, and yum. Divine." Divine crustaceans, divine blue-nailed Jeff, divine sunburned girls on sunbaked roofs.

I pointed at the bridge. "I have to go home." She lived on the north side, not far from her brother.

"Do you want to talk," she said, "or what?"

"I have to get some drawing done. I want to finish those last pages you wrote. That's what's important. Our relationship. Our book. And I'm going to bed at like eight. Your brother wants to go in for four."

"Oh, Noel. The drawing? Four o'clock?"

"I love you, Monique."

"Oh, Noel. Stop it. *Please*. What you trying to do? Four o'clock?"

"In the morning."

"To *work*?"

"Because then we can leave at noon, and we get the whole afternoon. He has this plan, all charted out."

"That's insane. You won't get the whole afternoon. You'll just end up sleeping."

"Tell Arnaud."

"Well," she said. "When can we talk?"

"Ask your brother. He owns me, remember?"

I drew until six, then ate a can of mushroom soup and went to bed. I dreamed of Jeanette, with the bra and the porn-star breasts and the long tissue-paper skin strips. We were on a metal roof, and all the binders were up there too, and I was letting her have it against the shelves, grabbing her ponytail for extra leverage.

"Give 'er Noel," she said. "Oh yeah, give 'er."

I wasn't turned off by the skin sloughing off and flying around us like streamers, but when she said that, I laughed. Jeanette grabbed my throat and pushed me backwards. My garbage bags tipped as I hit the ground, and she stood over me, her bare foot on my chest as my recyclable paper poured off the roof like a waterfall.

Wednesday

Arnaud was dangerously obsessed with the flexible-hour system. He was obsessed with it like a gambler in a diaper is obsessed with the slots. He had explained it to me many times: eight hours must be worked out of every twelve. Any eight. Extra hours counted toward vacation time or overtime, but not both. A riddle, he said. Each week was a Rubik's week, and he would find a way to shuffle the hours until time and dollars were wrested from each other's grip and stood in straight rows and columns, lined up for the taking.

I set my alarm for two-thirty, but woke up before it even went off, to the sound of someone crashing around downstairs. My roommate, Patrick, had spent his high school years Christian and sober, and as a result was spending his undergrad years drunk and high. Sure enough, his bedroom door was wide open with no one inside.

"Patrick?" I said. As I started down the stairs, I heard a smash.

In the kitchen, I stepped on something sharp, swore, and turned on the light. Monique's green mug, the big one with the daisy, lay broken on the floor. I picked up the handle.

I looked in the living room, and there was one of Patrick's friends passed out on the couch, the blanket pulled right over his head.

"Hey, asshole," I said. "That was my girlfriend's mug." I wanted to rip the blanket off him and explain what he'd destroyed. The one thing of Monique's that she kept at my house, the only proof she was coming back.

The guy didn't move.

"I don't have time for this. I have to get ready for *work*."

I checked for an unconscious Patrick on the porch. Door unlocked, but no roommate. Instead, leaning against the wall like the worst kind of miracle, was my bike. I stepped outside and touched it, then just stared at it for a while. Definitely my despised travesty of a bicycle. Must have been Patrick, I decided. Or some other joker. They saw the piece of junk outside D-Side, and took it, and then brought it here, just to make me paranoid. I looked around, but it was the middle of the night and there was no one. "I'm not in the mood for this," I said out loud, just in case.

I took a shower — the bathroom smelled distinctly of puke — then staggered around for a while, getting dressed. I pulled on my jeans and a clean T-shirt, and the same blue sweatshirt I always wore to work. At 3:35, I dumped the bike in front of Arnaud's building and got in his car.

He smelled like hair gel, and his coffee made my stomach clench. "You should really get a bike light," he said. After a while, he added, "I'm getting an Egg McMuffin. Want one?"

"No meat," I said.

Normally, I didn't buy things from exploitative corporations, but something about the time, about being out in the sprawling suburbs in the middle of the night, told me all bets were off. Besides, Arnaud paid for it.

The storage attic was exactly the same at four in morning as in the middle of the day: the kind of place where spiders make themselves at home. One of Jeanette's office supply boxes had been knocked off her desk and the contents strewn across the floor. I considered picking it up for her, but decided it wasn't my problem. There was a shitload more binders emptied than I remembered doing. The second wall was done, but I knew I'd only gotten halfway through it. I counted the full garbage bags a couple of times, and there were way too many. I was obviously going insane, just as Arnaud wanted me to. I felt like someone was following me around, nudging things out of place. One of the first signs of psychosis.

Jeanette arrived right on schedule, at nine.

"Hot enough for you?" She leaned against her desk and took off her cardigan. Underneath was a tight black tank top that didn't quite meet the tops of her camouflage-green slacks.

"My eyes ache," I said.

"My sunburn's better today," she said, starting to pick up the scattered office supplies around her desk. "It's like something came along and healed me."

"Sorry about your box. I mean, that I didn't clean it up."

"Ha," said Jeanette. She got to work picking up the pens and paperclips and recataloguing them. I got into my rhythm: open binder, open rings, dump paper, snap rings closed, close binder, stack binder. Open click dump click snap stack open click dump click snap stack.

"So," said Jeanette. "Is this job fun enough for you, or what?"

"This job is a joke. My girlfriend's family tricked me into taking it. And get this — I already had a job for the summer, working at a diner. Part time, so I had time for my own stuff."

"What stuff was that?" Jeanette kneeled to collect some pens under the desk.

"I'm working on a graphic novel."

"Oh, yeah?" On her hands and knees, now, she definitely thrust her ass noticeably in my direction. "How graphic is it?" she said. "Need a model?"

"No, not like that… Like, a comic book, only serious."

"Oh." Pens in hand, she eased into some kind of cross-legged yoga pose on the floor, facing me. "What's it about?"

"Retelling of Dostoevsky's *Notes from the Underground*. He's this Russian writer and —"

"Yeah," said Jeanette. "I'm not actually retarded."

"It's called *Another Ungrateful Biped*. Our book. Because that's how the Underground Man defines a human — a creature that walks on two legs and is ungrateful."

"Gawd," said Jeanette.

"My girlfriend's doing most of the writing, I'm illustrating it. She works at a comic book store."

"Was the book her idea?"

"Initially, actually, yes."

"Uh huh. Let me tell you something, Noel. I may not be your girlfriend, and I may not want to be, but this chick is a one hundred percent downer."

I finished the third shelf-wall just before noon. My brain felt like it had been wrung like a sponge. The evil Arnaud was obviously fucking with my circadian rhythm and depriving me of natural light as some part of a top-secret military experiment.

"Would you date a guy with sparkly blue nail polish?" I asked Jeannette. "I mean, as a girl — what would a girl see in that?"

She didn't bother to answer.

"Hey," I said. "Do you feel emotions?"

"What? Yes...." She stopped and faced me.

"What do you like?"

"You seem to know."

"Seriously. I mean, what do you like. Doing."

"Like, hobbies?"

"What's the last thing where you said to yourself, hey, yeah, I like this?"

Jeanette thought about it. "Corn. Yeah. It's peaches and cream season. My favourite corn. Barbequed."

"You have a barbeque?"

"On my roof."

"Where you sunbathe."

"Oh, right, yeah. Sunbathing. I love sunbathing."

"Yes...."

"Weekends. Friends. Those drinks with the vodka — the hard lemonade. I like partying, nothing hardcore, just low key. Having a good time. The stuff everybody likes."

I dropped a binder into the recycling bin and didn't bother fishing it out, just dumped another few hundred pages on top of it. Then the guilt caught up with me, and I leaned over, pushing pages out of the way. "Dang!" I said. "Ungodly paper cuts."

"Why do you always talk like someone else?" said Jeanette.

"*What*?"

"Nothing, just saying."

"Just saying...."

"Nothing. It's just. Your act. The way you talk, the music you listen to." Then Jeanette's brain skipped like a kicked Discman back to a previous track. "Blue nail polish?" she said. "I may not be your girlfriend, but trust me. What you're needing is *less* of that kind of thing, not more."

Wasn't her fault she didn't get me. Just a hick with a pickup truck full of corncobs and nothing better to do than work for weekends of scorching her objectified flesh under a carcinogenic sun.

I started down the stairs, and Jeanette followed.

"Okay, tell me this," she called after me. "If a guy and a girl had really hot sex one day — hot, badass, sucking, fucking-every-hole sex, then why would that guy choose not to repeat the experience?"

"I don't know...."

"Well, you have to *know*. I mean, you must have some idea why."

"I guess, maybe, does the guy have some reason to feel guilty?"

"Right."

"Does he?"

"Right, yeah. I get it."

"Okay, so. Bye, Jeanette. I'm going home to draw the Underground Man."

"It's really too bad, though," said Jeanette. "If the girl really didn't want any strings anyway, and was just craving the guy's cock."

"Yeah. I have to agree with you there."

"Well, shit," said Jeanette, but she smiled as though what I'd said made her feel a lot better.

"I need you back at my place at eleven-thirty tonight," said the malevolent Arnaud, when we were halfway home. "We're starting work at midnight."

"No."

"Hey," he yelled, and waved frantically out his side window as a Jeep raced past us in the other direction. "Yes! YES! Sweet Jesus, yes!" The Jeep's horn honked as it disappeared into a cloud of dust.

"Who was that?"

He laughed like a maniac. "Who was that? *Who was that?* That was the face of destiny, my friend. The face of destiny! I could kiss you right now. I swear to God, I want to grab your face and lick it. Nooel!"

"I don't get it."

He just grinned to himself until he got to his place, then said, "I love you, man. You're the most beautiful thing I ever laid my eyes on, and I'll see you at eleven-thirty."

There wasn't much point staying awake. I checked my phone messages and there was something from the bank saying my credit card had been maxed out overseas. "We've deactivated your card and await your direction," the voice said. Sure enough, my back-up card, that I kept at the back of my wallet and rarely used, was missing. I got in bed and squeezed my skull and tried to think, but it didn't work, so I set my alarm clock for ten and went to sleep.

Thursday

It was nine in the morning, and we were done for the day. As we pulled out of the parking lot, I saw Jeanette's pickup truck pulling in. I waved at her, but she didn't see me.

"We're almost there, man," said Arnaud. "Almost there. I'll pick you up at ten tonight, then we work till seven in the morning."

"Jesus."

"And then...."

"And then?"

"Trust me. You won't believe it."

"We get the day off?"

"This is why I'm the engineer and you're the — whatever you are. Use your imagination. Think outside the box. After our next shift, that's when the magic happens."

"Maybe I'll just stay home."

"No, no. Just do this one last shift. And it'll be worth it. I promise."

"Can you just explain–"

"One more shift. And then you'll see."

So I slept all day and was back at Arnaud's at nine thirty, at work by ten, and when I got to work, my progress seemed to have doubled again. The first full binder on the shelf was red, with a black "N" written on it with marker. Had Jeanette been doing my work for me? The girl was crazy. I obviously wasn't even her type, but she looked at me like she wanted to eat me. A girl like Jeanette. I'd never even imagined what it would be like with a girl like Jeanette. At least, I'd never imagined I'd ever find out.

I worked all night, alone,

Friday

and at some point, I emptied my last binder into the garbage. On Monday, they'd have to find something else for me to do, or fire me. Thank God — it was the end.

NOEL2

The phone. I'd never been so fast asleep in my life; the ringing dragged me from a deep dark nail-studded pit.

"Noel?" Only one person pronounced my name that way, in two syllables, the French word for *Christmas*.

"Who is this?" I said, anyway. I'd been dreaming about a tunnel, about a drive and then a bike ride. The High Level Bridge stretching like an elastic to the length of the North Saskatchewan River.

"*Mon ami*! Now we have truly done it, no?"

"Arnaud?"

"Of course. You're very tired, I know. I know."

"I'm going back to sleep now, okay?"

"It's time to get up. I'm on my way over. Get up, get dressed, have a cup of coffee. Trust me. I have all the materials for you, now." He hung up.

It was eight-thirty. In the morning. Only half an hour had passed since I'd come home. Or was it twenty-four-and-a-half hours? Either option was equally fucked, and when I noticed how hungry I was, I suspected the second. I pulled on some jeans and a plaid shirt, splashed some water on my face and sat on the sofa in a state of profound disorientation until the doorbell rang.

"Did you have your coffee?" Arnaud was grinning like the fiend that he was, his eyes staring out of his head like a hungry reptile's. He hadn't shaved and his skin didn't look too healthy, either.

"No...."

"That's what I thought." He handed me a cup of Tim Hortons. "Rise and shine. Time for work. I know you feel like ass now, but you'll feel better than ever in just a few."

"You're fucked," I said. "I quit, okay? And it's Saturday! I finished the binders last night, and now I quit."

"Last night," said Arnaud. "Last night!"

"What fucking day is it, man?" I couldn't seem to stop swearing.

"It worked," said Arnaud. "*It worked*. What day is it? *What day is it*?"

"What. Day. Is. It."

"Okay, wait for it. It's — Thursday."

I shook my head. "You're saying I slept for a week?"

"No. I told you. The flex hour system — I worked it. We turned around, and now we're facing the other way."

"I don't get it."

"It's Thursday *again*."

Thursday

"I'm Noel2?" I said.

"Ah," said Arnaud. "Drink that caffeine, would you? Listen close. You became Noel2 as midnight on Friday became midnight on Thursday, again. You're lucky you slept though it." He pointed at the "Tips" sheet he'd made up for me. "Try to be asleep between eleven and one at night this week. I think it's hard on the system. The jump-back. That's why you slept so long. I mean, though, we'll have to be awake at midnight on Tuesday, when it becomes Monday, and then we head straight for the airport. There's no helping that. Now, look at the chart. Look at it."

Arnaud had made up a chart with a row for each workday, and columns labeled *Noel1*, *Noel2* and *Noel3*; he had another with an equal number of *Arnaud*s.

"Now, here I've tracked all the work-related movement of Noel1. You add in stuff I don't know about. And make sure you write down everything you do in the Noel2 column. The point is, avoid home, work and anywhere else when Noel1 is there. That's super important. Also, make sure you don't run into Arnaud1. We don't need that kind confusion. Try to avoid people, period. Don't answer your phone. This week, man, we got to make ourselves scarce."

I nodded. I was pretty sure I was still dreaming.

"Look, please, where I am pointing. I've written down what time we're going to work today. Wednesday. Tuesday. Monday. We work the hours we missed the last time through the week, well only for three days because the Friday and Monday are the days we use as springs, and you see? Three extra days' worth of hours. *Then* we live the week forwards again. That's when you're Noel3." He pointed to the Noel3 column, which had the single word *PARTY!!* typed carefully down its length. "What you do for that week is, you leave town. Go to an all-inclusive somewhere, right? This is the dream. Noel1 and Noel2 are back here in Deadmonton doing all the work, and Noel3 with the overtime pay is living the easy life."

"You did this for a week's vacation?"

Arnaud ignored this. "Is that what you're wearing to work today?"

"I don't know where I put my clothes last night...."

"Of course," Arnaud sighed. "Noel1 is wearing them. You'll catch on." He looked at his watch. "We have to go. Noel1 will be home any time now. It's super important that you don't cross paths with him. *Super important.*" He shoved my copies of the chart and tips sheet into my hand. My keys and wallet were gone, so I took two twenties from the stash in my underwear drawer and went outside.

"What's this?" I said.

"My new ride. Like it? It's a rental."

"A Jeep? But where's your car?" As soon as I asked, I knew the answer. "Arnaud1 has it."

"Correct! You're not as dumb as you look, eh?"

The sun was extra bright, and my ears ached. I fished my sunglasses out of my backpack and put them on. Arnaud turned on the radio. "Listen for the date," he told me. But I didn't need proof. It was Thursday. I knew it like I knew a triangle had three sides. The air, the sidewalks, the sky were all Thursday all over again.

"This makes no sense." I looked at my chart. "This makes zero sense."

"Tell that to Noel3."

"I can't wait to tell Monique about this," I said. "She loves time travel. She would give anything to time travel."

"You can't tell her."

"Why not?"

"One, because she'd tell our parents, and they'd be pissed. Two, because chicks can't time travel, and it's better if they don't know about it, either."

"What? Why?"

"I don't know. They just can't do it. Have you ever seen a time travel movie where the chick time travels? Think about it. Terminator goes back, Linda Hamilton stays put. Bruce Willis in *12 Monkeys* goes back. Brown-haired chick stays put. There's always some babe *waiting* for the time traveller, but it's the dude that does the travelling."

"What about the girlfriend in *Back to the Future*?"

"*Ah, oui*, perfect example. In Part Two, Doc and Marty take Jennifer to the future. Huge mistake. She throws the fit and they have to knock her out and leave her on the porch."

"Yeah...."

"Before she causes some paradoxical shit."

We got to work at ten. I went to the washroom and examined my face in the mirror. My skin was rough and grey, just like Arnaud's, and my eyes had the same too-white glare.

When I stepped back into the hallway, there was Roger, my supervisor.

"You," he said. "Do you ever stop working?"

"I guess not. Hey, I finished the binders up there. I was just wondering —"

"I don't think so," he said. "I just took a look. I think you forgot a wall."

I shook my head. Then froze. I'd finished the binders on Friday morning. Now it was Thursday morning.

"You don't look so good," said Roger. "Are you getting enough sleep? By the way, Jeanette asked to work down here today, so you'll be on your own."

I walked up the stairs slowly, almost afraid of what I'd see when I reached the top. Sure enough, all my last shift's work, plus a whole lot more, sat waiting for me. On Jeanette's desk was a folded page with my name across it.

Noel, it said. *I can't be in the same room with you. I'm sorry about your girlfriend, but I have feelings, too.* Her handwriting was long and thin, the letters reaching high before looping back down. I sat and stared at the wall of binders for a full half hour before I moved. Sometime in the afternoon, I bought a vending machine sandwich for lunch and ate in the parking lot, then emptied, emptied, emptied. Just before six, I reached a bright red binder, the only one on the shelf. I opened it, and clicked the metal rings open. I closed them again. I picked up a black marker from the desk and wrote an "N" on the cover. *Don't sleep tonight,* I wrote on the first page. I ripped it out and tossed it. *Go home right now!!* I wrote on the next one. *Just call a cab and go home, before it's too late. Noel, I'm talking to YOU.* I put the binder back on the shelf, then pulled it off again and opened it. My note had smudged illegibly across the paper.

I met Arnaud at the car.

"I can't take you home," he said. "Noel1's there until nine. Where do you want to go?"

"Where are you going?"

"Home. Arnaud1's out for a drive. I planned for this, right?"

I got him to drop me off at the bridge, and walked the rest of the way to the university. Monique's logic class got out at seven, so I had a coffee in the HUB mall, then wandered the Humanities building looking for her classroom, which I'd only seen once before. Third floor; through the door, I could see all the logic symbols written across the board. Almost everyone was failing the class, Monique had told me. Even the computer geeks. She, of course, was acing it. I waited out in the hallway, sitting against the lockers. Screw Arnaud's tip sheet. I was going to tell her. I was going to tell her everything, and she was going to save me, using logic and existentialism.

Right on the stroke of the hour, the professor opened the door and came out, leaving the students to gather their things. He was small and thin with a long white beard and blue Converse sneakers.

Logic professor.

"Excuse me," I said, standing.

His expression reminded me of how Jeff had stared at me in his store, days ago. He nodded, leaning slightly away from me, like I might blow.

"May I ask you a question?" I said.

"Are you the young man who's been phoning me?"

"No — I've never phoned you — I've never talked to you before in my life."

"Yes, you have. "

"No, I —"

"You don't look well." He took a slow step closer to me, gentle so as not to alarm me, and peered up into my face. "You've contracted something abroad; you did the right thing coming home. You need a doctor."

"I haven't been...."

"This is not a matter of logic, I'm afraid. What you've got on your hands is a medical problem."

"Please, just tell me one thing."

"I already answered your question. Time runs in one direction only, and travelling into the past is logically impossible for a number of indisputable reasons. What will be is not yet determined, but what will be *will* always have been going to be. Now, as for your financial problems, you did seem to have made a big mistake, and I'm relieved to see you sorted it out and got yourself back to Canada."

"What? What mistake? Please — I need to know —"

"Young man. I'm not a mad professor from a movie. I can't ease your anxiety. And I don't want to have to point out that you're stalking me. Please tell me you'll see a doctor."

"Wait," I yelled. "Where was I when I called? Where was I when I called? What financial problems? What huge mistake did I make? *What huge mistake?* You bastard! Tell me!"

"Noel?" Monique was wearing her overall dress with the big splotches of colour. Her blue Converse shoes matched the professor's shoes and Jeff's nails, and her hair and her eyes, and Arnaud's eyes. I threw my arms around her, mashing her face into my collarbone, and she, hands on my arms, wriggled free.

"What's his name?" I pointed down the hall.

"Professor Ball? Were you yelling at him? Aren't you supposed to be working tonight?" She didn't look angry or embarrassed despite all her classmates milling around; she just seemed worried and sad.

"I need to talk to you." I clung to her dress.

"I have to meet my existentialism group in exactly ten minutes. I'll call you later, okay? Or in the morning? What time are you going to work?"

"No. Don't. Don't call me, please." Who knows which of us would answer. "You know whose fault all this is, right?"

"I know whose fault you think it is. Look, you can't blame him. I should have told you a long time ago. It's just that we have a lot in common; we're both twins, and. Me and Field, we —"

"Field? *Field Onion?*"

"Shh. Who were you going to blame, then? Me, I suppose?"

"That hadn't occurred to me, but now that you mention it…"

"Noel."

"*Jeff Onion?*"

"Why are you playing dumb? I know you saw us. I saw you looking through the window."

"The window? You saw me? Window?"

"You know I did. *Oh*," she wrung her hands. "I didn't mean this to happen. Field feels so bad. This is so bad. This is so not me…. Please, please stop looking so freaked out."

"But. Our plans to go to Scotland. Our book…."

"Oh, Noel. The book. It was my idea, and. It takes you days to draw a single frame."

"It doesn't take me *days*."

"And the characters look different in each one."

"You know I'm improving."

"Field's illustrating *Another Ungrateful Biped*. I'm sorry. I'm sorry; it's just he sees my vision; he brings it light, and. Noel?"

When I got home, Patrick was in his room, screwing some girl. I sat on the sofa and listened, then locked myself in the bathroom to rub one out. I felt a tiny bit better after that, and worse at the same time. I ate some pizza from the fridge and wished I'd never convinced Monique to take that Russian literature course with me. She wouldn't even have known about the Underground Man if I hadn't. Eventually Patrick and the girl went out, and I sat on the sofa again in the dark.

Wednesday

I made it into the bathroom just in time to puke in the toilet. My head was throbbing, and I lay on the floor for a while, wondering if I was going to live. I'd eaten bad lobster once, and that had felt better than this. I curled into a ball and tried to remember. I'd been sitting on the sofa, and then everything had stretched out like gum, slower and slower. I remembered green numbers of the digital clock stretching thinner and thinner.

I put my hand on the toilet seat and pulled myself upright, slowly. I reached for the handle and flushed. I grabbed the seat again and it crashed down. The sound hit my head like a mallet; if I could have vomited again, I would have. Water. I needed water. I fell against the wall twice on my way to the kitchen. 2:20, the clock said. It was dark out. 2:20 in the morning. Without turning on the light, I opened the cupboard and felt for a cup, filled it from the tap and drank. Breathed. Drank and breathed.

Someone was moving around upstairs. "Patrick?" a voice said.

The mug fell out of my hand and smashed on the floor. My body was stabbed in a million places by a million invisible knives. I staggered into the living room and fell onto the couch, pulled the blanket over my head. When Monique and I were first dating, she'd told me that she was always afraid to phone her own house. "I have this fear that someone will answer," she'd told me, "and that I'll realize it's me. Can you imagine anything more horrifying?"

I heard him say something in the kitchen, and then come towards me.

"Hey, asshole," he said. "That was my girlfriend's mug."

I didn't move. I'd never realized my voice was so annoying. I vowed to stop swearing. It sounded terrible.

"I don't have time for this," he said. "I have to get ready for *work*."

I heard him fumbling around at the front door, then out on the porch. He left the door open, and breeze came through the apartment. "I'm not the mood for this," he said. He shut the door again, went back upstairs, came back down, and finally got in the shower.

I fought to think through the pain. Could I warn him? Could I tell him the sinister Arnaud's plan, and stop it all in its tracks? Arnaud was definitely opposed to any such effort, but I had a feeling he'd picked up most of his rules from his time traveller's bible, *Back to the Future*. I approached the bathroom door, and the headache intensified. A wave of nausea came over me, but I forced myself to keep going. When I put my hand on the door, the pain in my head swelled to such intensity that I staggered backwards to the staircase, clutching my skull.

My wallet was sitting there on the stairs. Money. I needed money. I found my backup credit card behind the others and put it in my pocket, then went back to the couch, pulled the blanket over my head, and fell into a coma-like sleep.

Arnaud phoned me before eleven and ordered me awake. He was on his way to pick me up. Noel1 had already left the bike outside his place, and the success of his plan was making him oddly generous.

"Are you sure we'll start going forwards again at the end of the week?" I said, after his customary slap on the shoulder.

"Brother. Yes. I am sure. Did I not show you the charts?"

"I didn't completely understand the charts."

"Have you been sure to avoid Noel1? To sleep between eleven at night and one in the morning?"

I balled my fists into my sleeves. I nodded, barely.

"Okay, well let me put this in a simplified way, let's say. The same mechanism that sent us backwards? It will send us forwards again. This week is like a tube with springs on both ends, okay? You can't go through the spring; you can only bounce off it. You see this?"

"Kind of."

"I'll be fucked if I'm going to be fucked out of my two-week vacay. You think I'd set up some shit that would fuck me out of my vacay?"

"No."

"Hell, no."

"But how do you know we won't bounce back again once we reach the end of the week a second time?"

"Eh?"

"And create a, you know, Noel4 and Arnaud4?"

"What? Yuletide, my brother, we won't be at *work*."

"No."

"The system is the springboard for the springs."

"The flex hour system."

"Right. It's like *Back to the Future*. The flex capacitor."

"That was a *flux* capacitor."

"Yeah — sure. It's just an analogy. Okay, think of it this way. Outside the flex-hour system, hours are not flex, are they? They are *in*flex. Cancun," howled Arnaud. "Girls gone freakin' wild. Arnaud3's gonna be getting some pussy. *Is* getting some pussy. Yeah. Okay, think of it this way. If there were infinite Noels and Arnauds running up and down this week like a zipper, don't you think we'd have noticed? All those Noels and Arnauds spending our money and fucking our girlfriends?"

"That's true."

Then we both remembered that my girlfriend was Monique and looked away from each other, and then I remembered that Monique wasn't my girlfriend anymore; at least, I was pretty sure she wasn't. And that severed my obligations to Arnaud.

"Wait a second," I said. "That looks like your car." I looked out my side window as the grey Honda Civic passed us. Arnaud1 was at wheel, waving at me like a psycho. I caught a glimpse of the figure beside him. I screamed.

"Right on time!" said Arnaud2, punching the wheel and honking the horn. "What a ride. Woo!" He didn't seem to mind that we'd just broken his number one rule.

It was ten past noon when we turned onto the rural route to the base.

"What would happen if I just stopped coming to work?" I said.

"I wouldn't try it," said Arnaud.

Jeanette came back from lunch half an hour after I started emptying the binders halfway down the second shelf.

"What are you doing?" she said. "I thought you went home. And you changed again?"

"One thousand binders of paper on the wall," I sang, "one thousand binders of paper. Take them all down, put two thirds of them back...."

She stood close to me. Too close. "Why'd you come back, Noel?"

"It's Arnaud," I said. "He's got this thing with the flex hours."

She went to her desk and sat down, kicked off the sandals. "Arnaud Bontemps? Your girlfriend's his sister, right?"

"Wrong. We broke up."

"What — when?"

"Yesterday. Tomorrow. Whether it happened or it's just about to happen, it's done."

Jeanette looked like she was about to cry. "Why?" she whispered.

"Cheating. Okay? Cheating at work."

"Oh my God. I'm sorry. I. What do you want me to do?"

"It's not your problem. Let's just do our jobs."

"Look," she said. "At least a bit, it is my problem. I feel responsible."

"Are you delusional? Trust me. You're not responsible."

"Go to hell," said Jeanette.

We left work at nine that night, and since Noel1 would be sleeping until five-thirty, Arnaud dropped me off at a hotel downtown. When I used the credit card to pay, I felt guilty, like a thief, like nothing I touched was my own.

Tuesday

I woke up late and ordered room service. I knew it was my own credit card I was using, but somehow I couldn't convince myself of it, couldn't shake the feeling I was living it up on someone else's dime. I ate my eggs in bed, and studied the chart. I made a few additions to the Noel2 column, in case I wanted to remember, later. According to the chart, Noel1 was working until three, and I was starting at five. That gave me a few hours of sweet freedom. I stretched out for a few hours and watched TV, then took a long shower. I washed my hair twice and scrubbed my face. I could feel pimples starting under my skin and wished I'd bought some acne wash. I turned my underwear inside out and put my clothes back on. I'd have to go home and steal a clean shirt while Noel1 was still out.

I took my time brushing my teeth with a hotel toothbrush and made my way downstairs to settle up. I checked the clock in the foyer as I settled up. It was already after three. I'd wasted the whole day. It felt great. Then it hit me.

I booted it down seven blocks down Jasper, and stopped in front of D-Side. I could see in the window, but there didn't seem to be anyone there. I walked around the block and found the alley between the stores. Monique loved alleys for some reason, always wanted to walk home through them, trying to see in people's back windows. The alley behind D-Side was dusty and full of potholes. All the business owners just dumped garbage back there.

Jeff had gotten someone to spray-paint "D-Side" across the back of his store, graffiti style, so I had no trouble figuring out which one it was. The door was slightly ajar, and I heard a laugh from inside. Monique's laugh. There was a small window high on the wall, too high for me to reach, so I dragged a rickety, abandoned desk chair over from beside a dumpster a few feet away. I hoisted myself up. And there was Monique on an old grey sofa, with Field fucking Onion kneeling, bending over her foot, which he held in both hands. I pressed my face against the glass. Jeff leaned forward and Monique put her leg over his shoulder. She had little balls of cotton between her toes. Jeff was kissing the inside of her thigh. I slammed my fist on the glass, and Jeff jumped back. He and Monique both looked right at me. Monique jumped to her feet, eyes wide. I stepped off the chair and sat in the dirt.

Even though I'd known what was coming, it still hurt just as much; that was the weird thing. I wiped the tears across my face and breathed hard. I stood up and kicked the wall, paced the alley, and walked around the block back to the sidewalk, not sure what to do next. I looked in the front window of D-Side again. There was Jeff, facing the door and talking to someone beyond my line of vision. Monique stepped into the room, her newly painted toenails now safely tucked away in her motorcycle boots. *Shit.*

I turned to run, and there was my bike, leaning against a tree, unlocked. I grabbed it and took off down the street as fast as I could, toward Arnaud's.

I went up to the storage attic at five. The first wall of binders wasn't even finished, and Jeanette sat in the roller chair, legs tucked under her. She was in the khaki capris, and her white flowered blouse was tucked up under her bra. She was peeling skin; she looked up and smiled.

"Still here?" I said.

"Just about to leave. You're back? Why'd you change your clothes? Are you okay? You look kind of...." I sat on the desk on front of her; she motioned to pull her shirt down, but I grabbed her wrist.

"Can I pull one?" I said.

Jeanette gave me a long look. She didn't say, *give 'er*. She said, "Sure."

I sat on the edge of the desk and looked down at her.

"Is this what you came back for?" She unbuttoned her blouse.

SWEAR IT

"Every now and then," said Mia, "usually late at night, I wonder how I ended up here."

"Aha," said Hayato. "Ha. On occasion."

"Exactly. Now you do one."

"Every now and then...." He leaned back, mouth open. "Ahm...." His head snapped forward again, long bangs falling into his eyes. "I sleep through the night and the day, and the next night."

"Yeah."

"I'm not joking. I do that."

"So tired, huh?"

"Sometimes so tired. I do it on occasion. Every now and then."

Mia tutored Hayato in a private room in the university library so they wouldn't disturb people studying. She'd met him through her roommate, who was also Japanese and knew him from the foreign students' centre; the roommate had said Hayato's English was good, but that he was an aspiring translator, and needed help with idiom.

Every time they met that winter, Mia stood outside the library doors at the allotted time, and ten or fifteen minutes later, Hayato came shuffling up the slope draped in a huge jacket and speed-smoking a cigarette, his shaggy hair parted haphazardly with the thick bangs pushed to either side. He walked bent almost double so he wouldn't slip backwards on the ice — the town was built on a series of steep hills with the university on the most dramatic one. Almost a foot shorter than Mia, he seemed neither young nor particularly old, but simultaneously round-faced and haggard.

"I'm sorry," he'd say, smiling widely. "So sorry. Mornings are my Achilles' heel. Yes?"

"Yes — good — Achilles' heel. Mine, too."

They usually met at noon.

Hayato was a quick student and paid Mia at the end of each lesson, in cash. After a few months, he thanked her, and she didn't hear from him again for over two years.

In the small city and at the smaller university, Mia hadn't seen Hayato around. She didn't know he was still in town until she received his email near the end of June.

"Listen to this." She read from her computer screen, "*I need to talk to you about something. Please meet me for coffee.*" Steve was on the sofa behind her, waiting for his bagel to toast. "Weird," she said. "What do you think he wants?"

The toaster oven pinged, and Steve disappeared into the kitchen. She called after him, "*Meet me tomorrow*, he says. *Mister Tea. Noon.*"

Steve walked past her, heading back to his office with the cheddar-covered bagel. No plate. Mia averted her eyes from the menacing cascade of falling crumbs, promising herself she'd sweep them up later. In theory, Steve had the second bedroom as his office because he was more introverted than she was, but she'd agreed to set up her desk in the living room mostly so his spread-out papers, dirty socks, dust bunnies, and books would be contained in an enclosed space. He'd complained that the apartment outside his office felt like her space rather than a shared one — he was sequestered into a miniature version of his former basement pad, minus the tumour-reeking ashtrays since he had agreed to smoke outside.

"What do you think?" she called after Steve. "Do you think I should meet him? What could he want?"

"I don't know, babe." Steve had already covered the apartment's 600-foot length and was inside his office. Before the door clicked closed, he said, "I mean, sure. Go for it."

Hayato was sitting in Mister Tea when she got there, a steaming cardboard cup in front of him. He wore the most serious expression she'd ever seen on his face. A small, tense smile. He watched her buy a cup of coffee, nodding with a lacklustre impersonation of his usual enthusiasm both times she glanced over and met his eyes.

"So," she said, sitting down. "It's been a while."

"Long time no see," said Hayato.

"Yes."

"I've never seen you in summertime. Hair's too short. Wait — I don't mean that. I mean to say, hair's so short. Not too short, not too short." His face cracked into the familiar grin. "Ha ha!"

Mia clasped her hands in her lap to resist touching her head. "Was even shorter," she said. "I shaved it off."

"Shaved?" He mimed a razor against his face, eyebrows high.

"Yeah."

"This is crazy!" But the tense expression was back. "Thank you for taking this time to meet me," he said. "I have something to tell you. My sister-in-law has died."

During the sessions in the library, Hayato had never mentioned his sister-in-law, or any member of his family. "Was cancer."

"I'm sorry. She lived in Japan?"

"Yes. She was married to my brother."

"How sad."

Hayato put his hands on the table, palms down, then took them off again. He looked out the window. He was wearing a grey T-shirt, and had a jean jacket over the back of his chair. His hair was still as plentiful and unkempt as ever, his skin a little shiny with the heat of the day. Hers must have been the same. His eyes settled for a moment on her collarbone, then on her shoulders; she was wearing a tank top. Her hands twitched to cover herself, but she clasped them tighter.

"Mia," he said. "I would like for you to tutor me again."

"Oh, really? The same as before?"

"I've applied for translation work. I need to make sure I'm ready. I can pay more than last time."

"That's great," she said. "Because I'm taking an extra semester to finish. I'm supposed to be done. So my funding's run out."

"So, you need a job, I need you."

"Right."

"And you finish your MA in...."

"August."

"And then you...."

"I'm moving out west with my boyfriend. He's starting his PhD."

"You have a boyfriend now."

"I do. Yes."

Hayato looked at her forehead, her shoulder, his cup on the table. "One more thing I have to tell you. I have a laptop for sale. A year old. I'll sell it for four hundred dollars. You know anyone who needs a laptop?"

Mia pictured herself writing in the library overlooking the river, in Mister Tea's and Sally's Café, in the grad bar that occupied the famous dead poet's old house. With a laptop, she could put the finishing touches on her thesis in the poet's former living room, instead of in her own living room, where the sound of typing woke Steve and tormented him, reminding him he wasn't working on his novel.

"But I can't afford four hundred dollars," she said.

"Three hundred and fifty — as low as I go."

"How about if I pay you two hundred, and work off the rest?"

"Work off?"

"I'll pay you in work instead of money. I'd work off the hundred and fifty dollars by tutoring you for the equivalent number of hours."

"Ahh! Work off. Yes. Yes, all right. You work off."

"Work it off."

"It. Aha. One question." He pulled a squashed cigarette from his back pocket and tapped it on the table, trying to reshape it. "There's a phrase I read recently that I don't understand. May I ask?"

"Sure."

"It's *just fucking with you*. What does this mean?"

"Oh — that's a colloquial expression meaning, *just kidding*. I'm just playing a trick on you. Trying to confuse you." Mia moved her finger in what she imagined was a universal sign of insanity, in a circle beside her temple.

"Ahh. I see. Very colloquial?"

"Yes. Remember, *fuck* is considered a rude word? Until recently, it was considered the worst word in the English language."

"It means — sexual intercourse."

"Most swear words have something to do with bodily functions or sex or religion. Taboo things, right? In Japanese, too?"

Hayato moved his head in a motion that could have been nod or a shake. "What's considered the worst word in English, now?" He squeezed both sides of the cigarette, and it sprung a leak. Little shreds of tobacco scattered across the table. He tapped it again, slowly, as though to be sure.

"I don't know. I'll think about that one."

That evening, when Steve woke up for his night shift, Mia climbed into bed with him, and said she'd found a new source of income and a laptop.

He pumped his fist sleepily and said, "Woo hoo," in a tone that sounded sarcastic, but wasn't.

"It'll help pay for the movers," said Mia, rolling on top of him.

"You're awesome." He wrapped his arms around her lower back and ground his erection against her hip.

The next day, Mia met Hayato again to pick up the computer, which he handed over in its own shoulder bag, in exchange for her cheque. The bag was heavy enough that it bent her body sideways, and she struggled back up the hill, her back aching, the shoulder strap digging into her shoulder.

At home, she immediately turned on her computer, saved her thesis onto a disk, and transferred it to the laptop. She ate her lunch, and when she came back, the laptop's screensaver had turned on: a single phrase, in white text on a black background, moving across the screen from right to left, again and again: *Just fucking with you!*

He emailed a week later. Mia nudged the door of Steve's office open, holding her laptop. "Listen to this," she said. "My student wants me to meet him at Chapters, up at the mall, so I can help him choose novels. Two of them. He says he wants ones I've read so we can discuss them."

"Uh huh."

"What do you think about that?"

"I don't know. I'm concentrating."

"On Minesweeper."

"Thinking."

"Okay, but listen to this. *I believe reading is living. So reading the same is living together in a way.* "

"So?"

"So what do you *think* about that?"

"I don't know. Nothing, I guess."

It turned out Steve needed to sleep, and couldn't relax in her presence, not with her tendency to stand in his office doorway, asking, "Why do you want me to move out west with you, again?"

So Mia left an hour early and trudged up the hill toward the mall. Dark and cool, the sky full of low, grey clouds, the kind that usually gave her migraines.

"What do you want me to do?" Steve had said. "Take an oath? I don't know when I'll stop being depressed. That's not how love works; you don't stop loving someone because they're working as a taxi driver and having a hard time."

"I'm sorry."

He concentrated on his clicking.

"What can I do to help? Do you want a massage?"

"You know what I want."

Mia stepped into the room, put her arms around his shoulders, and leaned her forehead against his cheek. "Come to bed and let me make you feel better —"

He snapped forward, away from her, and clicked on a mine. "*Crap*," he said. "Oh, not *that*."

By the time she reached the mall, Mia had replayed the whole scene at least ten times. The problem was, Steve was right. She'd declared her love when he was cheerful, adoring and over-sexed, eager to take her on drives into the forest, to stop during walks by the river and pick her up to swing her around. Watching his broad shoulders at the computer, she'd been thinking of getting his clothes off, getting his hands on her, not about his feelings.

"If you need to get laid," he'd said, "just find someone else. You're a girl; you shouldn't have a hard time. I told you, I can't be responsible for your sexual needs."

"You're a — you're crazy. Turn around! Look at me, at least. Steve! Stop playing that fucking computer game!"

"I'm not talking to someone who's yelling at me."

"Are you insane?" Her throat ached with the volume of her voice. "You want me to fuck someone else?"

"I want. You. To leave me. Alone."

She stood outside waiting for Hayato, for half an hour this time, her English teacher face twitching, her shoulders back. As he hurried across the parking lot, dragging viciously on the last scraps of a cigarette, she felt the first raindrops on her arm.

They found the fiction section and started with the A's. She pulled out books she'd read and enjoyed, summarized them for him, and described the writing style.

"How about Martin Amis? Margaret Atwood? JG Ballard?"

Hayato turned each volume in his hands, shaking his head. "I can only read a book that gives me a feeling — a certain feeling when I touch it," he explained, after listening politely to her pitch for *Empire of the Sun*. "No feeling, no good." He shrugged; he couldn't help it. Nothing she could say would give him the feeling if it wasn't already there. She resisted looking at her watch. She would find books that gave him that special feeling. She would earn that laptop.

"What about this one? It's great." One of Steve's favourites, too. "It's about the absurdity of war and bureaucracy. A classic." Hayato held out his hands, and she lowered the book into them.

"Oh!" His fingers closed around *Catch-22*. He held it at arm's length, turned it from side to side, examining it. "Ahh!" he said. "Yes!"

"Yes? Yeah?"

"Yes! *Catch-22*. Joseph Heller. Yes, yes. This is good."

"Great!" she said. "You'll love it. Terrific!"

They continued through the I's, J's, K's, and L's. At least Steve would be working all night. Mia could go to bed as soon as he left the apartment and lie right in the middle, with her arms and legs spread out like a starfish.

"Oh," she told Hayato. "How about this? I just read this for a class."

"*Atonement*?"

"By Ian McEwan."

"You like it?"

"Yeah, definitely. It would give us lots to talk about."

He reached for the book, slowly, bracing himself, and as his fingertips made contact, his eyebrows shot up. Thank God: the feeling.

The mall's foyer was darker now, though it was still mid-day, and smelled of ozone; the rain was pouring. Mia called a taxi from one in the long line of payphones. In this town, taxis didn't just hang around malls, not even in bad weather.

"My boyfriend's a taxi driver," she said. "Maybe it'll be him." Steve would not have approved of her using him that way — mentioning him to provide a buffer between her and a man eyeing her with an expression that could have been affection, amusement, fear or something for which there was no word in English. Maybe he was just thinking about his next cigarette. She calculated in her head how many tutoring hours she still owed before the laptop was officially hers.

"It's difficult to make friends in Canada," Hayato said.

"Is it?" said Mia. "Yeah. I don't really have any friends in town, either." She led him past the phones and jumbo movie posters, and pushed through one of the mall's inner glass doors to lean against an outer one.

He said, "Lonely." It sounded like a question.

"I'm not lonely. I have a boyfriend." The black asphalt parking lot was clean and shiny in the rain. A yellow car turned onto it from the road, way off by the Boston Pizza.

"You consider me as a friend?" said Hayato, looking at her instead of outside.

"Sure...."

"Oh, good!" he said. "That's what I thought. Friends, out for the day."

Only as they jogged through the rain to the cab did his meaning dawn on her. The two hours at Chapters had amounted to friends hanging out, not to tutoring hours. She still owed him the full hundred and fifty dollars. Over ten hours. Ten long hours that stretched out ahead of her with the laptop visible in the distance, its screensaver blinking at her: *Just fucking with you! Just fucking with you!*

The taxi eased down the long hill toward the river and downtown.

"Will you marry your boyfriend, the taxi driver?" said Hayato. He was already holding a cigarette, ready for when the car stopped, so he could stand in the rain, smoking it.

"I don't think so."

"Why not?"

"We don't believe in marriage."

"Why?"

"Don't believe in making institutionalized promises that humans are constitutionally incapable of keeping."

If any of her words were ones he hadn't learned yet, he didn't show it. "*You* don't believe?"

Mia did a half-nod half-shake, Hayato-style. The sad thing was, when Steve had applied for the cab-driving job, she'd been excited. Partly because she'd looked forward to phoning the dispatcher in the middle of the night and pretending to be a customer, and to Steve picking her up and screwing her in his taxi. At least once. For godsake. You have your own taxi, and you're not going pretend your girlfriend's a customer and get it on with her in it? Sometimes when Mia looked at Steve, she wanted to say, *Stop being such a pussy*. Insane, considering her thesis was about effeminacy and chivalry in seventeenth-century English literature.

"Are you and your boyfriend on a rock?" said Hayato.

"Hmm? Oh, on the rocks. No, no...."

When Mia got home, the vinegary egg-smell of mayonnaise told her Steve was in the kitchen making his midnight lunch.

She stood beside him at the counter, and he said, "Hey, babe." He spooned mayonnaise into a bowl of something pink.

"How's it going?"

"Ehn," he said. "You know. Just woke up."

"I'm sorry we fought."

She put her arms around him from the side, and he turned, gave her a solid squeeze, and let go.

He said, "You know those scenes wreck my whole day. I don't just snap out of it like you do."

"I don't just snap out of it. I felt awful all afternoon. I'm sorry."

Steve always made the same thing: a bagel sandwich containing some kind of canned fish or meat salad. Sometimes the canned substance was tuna, sometimes salmon or ham.

"Why don't you try those Montreal-style bagels I got?" she said. "They taste so much better than those puffy ones."

"These are fine. They fill me up. Why do you care what bagels I eat?"

"I just don't see why you'd eat a grocery store bagel when you could eat a real one."

"These are fine."

"Like how you could really not care one way or the other —"

"Drop it."

The week before, she'd suggested throwing some chopped celery into the sandwich mix, and had once offered to make him something else. He'd said she didn't respect him because he was a working class Joe.

"You have a master's degree and teach at a university —"

"*And* drive a taxi. And you don't have to work at all, because of your *scholarship*. You're *privileged*. And I keep my earnings in a jar, and you can't stand it."

He gestured toward the table, where the jar sat, its lid off so he could count out his float for the night. He was right. The jar really got to her. Especially when, every few days, he dumped its contents onto the table to count it.

Now, she said, "Why not take an apple?"

"Christ."

Steve tucked plastic wrap around his sandwich to hold its shape, put it in his backpack, and sat down at the table to make cigarettes.

"Anyway." Mia sat down across from him. "I just had a strange experience."

He packed tobacco into the little machine, worked an empty paper tube onto the end, and then slid the sprung contraption to form a perfect smoke.

"That guy is *obsessed* with smoking," she'd once heard someone comment at a party, pointing over at Steve with his cigarette-maker on the sofa. "Look at him. He would *eat* smokes if he could."

"I think my student might have a crush on me," she said.

"Right."

"Maybe not. I'm not sure." Mia told Steve about the Chapters outing, and he rolled his eyes.

"So what do you think about that?" she said. "Does he want to be friends, or just not to pay me, or does he have a crush on me?"

"Can you please stop talking?" Steve pressed another wad of tobacco into the machine, and arranged another paper tube. "I don't like to talk right before going to work. I'm trying to think."

"Steve." Mia closed her hand around his wrist, a thick, muscular wrist, weighty in her hand. "Why do you want me to move out west with you if you're so unhappy?"

He sighed. "Not again. I'm not unhappy because of *you*." She let go of him and he cranked the machine, laid the smoke beside the first one. "I'd probably feel even worse without you. I can't stand this — your constant demand for attention. You say you love me, but you won't give me what I need."

"Which is to be left alone."

He reached into the tobacco pouch for another wad. "Yes."

"But not to be *left*."

"No."

Mia picked up Steve's two perfect cigarettes and crushed them in her fist. They didn't come apart, but a bit of tobacco squeezed out their tips. She let go; they hit the table, wrinkled and deflated.

"Not cool," said Steve.

"Why don't you just dump me?"

"I'll never dump you. I told you."

"*Why?*"

"Shh — just talk in a normal voice."

"Why."

"Sometimes I wonder."

"I'm sorry." Mia put her hand on the table, her fingertips almost touching the mangled smokes. "I'll make you some new ones."

"I'll do it." He swept the tobacco she'd wasted off the table and back into its pouch.

A week later, there was a heat wave, the kind that melts lip balm into a puddle in its little jar. Mia was sitting at her desk with a fan two feet away.

"Hey, Steve," she called toward his office. "My supervisor says one more set of revisions and I'm done."

"You rock," called Steve.

"Oh — and. Oh, weird. Listen to this. It's Hayato. He wants to discuss the books now, and then he says, *It is so very hot. Are you hot? Damn, yes!* What do you think he means by that?"

Steve stepped into the room and stood behind her for a moment. "I don't know. Nothing."

"So he's just referring to the weather?"

"Obviously."

"Should I explain to him that *hot* has another meaning? I guess it's my job to explain stuff like that, but it's awkward. You see what I mean?"

"I don't know. He's your student."

"Maybe he chose *Catch-22* as a message to me, that he was planning to put me in this position where I'm damned if I do, damned if I—"

But Steve had left the room. He was two hundred square feet away, mashing mayonnaise and canned ham.

To discuss the books, Mia suggested Sally's Café, the teahouse run by a couple renowned for their rudeness. "Their rudeness is their charm," Mia convinced Hayato. The first time they planned to meet, he didn't show up.

Give me one last chance to keep my word, he wrote to her that evening. He just hadn't been able to wake up, he explained.

The second time, she sat for five minutes with the grey-bunned Sally glaring at her over the counter before Hayato appeared outside, pacing the window. Finally, he dropped his cigarette butt, came inside, and ordered tea for both of them.

"The note," he said. "What do you think about the note?"

Sally slammed teapots onto the table, her husband peering in from the patio to eye his only two customers with bald contempt.

"Note?"

"The *note*. That Robbie sends to Cecilia."

"Oh. Right."

"By mistake, and then they meet in the library, and, ahh…"

"What do I think of it?" she said. "Well, it's pretty amazing how that little mistake affects all the character's lives so deeply isn't it? And how something seemingly profane becomes profound…."

"Yes," said Hayato. "But what would you think if someone sent you a note like that?"

"Um," Mia said.

Steve had sent Mia notes like that; for the first six months of their relationship, her email inbox had been full of them. That's how she ended up in this mess.

"You wanted to know the most offensive word in the English language?" Mia said. "That's it. That's why it works in the novel. To shock the characters and the reader — do you see?"

"What word?"

"It's so rude, I don't want to say it. That's how rude it is."

Hayato had deep grooves in his cheeks; would he be offended if she asked his age? He said, "But what would *you* think if you got a note like that?"

"For anyone, it would depend. But what did you think about the ending?" she said. "What Briony reveals at the end?"

"Not so interesting for me."

His hair flopped over his forehead, and his grin threatened to crack his cheeks.

Mia said, "This counts as tutoring hours."

"What?"

"Just so we're clear. This is tutoring. Hours."

He didn't care about metafiction, about Briony's tortured quest for atonement. He probably didn't even care about Yossarian and that dying soldier in the plane.

"Tutoring," he said, "Teaching words. But you won't say the word I want to learn about."

Sally stood behind them and frowned at their mugs. "Are you ordering something else?" she said.

Hayato stared at Sally like he didn't speak English, and her eyes widened. She backed away.

Hayato leaned toward Mia, just a little. "Just fucking with you," he said.

Mia didn't have to avoid Hayato for the next three weeks; he didn't contact her until a few days before her departure. By that time, she and Steve had packed their apartment apart from a few sets of clothes and enough dishes to get by.

In his email, Hayato apologized for bothering her when she must be busy. He wanted her to take some photos of him on campus, he said. He had no one else to ask, and he wanted to show his friends in Japan.

"I can't believe you're going to meet some student the day before your defense," Steve said. "The day before we're *leaving*."

"This guy doesn't have anyone else, maybe," said Mia. "I think I need to do this. Listen." She squeezed onto Steve's lap on the sofa, between the boxes. "Can we take a shower together when I get back? I feel like we shouldn't leave this place without taking one shower together."

"Yeah," said Steve. "Okay."

"I'll wash all that moving sweat away." She lifted his arm and pushed her face into his armpit. The smell made her dizzy.

Hayato was waiting for her outside the library, as they'd planned. Mia stopped, and he stepped closer to her. "You're so tall." He looked up at her chin. "You have a pimple."

"Stress. I'm defending my thesis tomorrow. That's rude, by the way."

"What?"

"Pointing out a pimple."

"No. No — not… I meant. You're young. I meant you're so young. And I'm —"

"I'm 29."

"No."

"Yes."

"Still, young. Too young for stress."

"I'm moving across the country with a man whose most prized possessions are a jar of coins, fifteen years worth of his own journals, and a second-hand Oxford English Dictionary — the multi-volume kind that comes with a magnifying glass."

"Why?"

"Love."

Hayato gasped. "Love," he muttered, like he was embarrassed to say it. Then he said, "I. I will move to Texas."

"Really? When?"

"Next year."

"Oh...." said Mia.

"By myself."

"Why Texas?"

"Texas — because — the work is there."

"The work."

"Yes."

"Right, well. You wanted photos? I only have about ten minutes."

Hayato posed in front of the library and then with his back to the hill; the town, spread out behind him, looked like a lush forest dotted sporadically with houses. He sat on his favourite bench, spreading his arms to invite his family? friends? in Japan to take a look.

"All done?" Mia said.

"Wait! Us together." He stood beside her and took a shot of their faces.

"I'd better go," she said. "I'm packing today, and my defense...."

"Wait, wait. Please. One photo of you, please. To remember my friend. Sit on the bench?"

Mia sat on the bench.

"I can see your underwear," said Hayato.

She followed his gaze to her shoulder, and pushed her bra strap into her shirt.

"Okay, now. Yes. Turn your shoulders like...."

She smoothed her hair.

"You look like a Playboy model!" said Hayato. "Now just lean back a bit, look at the camera...."

"That's enough!" She stood. "I have to go."

"No, no!"

"Yes. I have to get ready for my defense. My boyfriend's waiting for the movers. I have to help him! I'm really busy. So — goodbye, Hayato. Good luck."

Mia stepped backwards, downhill, and they faced off, both panic-stricken. He looked as if he might do something desperate. Hug her, maybe. She stepped back again and waved her hand, nodding manically to encourage him to do the same.

"I want to kiss your cunt." He mirrored her open-mouthed expression and then reassumed his trademark grin. "Like in the book!" he said. His smile twitched.

"Ah," he said. "Um?"

"That's not cool."

"It's not? Wait — I'm sorry, I'm sorry!"

Mia resisted running, but speed-walked along the path that led her to the grad bar, where she ordered a pint and sat in the dead famous poet's living room.

Mia took the laptop, which was technically half hers and half Hayato's, from its bag, flipped it open, waited for it to boot. Hayato had managed to email her already; from the library, she supposed.

I deeply regret that my joke was not funny for you, he'd written. *It was a joke and I never meant it. I swear it.* He said he hoped and prayed that Mia's defense, and the rest of her life, would be a wonderful success.

Hayato, she wrote. *Aren't the Japanese supposed to revere teachers? I know I live with my boyfriend, who I don't intend to marry. I look young for my age. I made too many jokes, maybe, while I was tutoring you, and I recommended* Atonement. *But you have the wrong idea.* She paused, her fingers still on the keyboard. *I'm a serious person,* she wrote. Then she deleted the whole message.

She wrote, *You misunderstood,* and pressed send.

The next message from him appeared in thirty seconds. It said: *You.*

No need to answer. She was leaving the next day. She would never see or think about Hayato again. She shouldn't have gone to meet him in the first place; what was she doing, taking time out of the busiest day of her life to meet someone she barely knew? She should have been at home, helping Steve, getting ready to leave, getting ready to begin their real lives together.

She left her pint glass half full, and jogged toward home, downhill and then uphill again. When she turned onto their street, she saw the moving truck. Four strangers were carrying boxes into it, marching with their burdens like a line of ants, one with her unassembled futon on his shoulder. They would leave only an air mattress and a couple of suitcases. Steve sat on the front steps, smoking. He lifted his head, and Mia waved. He stood, and she broke into a sprint. She imagined how she must look to him, running up the hill; her hair was too short now to lift and fall much, but he'd see the involuntary smile transforming her face. He'd remember two years earlier, the first summer they dated, how she used to run the last block to his basement apartment and arrive breathless, how he'd open the door and pull her inside, his hands already in her clothes.

"*Steve!*" she yelled.

She was close enough to hear the creak of the moving truck's ramp as a teenaged boy carried her bike inside it. None of the movers glanced at her. Likely, they didn't know Steve was moving with a woman; it wasn't the type of thing he'd think to mention. He reached into the nook in the brick wall beside the mailbox, where he and some other tenants kept a coffee can for their cigarette butts, to prevent litter. He was freeing his hands so he could grab her, lift her and swing her around. He'd say, "Hello, sexiest woman on Earth," just like he used to, and they'd go inside to shower together, to make love in the empty apartment cleared of everything that had obstructed their happiness. Afterwards, they would smile and smile, faces close together, savouring the end of their difficult year. Mia laughed and ran faster, beginning to spread her arms. Brushing his hand against his jeans, Steve looked over his shoulder; one of the movers said something, and Steve lifted his hand in response, then turned away again. Mia was halfway across the street when he stepped inside and shut the door behind him as though he had never seen her in the first place.

EYE

When I was a boy, fourteen or sixteen, my parents moved us to the prairies. They called it "God's kingdom." They meant that literally. It was a religion they'd joined.

I was a stranger to the colonies, as we still thought of them then, though technically the empire was already long defunct, and I had never, in all my short life, entertained the slightest notion of leaving the great city of my birth, once the centre of the civilized world. On these prairies, we lived in what passed for a city. I began crashing my bicycle into every bit of God's kingdom I could find. After a few less dramatic smash-ups, I sped into a statue of two businessmen conversing on the pavement. I launched over my handlebars and into their arms. The plaintive one with the briefcase had two fingers raised, to emphasize a point. Which was how I got this scar on my neck, how I became disillusioned with religion, and how I ended up estranged from my parents and living on my own in the wild west by the age of seventeen-and-a-half.

You would not believe how many people said to me, back then, "You're lucky you didn't lose an eye." And that was five years before I met my first wife, Lila.

When my second wife said she was leaving me, you know what I told her? I said that if she expected to see me broken hearted, she was in for a disappointment. I said I was too old for that kind of thing. I was thirty-two. That's a bit of a private joke for me these days, because, of course, I am broken hearted now, and a whole lot older than thirty-two, though I won't say by how much. My currently broken heart is what's prompted me to tell you all this. The point is, after what happened with my first wife, my heart was such a collection of shards and smithereens that breaking it again was out of the question for some decades. The other point is, life is long, and a second instance of heartbreak feels entirely different from a first.

So, Lila. Like most people, she talked about her childhood; hers had transpired in a forest by a lake.

"We tapped the trees, and we had so much maple syrup, we used to fry our eggs in that instead of oil."

"Did you ever pour it on the snow to make candy?" I said.

"Yes."

Incredible, I know. How could a child privy to that much syrup — who squeaked her little boots under towering mid-continent maples, collecting buckets of sap from the tapped trunks, who boiled it down in one of those giant cauldrons, standing in the cold, breathing the sugary steam; how could she go and grow into her twenties to be such a, excuse me but, cunt?

Me and Lila, we were never married; no, not in the sense of being legally married. But I've always thought of her as my first wife, and for a number of compelling reasons. Number one, because she pulverized my heart. Number two, because I gave her my eye. Number three, because after she left, I stood in the snow outside her trailer. If nights find you standing in the wispy prairie-snow outside the trailer of your ex-wife, it's that some part of you is still in there, and you're drawn back to it, the way a ghost is stuck haunting the site of its murder; but if that trailer belongs to someone you were never married to in the first place, that makes you a stalker. I can tell you for certain, I was no stalker.

I know what you're thinking: Eye?

It began with a wish I made in the heat of passion. We'd been out dancing and drinking and sweating and smelling each other's sweat while we danced. Then back at her place we're already kissing on the stairs, throwing each other against the walls, and then, finally through her apartment door, shedding clothes on our way to the bed. (That's right; she lived in an apartment on the third story of a house. Not in a trailer. We lived in what passed for a city, and she lived in an apartment in a house, and when I would stand in the snow at night, it would be in the small gap between Lila's house and the one next door.)

I said, "I wish your organs would fail so I could prove how much I love you. I wish I could give you my lung, my kidney, a piece of my liver. Some part of me working inside your body, its vessels pumped through with your blood."

"That's a weird thing to wish," said Lila.

"I would do it, I promise you. It would be a tattoo of my name, only more so. A hundred times more so." All the while, I traced my fingers over her bare skin and mine, imagining where the incisions would be.

I know what you're thinking. But those are the kinds of things we say when our hearts are young and plump and dented only by the unwilling move across an ocean to a land of interminable wheat fields and jarred cheese. Even the loss of a country with millennia of culture can't compare to the loss of a twenty-three-year-old's first love, a rosy-nippled woman with black fruity-smelling hair. And eyes — well, eyes that started out nut-brown, but were destined to be green with brown rings around the pupils, exactly like mine. Not *like* mine. Mine.

My dear Helen, who of course I lost just recently after thirty brief years, found it deeply disturbing that someone, Lila, namely, was walking around out there with my eye in her head. (The word 'deeply' was a bit of private joke between Helen and me since depth is exactly what you can't perceive after giving away one eye.) What bothered Helen most was the scene in the hospital, which she sometimes dreamed about, though she hadn't been there of course and only had what I'd told her to go on — the doctor peeling the bandage from around Lila's head, and she on the exam table, blinking into my face with my very own eyeball now wired to her cortex.

Lila opened my eye wide and we examined each other — real eye to glass eye, glass eye to real eye.

"I'm just not sure I love you, though, Hank," she said. "My sense of love feels kind of empty."

If I had been older at the time, I'd have known the Hank thing was a bad sign all along. She called me that because she thought it was a suitable name for someone who wore plaid shirts, drove a pickup truck, and had a big black dog. I did none of those things. But she kept calling me Hank, hoping the shirt, truck, and four-legged companion would follow. I told her I was born abroad; I showed her the scar on my neck. I repeated my given name. She was not convinced.

Does it seem strange that so soon after losing Helen, I'm telling the story of Lila and my eye, instead the story of Helen and my life? That I want to explain how we were fighting when the accident happened? We were driving beside a spruce grove on one side and a canola field on the other, and I wanted Lila to turn into the yellow and stop the car so I could work myself up into her skirt. Like she'd let me do a year before.

"Give me, give me."

"No, no, no."

"Your breasts. Your mouth. Your underwear around your ankles."

"No."

"Why, why, Lila!"

"I don't love you I don't love you!"

I grabbed; she shoved. Her other arm wrenched the wheel away from bright paradise and into the cool dark trees. Smashed glass, little jewels of it, the branch in the car, blood everywhere. Most of it hers. Two weeks later, I got the test; I was a donor. I came to, and my eye socket wasn't empty, but brim bursting with pure agony. Is it too obvious to point out that having your eye removed and your heart ripped out hurts? Some things are describable, that's all, and some things aren't. I'm telling you what I can.

DIGGING A HOLE

Bill had visited James and Angela in Fredericton just a few months before she took the bookshelves, the armchairs with their grandmother-knitted afghans, the oak table, the blue plates with the daisies in the middle, the red paper lanterns, the vacuum cleaner, the son, and the daughter to Halifax. On the second and final night of the visit, Bill, James, and Angela drank two bottles of wine, and by midnight, James was stretched out, almost strangling on each of his long snores. Angela rocked the wooden chair forward to plant her wool-socked feet on the floor. She told Bill, "I want to show you something."

He followed her past the antique desk on the landing and up the narrow stairs, stepping carefully like she did, heel-to-toe, so as not to creak the ancient hardwood and wake Roche and Honey. When she stepped into the bathroom, he hesitated, but she pointed meaningfully at the door, so he followed her in and eased it shut behind him.

The room was oppressive, with slanted walls, so no space for a shower, just for an enormous claw-foot tub. Angela was just about

Bill's height, and she stood uncomfortably close, her pale hair the colour of spaghetti-sauce stain against the white cloth of the dress shirt she'd worn to work, her face tired as a bleached-out napkin. She'd been beautiful the other time he met her, at the wedding, but tonight the red wine in the dry lines of her lips matched the small veins in her eyes.

"Tell me something," she said, just a little louder than a whisper.

"All right."

He'd never been alone with his friend's wife like this. The desperation in her face made him want to run, to get in his car and drive all the way back home to Quebec City, to Emile, who did not understand why Bill persisted in his friendship with James, with whom he had nothing in common, who always managed to upset him, who appeared as instigator in each of Bill's most cringe-worthy childhood and adolescent stories.

"You've known him the longest," said Angela. "Has he always been this way?"

"James?"

"Yes. *James*. How is he so *forgivable*? How does he *do* that?" She leaned closer still, and Bill's hand moved behind him to the doorknob.

Perhaps sensing he was about to bolt, Angela edged away, around the toilet, and peered into the red plastic bucket beside it.

"Come on," she said. "I want you to see this."

Bill stepped closer. The bucket was filled halfway with clear liquid, and in the liquid were three soiled cloth diapers.

Angela said, "I leave this bucket full of vinegar every day. All I ask is that he scrapes the diapers into the toilet and then leaves them to soak in here. But instead, he just drops them right in the bowl, so when I get home from work, I have to fish them out. Sometimes I have to hold it in until I've done it. One time, I went on top of them, and *then* had to fish them out."

She looked at Bill as if he knew the answer to the question of James. As if he might hand over some secret stuff that could be packed into the void between James's dizzying potential and the dirty-diaper reality of him. She looked at Bill as if maybe it was his fault James turned out the way he had.

A year and a half later, Emile said, "He'll be the same. *Mais pire encore.*"

But Bill just kissed him and said, "I think he needs an old friend right now," and, "he's like a brother to me," filled his thermos with one eighth espresso and the rest hot water, and left Quebec City after breakfast. He drove east, all the way through the province and into New Brunswick.

Fall was the only season for the drive; his eyes ached with the reds and yellows and oranges. He reached Fredericton at twilight. James lived on a section of road with few homes, in a house so close to the highway exit it seemed in the middle of nowhere. The dirty brown, red-roofed rental looked close to collapse, and so did the pine-coloured storage shack behind it; but the yard's two yellowing willows and four livid-leaved maples steered the property away from decrepitude, and lent it a cottagey, rustic air instead. Beyond the trees the St. John River raced by, frantically resisting the inevitable freeze. James was standing on the rotting wood porch with the girlfriend he'd mentioned, who clasped her hands and jumped up and down a bit as Bill pulled up. She had shiny brown hair cut in a bob, and wore a beautiful wool sweater, turquoise with big brown buttons. As though unable to contain her glee, she ran down the steps and over to the car, with James, a foot taller than her and twice her girth, a few paces behind.

"Oh, my," the girlfriend said, as Bill stepped out of the car. "Billy. *Billy. Welcome.* I'm Miranda." She unclasped her hands and held out her arms. "I feel like I know you. I just have to hug you." On tiptoe, she held Bill tightly around the shoulders, and he smelled floral soap and cigarettes. "Whenever James talks about his childhood, it's Billy this, Billy that." She stepped back and clasped her hands again, at hip-level. "I don't even have a childhood friend I *remember* all that well, and meanwhile James talks about you more than his own family."

Her eyes were cartoon-big, and blue, almost as blue as the sweater. That she couldn't remember her childhood friends seemed a preposterous claim, since she was barely out of her teens.

"Okay, okay," said James. "Jesus H. Christ. Our Miranda has a penchant for exaggeration. Is that gel?"

Bill dodged James's reach, covering his hair with his hand. "At least I don't cut my hair with a bread knife."

"Careful," James said. "This is Miranda's handiwork you're looking at."

"Billy." Miranda crossed her arms in front of her chest, the breeze lifting her hair, which looked soft as a kitten's. "Maybe you could convince him to pay for a proper cut."

"I've never been able to convince this guy of anything."

"It's great to see you, man." James hugged him, a quick two-armed crush and release. James looked fine, the same as ever. He wasn't falling apart. The plaid shirt, the jeans, worn and loose on his broad hips. The small gap between his front teeth. And just a hint of two more years gone by around the jaw line and the eyes.

"Come inside," said Miranda. "It's freezing out here."

The kitchen was a disaster, squash entrails everywhere, onion peels on the floor.

"It smells amazing," said Bill. "Cinnamon."

Miranda lifted the pot's lid and stirred a bit, and James leaned against the counter, knocking more vegetable peelings onto the floor. She said, "Butternut soup, and you won't believe this rye. Local bakery. Jamie says you're a foodie. Let me get things in order down here. The guestroom's upstairs on your right. Grab the broom, would you, Jamie?"

"Don't look up," said James.

"What is that?" said Bill.

"I said, don't look up."

Bill craned his neck. The ceiling's biggest crack was at least a metre long, the plaster around it yellow and bubbled.

"It's the bathtub. That iron thing. It's sinking." James was still smiling. He held his arms out, fists clenched, let them fall against his sides.

"We do our best," said Miranda, lifting a small trashcan and using a grey dishrag to push some of the squash slime off the counter's edge, into it. "That's all anyone can ask."

"You use that bathtub, though — you sit in it." Bill reached his hand toward the crack. All that iron, plus two hundred pounds of barrel-chested James.

"I'm trying to help him live in the present," said Miranda.

Last time, Bill had slept in the living room. Now there was a guestroom half-filled by the double futon mattress on its floor. The Little Engine That Could raced around the tops of the walls. Bill set his bag beside the tiny blue dresser and ran his finger over the label on its side. James's son had stamped it with his name: *Roche*. From one of those label makers kids love. Honey's pink dresser was gone. The hardwood floors were old as the house. Gorgeous old pine, though scratched to hell and all the varnish long gone. Bill could easily picture the wood restored, though he knew the house's drywall and wiring would inevitably disintegrate, taking the perfectly good floors with it.

Every evening and weekend, James had been working on his dissertation, only it turned out he was playing computer games instead, hadn't written a word in over nine months. They'd been paying a babysitter. That's when Angela boxed up her books and left James's in three tall piles against the wall where the bookshelves had been. She'd applied for the Halifax job months before; she'd even found a school and daycare for Roche and Honey.

"As if my PhD in Maritime poetry was really going to make any difference to anything anyway," James had told Bill quite recently over Skype. Then he said, "I fucked up. I know it. She's a winner and I'm a loser. I miss my kids. I've got to get her back, man. Listen," he said, then. "I've gone and got myself in a bit of trouble, here. This chick. This young girl. Like a peach, you know? Fresh, sweet. She does this thing where she packs every big word she knows into a sentence. Just like a kid, you know? Makes me feel like a dirty old man. Sometimes I envy you, you know that? I mean, I get how you'd want to love a dude. I mean, *I* love *you*, and you're a dude. I mean, *girls*. I'm in trouble, here, Billy."

Bill was grateful Emile was not home, and had not overheard this conversation.

The phone rang once, then twice, and the stairs creaked, and then Bill heard a few quick footsteps in the hallway. He stepped away from the miniature dresser to rest uncomfortably on the windowsill.

"Oh my God." Miranda's face was a little shiny from the soup steam. "Just a minute. I'll get the duvet cover. James said he got the room ready for you. *James.*" She turned to the empty hallway. "You didn't put a cover on the duvet." James didn't reply, and Miranda said, "He's on the phone." She turned back to the hallway. "Oh, *James. Really.*"

She reappeared in minutes, holding a bundle of flowery white fabric, and shook her head as Bill reached for it. He returned to the windowsill as she set about shoving the duvet into the cover.

"The first time I saw this place, it was so austere. Downright ascetic. I managed to put a breakfast together the next morning, and, as we ate it, I told Jamie, Your place is very masculine. And Jamie said, Thanks, and I replied, You're welcome, just like that, in that tone. And Jamie remarked, There's nothing like dramatic irony first thing in the morning."

"Hey, kids." James leaned into the doorframe, and Miranda leapt over to him in two steps, abandoning the duvet more or less inside its cover. She put both hands on James's chest and stood on her toes, looking at Bill over her shoulder.

"That morning," she said, "the snow lay thick as a blanket, fresh and untouched except for one set of rabbit tracks diagonal through the yard. Everything was fresh and new, a blank slate." She lifted her arms, ballet-like, then leaned her cheek into James's ribs. His shoulders rolled forward as he studied the top of her head, as though charmed but baffled to find it there.

"You know my favourite story about you two?" Miranda licked the last of her soup from her spoon.

At the counter, James opened a second bottle of red wine.

"It's that line in Jamie's old journal," she said. "From when he was twelve. *Billy and I are seriously considering digging a hole,*" she recited.

Bill finished what was left in his glass, and James refilled it.

"Seriously considering digging a hole," she said again. "I *love that*."

"Oh yeah," Bill lifted his glass, which was filled to the brim, and took a tiny sip, just so it wouldn't overflow. The wine was too cold, not that it mattered much, from sitting on the counter near the door. "Yeah. The fort. We drew up designs for it and everything. That's hilarious. Seriously considering digging a hole. That's what you wrote?"

"I know, I know," said James. "To do our homework in."

"Too funny!" said Miranda.

"Was going to be on one of those islands in the river," said Bill.

"Right," said James. "Exactly."

"Man," said Bill. "You and your journals. Always writing. You still have those?

"Not a tree house," said Miranda. "Not a snow fort. But a *hole*."

"So, anyway, man," said James. "How's *Québec*?" He fluttered his fingers to indicate he meant the French pronunciation mockingly, though whether he was mocking himself, or the fact that Bill lived somewhere French, or French people in general, was not clear.

"It's good."

"And your guy–"

"Emile."

"*Em-ill.*"

"Emile's great."

"You guys speak French at home?"

"Quelquefois."

"And he's a lawyer."

"Sure is."

"Avocat en français."

"Bien sûr."

"French immersion was good for something, I guess. Are you a psychologist in French?"

"No. In French, I'm a psychologue. No, I know what you mean. Yes, I do have French patients."

The phone rang in the living room, and as James loped through the white swinging door to answer it, Miranda's smile faded for a moment.

"It's so cool you guys are still friends," she said, almost loud enough to drown out James greeting the caller.

"Almost thirty years," said Bill.

"Wow," said Miranda, sitting bone straight and shredding the paper towel that had been her napkin.

"No, no." James was perfectly audible through the door. He had always spoken too loudly on the phone. "It's important we talk about this," he said. "Who is this guy? Has he met the kids?"

Miranda stood. "Want to step outside for a little dessert?"

"Hmm?"

She took a joint and lighter from one of the kitchen drawers and held them out. "You smoke?"

Bill didn't, but he stood.

James' voice was getting louder. "I just don't want someone taking advantage of the situation. Does he have a key?"

"Better bundle up," said Miranda.

Surprisingly light out for dark. The stars. They sat on a dryish patch of ground past the trees, where the sound of the river made Bill close his eyes and breathe deeply through his nose. That earthy smell, and the cinnamon now in his hair and his clothes. He sneezed.

Miranda, bright in a yellow quilted jacket, leaned back on her elbows, holding the joint carefully and pursing her lips to exhale. "I didn't grow up here," she said. "But on a farm. I came here for college. Textiles. And bookmaking. I made a journal with rose petals in the paper. I have to show it to you. You'll love it. Are you surprised James lives with me?"

Before Bill had to formulate a response, she said, "I am. I know how amazing he is. I know how young I am. I used to see him around town all the time, and I thought, *that man*. That man is just so. Intriguing. The first time I talked to him, I felt like an idiot. I mean, I felt so stupid. Like he must have thought I was some airhead. Because of this thing I do, when I'm uncertain. This thing where I act all girly. It's an act. I'm not silly at all. And then one night, I was walking. Just walking on the walking bridge" — she pointed along the river's length; there were two lit bridges visible in the distance, glowing bands — "and James was standing there, at the edge, staring at the water. I said to him, What's down there? And he said, Things you'll never need to know, sweetheart, and isn't that *just* what James would say. And now look at us. We're common law."

Bill took the offered joint and puffed on it without inhaling too much.

"I was pregnant when I moved in, but that didn't work out."

Bill coughed. James had only said it was like holding a bird in his hands. He'd said he was afraid if he squeezed too hard, all the little bones would break. He'd said there was no harm in letting her bring some clothes over, and hang some art on the walls, was there?

"Sometimes I feel like I tricked him." Miranda leaned closer, so her arm rested against Bill's. "But it's not like I did it on purpose."

"Of course not." Bill passed the joint back. The smell on his fingers, which were numb partly from the cold, reminded him of long-ago camping trips. Sitting by the fire, watching all the boys and girls pair up. Panic tingled at the back of his tongue. He swallowed.

"Having a baby wouldn't have been the best thing for me, but I'm not glad I had a miscarriage. Was only seven weeks. But how could anyone be glad about a thing like that? Seriously. You're a psychologist, right?"

"I work with children."

"Well, it was horrible. It was my baby, and it hurt, and I vomited on the bathroom floor, and no one could be glad about a thing like that." She held out the joint again.

"No more for me, thanks."

She licked the pads of her thumb and finger, and pinched the roach. "Well, what would you say, if you were my therapist? I mean, I'm not a kid by the way, I'm twenty, I'm in my second year at the Craft College. But."

"I'd need to know a lot more about you."

"Like what?"

"Like what makes you tick."

"Okay. How about this. One time, in grade eleven, I went to this party, and I had sex with a guy up in the bedroom. And then he went and got all his friends, and they took turns screwing me while the others waited in line outside the door."

"Miranda? Jesus," he rested his forehead on his knees. "My head is spinning a bit. I don't smoke pot."

She put her hand on his back, right in the middle, a warm weight on his spine. "I'm sorry," she said. "I'm sorry. I shouldn't have brought that up. James told me about it, just recently. I was disappointed. Listen. I'm feeling a little strange. I'm sorry."

"I haven't thought about that in years. What a horrible memory."

"I'm sorry. You had sex with her, too, right? You don't have to answer that. He's on the phone with Angela, you know. You okay?"

Bill breathed deeply through his nose and exhaled through his mouth. "Yes. I feel a little silly. I'm not used to this stuff. It's okay. I feel better, now."

"I'm sorry I brought that up."

"It's okay. It was a long time ago."

"I know. You probably don't even remember who she was, her name or anything."

"Leslie."

"Ohh," Miranda breathed. "Jamie said he didn't remember her name."

"It was Leslie."

"Was she the only girl you ever —"

"No."

"Sorry, I'm —"

"It's okay."

Inside the house, James yelled something. Bill turned at the same moment as Miranda, and almost grazed her nose with his. Through the living room window, with its white lace curtains, James paced the room, turned around, and paced back.

"I'm embarrassed." Miranda hugged her knees.

"But there's no need. Not on my account." Seven and a half hours of driving, three glasses of wine, and a couple of tokes. Sleep. Sleep.

"Billy?" said Miranda. "I want to be here next time you visit. I want to be here every time you visit, from now on. I want there to be no question I'll be here." She laced her fingers through his, and clung. Her hand felt strong and not at all birdlike, and he squeezed it, tried to sound reassuring and avuncular instead of exhausted.

He said, "Well, you're living together. Wouldn't you say that's a pretty good sign?"

"He's talking to Angela." The words seemed to suck the breath out of her, and she waited a moment before filling her lungs again. "He's talking to Angela," she said again, sitting up a little straighter. Then she said, quickly, "He's always talking to her. She phones every day. She phones and phones. The other day, we were leaving for the store, and he said he'd forgotten his coat, and I went in after him, and he was on the phone with her."

Bill shifted on the hard, numbingly cold ground. His back ached.

She said, "Do you think he'll go back to her?"

"I don't know, Miranda. Listen. James has always been... You're young, and I just, well. James is my friend. So. I'm sorry — I'm quite tired."

"You mean I'm young as in, someday this won't seem important, right? Someday James will just be a blip to me, a memory. But *you* know what it's like to love James. You know."

"Hey, ladies!" James closed the screen door with a bang, and Bill tried to pull his hand away. Miranda held on for a moment before letting go. Mudlogged leaves squished as James walked under the maple. "Having a little party without me?" James lowered himself to ground in front of Miranda, and she wriggled backwards so he could lie against her legs. She handed him the roach and the matches, and he smoked the rest of it in silence, Miranda's hand in his hair, his arm hooked around her calf. Bill thought he'd just wait a couple of minutes and then get up and say goodnight. He pictured himself doing it. Two more days and two more nights. Maybe Miranda would go to class in the morning, and he could have a good talk with James. Ask the right questions.

"Did you guys ever start digging?" said Miranda.

"Hmm?" James pushed back until she opened her legs, and he rested his head on her belly.

Naomi K. Lewis

"The hole," she said.

James laughed his cave-chested tuba laugh. "The hole," he said. "We never got past considering it. Not so hot on the follow-through, eh, friend?"

"I started digging," said Bill. "When you were at camp."

"You're joking."

"No — I spent a whole day out there. Was no picnic getting the shovel to the island, either. I used my dad's canoe."

"You're friggen joking. Why didn't you ever tell me?"

"I don't remember. When you left for camp, you came up to my shoulder; when you came back, you were taller than me. You'd outgrown forts — I could see that the moment you opened your door."

"The summer I went to camp."

"You came back a foot taller, and all you could talk about was the girls you'd kissed and the dirty magazines you'd read."

"Yeah," said James. "Camp girls." He seemed to mull this over for a while before he said, "Miranda here was asking me if I knew about your gayness when we were kids. I didn't. You didn't tell me."

"I didn't know. I wasn't keeping a secret."

"That's what I said. If you'd known, you would have told me. Is that the phone?"

None of them breathed. It rang four more times, and stopped.

"So, a lawyer and a psychologist." James registered the volume of his voice, and lowered it. "You guys must do okay. I bet you have a sweet house."

"I don't know about you two," said Miranda, "but I'm freezing my ass."

James stood and pulled Miranda to her feet. He turned and offered his hand, but Bill was already halfway up.

Inside, James immediately started collecting the dirty dishes from the table and piling them in the sink.

"Listen," said Bill. "I hope this isn't rude, but I'm very tired, so —"

In the living room, the phone rang. Miranda and James both looked at the swinging door.

"Listen," said Bill. "Maybe —"

"Maybe what?" James wiped his hands on the tea towel he'd draped over his shoulder.

"Maybe you shouldn't answer the goddamn telephone when you have a guest," said Miranda.

"That's not what he was going to say," said James, over the next ring. "What were you going to say, Bill?"

"I think it's time for me to say good —"

"I have to get this," said James.

Miranda sat and stared at her hands on the table as James pushed through the door into the living room, and said hello three times. She spread her fingers as he reappeared. Her nails were dark red and short.

"She hung up," said James. "Happy?"

The phone rang.

Miranda stood. She flexed and unflexed her fingers. "You piece of shit."

The phone rang.

Miranda's picked up one of the soup bowls from the table, and pulled back her arm. James flinched. Miranda let the bowl fall from her hand onto the table. "You piece of shit." She stepped into the living room, and James followed her. The stairs were through there. Bill considered sitting down and resting his head on the table.

"Ange and I have children together," yelled James.

Bill cracked the door and peered through, his feet still in the kitchen. James held the phone, and Miranda held its cord, which she'd unplugged from the wall. Over the green upholstered chesterfield hung a beige and brown felt owl with stabbingly blue eyes.

"Does she know I live here?" Miranda asked James.

"Excuse me," said Bill. Neither of them gave any sign of having heard him. "I'm going to say goodnight now." He crossed the living room to the antique desk and the stairs, and took them quickly, creaking every one.

Bill took his black toiletries bag and black cotton pajamas into the bathroom, which was even colder than the rest of the house. He examined the floor around the tub, and wondered if he could wash himself in the morning without risking his life. Then he blinked at his bloodshot eyes in the mirror and brushed his teeth. He always brought a facecloth when he travelled, and he used it with facial cleanser, spending extra time on his nose. A habit, from the days when he'd fought acne. The sink looked dirty, but when he rubbed it with his thumb, nothing came off. The enamel was just chipping. That girl, Leslie Meaks. In his math class, she'd always worn her long pale hair in a ponytail. She looked around the room a lot. He'd noticed that. How she didn't look at the teacher or her work, but scanned the other students, one by one, seeking eye contact. Her chin always rested in her hand as though her head were weighed down with unprocessed information, and her voice, when she spoke, came from deep in her throat. He'd closed the bedroom door and turned to her. She was sitting, the sheet tucked under her shoulders. Naked. No ponytail. Clear eyed; didn't seem drunk or stoned. She ran her hands through her hair a few times, but it was still a ragged mess. A box of condoms sat on the bedside table. Outside the door, the others guys clustered like starved wolves. The room smelled like sweat and latex. Someone's parents' bedroom.

"You don't have to," she said. "I won't tell."

Maybe if she hadn't said that, he wouldn't have held her down by the hair the way he did.

On Monday, she'd approached Bill and James's lockers, smiling too much, hands clasped, but they'd dodged past her without saying hi; James looked a bit proud, but really scared, that way he did when you just couldn't blame him.

Leaning close to the mirror, Bill massaged skin cream into his face, with the pads of his fingers. He rubbed some over his lips, which hurt, and looked close to cracking. He'd find a glass downstairs, for water. Remorse was not exactly appropriate for something that happened so long ago. He was sad for everyone involved. He was an adult, now, looking back. He took off his jeans and sweater, and put on the pajamas over his undershirt and briefs and socks. Still not warm enough.

As he sat on his mattress, he realized he'd forgotten to take out his contacts, but when he stood to return the bathroom he heard its door close. So he stayed up for another fifteen minutes, drinking water and fighting the waves of exhaustion until the bathroom was free again. Emile had been right, of course. Bill would go home with knots in his back and a stress fever, and a pimple beside his nose.

Contacts out, Bill shut the bathroom door behind him.

"Hey," called Miranda, through the open bedroom door. In a futon resting a few inches off the floor on a wooden frame, she and James were propped up against giant, puffy pillows. They wore plaid flannel pajamas, his burgundy with grey, hers pale blue with white. Beside Miranda, a small black lamp sat on a milk crate, providing the only light.

"Do you need anything?" she said.

Instead of a curtain, a yellow baby blanket covered the window. Yellow with darker yellow ducks and blue flecks all over it.

"No, I'm okay," Bill said.

"Do you want to call home? To say goodnight to Emile?"

"Oh. No. Maybe it seems weird. We don't usually call each other when we're away."

"To see if he's okay?"

"He's always okay."

"Okay."

"Goodnight," Bill said.

"Night," said James.

"Come in here for a second," said Miranda. "And turn off that hall light, would you?"

"Yeah," said James.

After a glance back into the now-dark hallway, Bill crossed the blue rug, and when Miranda patted the futon beside her, he lowered himself to its edge.

She lifted the black and red Bay blanket and white sheet, and he slipped his legs under them, leaned back against the wall.

"Relax." She pulled at the pillow behind her back so he could lean against it, too. "I want to say I'm sorry. I don't want you to misunderstand anything. I was just saying to James, I don't want Billy to misunderstand anything. And he said he didn't want you to, either."

"That's true," said James.

"We'll start again tomorrow," said Miranda. "We'll go to Mactaquac. A beautiful walk. The leaves."

"Miranda has nothing to be sorry for," said James. "It's my bad."

"Don't worry," said Bill.

"Jamie loves you. We just don't want you to think anything," said Miranda.

"I don't think anything."

Miranda looked at him hard with her giant eyes. James was hidden behind her except for the lump of his legs under the blanket. Her makeup was gone. Bill hadn't realized she was wearing any. He said, again, "I don't think anything."

Miranda yanked the pillow flat on the bed, then leaned across him, the back of her arm touching his chest for a moment as she turned off the lamp. The duck blanket didn't make a good curtain. A leak of light crossed her fine brown eyebrow and the edge of her perfect little nose.

Bill closed his eyes and lay flat on his back, and Miranda lay beside him, her body heat amplified by the flannel. The blanket was itchy where the sheet pulled away from its edge, and part of his hand and the side of his neck were bare and cold. He was too tired to move.

James said, "What are you thinking, Billy?"

Two more days, two more nights. The rogue line of moonlight slashing his chest. The dormitory sounds of Miranda and James breathing.

"Billy." Miranda's kittenish whisper, muffled because her face was pressed into his shoulder. "Jamie loves you so much. You don't know how much."

Bill lay still, still, chest lifting and falling by its own power, as though anything his body did now had nothing to do with him.

Five years later, Emile would speak at a conference in Halifax, and Bill, bored during the day and wondering why he'd tagged along, would, on a whim, phone James and Angela. James would seem so upbeat and together, helpful and sweet to Angela, and jovial with Roche and Honey, who were lanky limbed and unrecognizable — even Emile would say so when they all had dinner in the suburban backyard that night, on the old blue plates with daisies in the middle. When they were alone by the barbeque, James would tell Bill he'd heard from Miranda. That she was travelling the world with another artist. "What a cool chick," he'd say, just like that, as he flipped burgers.

And Bill would certainly not have to turn away from James's broad face and the ashes that had stuck to his forehead and lip, and if he did, it would not be because of Miranda's flower and cigarette scent, and the way it had mingled with the damp-leaf chill of Mactaquac Provincial Park when they walked, Miranda pushing one arm through James's and the other through Bill's, absorbing not merely all responsibility for what had happened the night before, but all memory of it, so she could then step aside, taking it with her.

And Bill would not suddenly recall whether it had been she or James who had whispered, under the quicksand warmth of the wool blanket, "Tell us. You can tell us. What are you thinking?"

Naomi K. Lewis

"I told you…." Bill pushed his voice up, up, up to the faces bent over his.

"Tell us…."

"I'm not…." a bared shoulder, soft hands "…. thinking…." a rough cheek on his chest "….anything."

WEFT

Berry

Berry sat at the school desk behind Ben's every Tuesday and Thursday night all fall. She was twenty-four and he was twenty-five, and grade twelve English was the last credit each of them needed to finish high school. Berry hadn't finished the first time because, obviously, she'd had Izzy. Ben's story, which he told her over coffee after class, involved stolen cars from an airport parking lot, police surrounding a Denny's, and a year of incarceration. Hard to believe — Ben, with his vigilant posture, his symmetrical hair, and his navy wool pea coat. The English course ended. Berry was the one who looked him up and phoned him; they began the conversation by congratulating each other on the high-school diplomas they'd received in the mail.

"We should celebrate," said Berry.

"Definitely," said Ben.

That weekend Izzy was with her dad, and Berry and Ben had dinner together — Ethiopian on Bloor — and a night of drinking wine and sliding around in their boots on the hockey rink in Christie Pits, across from his apartment. They lay side by side in the middle of the ice. They kissed. Ben lay on top of Berry and pressed his body against hers, thighs to thighs, belly to belly, chest to chest, through the layers of long johns, jeans and coats. Berry thought: Yes. This person. I will do anything. A dangerous feeling. She knew the danger; she'd had this feeling about Izzy's dad, when she was seventeen. Dangerous, but she welcomed it. She was helpless to it, and she welcomed the helplessness.

Back at Ben's apartment, he made a big show of turning on lamps and positioning them just so, to cast a still, dim light. She sat on the sofa, but he sat in the armchair across from her, and they talked for a long time, though she couldn't have said later about what.

Eventually he told her, "Lately I've been questioning the dichotomy between intimacy and loneliness."

"Oh?" said Berry, waiting for her brain to catch up with what he was talking about.

"The thing is, what I'm really in need of is a friend. Things don't work out too well with people I date, and I don't want things not to work out too well between me and you. I like you a lot. Would you be interested in being friends?"

"Oh," said Berry.

Ben slumped, legs apart, feet in sheepskin slippers flat on the floor, arms dangling. The lamp cast a long, reddish glow, a skewed impression of itself that bent toward Ben's shadow, as though even light couldn't resist him.

"The problem is," he said, "no one should trust me."

"Why not? I trust you."

"You shouldn't. I can make myself cry at will."

"Do you do that a lot?"

"All the time."

The sleeves of his grey Shetland cable knit sweater hung over his knuckles. No acrylic in that sweater. His fingers were long and beautiful. The armchair was upholstered in a textured green weave;

in the lamplight, it was faded pine with small bursts of lavender. Berry imagined stretching a thin wool sheet on a wood frame and firing paint at it from behind. Would a paint gun work? She'd never actually seen one. She thought of popcorn, how the internal pressure made each tight kernel tremble in the pan until its surface burst apart. The sheer violence of it. She and Izzy liked to watch together through the glass lid, Izzy standing on a chair, Berry's arms around her daughter's waist. Each popped kernel was an explosion, a disaster frozen in time just before it dissipated. She and Izzy liked to toss the popcorn in butter and maple syrup and salt. Berry was drunk, her body still warm with the promise of Ben, the promise he'd just withdrawn.

"I went to my brother's place before I met up with you today," said Ben. "There were syringes everywhere. They're back at it." Tears pooled under his reddening eyes and he sighed through his nose.

"Are you serious?" said Berry. "Or faking?"

"Faking."

His voice shook, as if he were trying to regain control.

"How do you do it?"

"I just think about something really sad."

"Like what?"

"Like the syringes I saw at my junkie brother's place earlier."

So they agreed to be friends, and what that meant was, Ben phoned her almost every day. They had dinner together three or four times a week. Berry thought about Ben all the time, smiling at things he'd said as she walked down the street or cut vegetables for dinner. For quite a while she assumed they were working their way back to each other's bodies, but they never touched again.

That wasn't true, of course.

Not never.

Sometimes Berry and Ben slept in the same bed after a late night out, and sometimes there was a rough tussling, Ben pushing Berry's arms around, getting her thigh between his legs and pulling her hair. The chest-to-chest tenderness he'd shown on the skating rink did not return, but she knew he was capable of it, so she waited. They breathed hard, faces close together, and sometimes Ben whispered crazy things like, *I want to have a baby with you.* Ben's breath and skin smelled sweet, milky, even when they'd been drinking or smoking, and Berry chose to believe this was some sort of magic, rather than evidence of the toothbrush and toothpaste and face cream he always carried with him. Mornings, Berry took Ben's lead and told herself it had all been a dream. The small dense hold behind her sternum unfurled those days, and aching, long tendrils of sadness strained toward each place Ben's body had deigned to make contact with hers.

After ten months of this, Berry met a man in an upstairs living room in a huge house during a party. An entomologist, who was excited because he'd recently bought some prints of different insect species. He loved insects, and referred to them affectionately as "critters."

"I work at a yarn store," Berry told him. "I teach spinning classes. Not with exercise bikes. Spinning yarn."

"With spinning wheels?" Larry edged closer to her on the sofa.

"We use handmade drop spindles."

"I don't think there's a word in the English language less sexy than *spindle*," said Larry. "But somehow, when you say it…." He kissed her. He would explain later he appreciated irony to an extent most people, Berry included, simply couldn't grasp. That's why he was often misunderstood.

"I have a spinning wheel at home," Berry said. He kissed her again before she could say anything more. Izzy loved the spinning wheel, to sit there pretending she was Sleeping Beauty.

"Come to my place," said Larry.

"Not tonight. I have to pick up my daughter in the morning."

"Daughter?"

"Daughter. She's eight."

Larry tried to be cool about it. She had no way of knowing then that his facial expression indicated a disappointment so choking it was indistinguishable from rage.

Soon after that Larry was her boyfriend. A boyfriend meant no more Ben. Berry was busy with her job at Warp & Weft, and with Izzy, and with having sex with Larry whenever Izzy went to her dad's, and she barely thought about Ben anymore at all.

Ben

He could hear her typing. *Tap tap hesitation tap-tap-tap*. His girlfriend. Girlfriend. She'd said she just needed to read some stuff online and that she would use the mouse to navigate. No keyboard, she promised. *TAP TAP TAPity-TAP*. Fuck.

"Listen to this," Karen called from the living room. Ben tried to sink into the bathwater, but getting his chest and head under meant sticking his legs up the wall. Just before his ears submerged, he thought he heard Karen say, "A something something a beaver." Ben focused in disgust on his right foot, giant and obscene up there on the tiles. *Karen Mabee, please go home*.

No: she came closer and opened the bathroom door, and a draft cut through the precious warmth like a blunt knife through a loaf of bread, ruining it. He'd seen Karen do just that: mash a perfectly good whole-wheat loaf to a pulp, leaving crumbs on the counter and offering him a slice thin as paper as one end and thick as spite at the other. Ben lifted his head from the bathwater just enough to offer his ear holes. He frowned at her as fiercely as he knew how, and Karen ran a hand through her short apple-juice-coloured hair, making it stand on end like a mohawk. The reason it stayed in place like that, Ben knew for a fact, was that she hardly ever washed it.

She said, "A writer is like a weaver."

"You're letting out all my heat."

She stepped into the room and closed the door behind her.

"What's wrong?" she said.

"I forgot to cut the nails on that foot." He flexed the toes. "I did the other one."

"Because," said Karen, "he works on the wrong side of the fabric. He has only language, and thus suddenly he finds himself surrounded by meaning. Merleau Ponty."

"I just can't bring myself to cut the ones on this foot. It's been four months. I mean, look at it. Soon the nails will curve over and grow back into my fucking skin."

"So, just cut them."

"It's not that simple."

"Then there must be some good reason for leaving them." She sat on the counter beside the sink, legs dangling. She didn't look comfortable at all. "You just don't know what it is, yet. Four months. Let's see. What's significant about four months?"

That was typical of Karen, to make everything about her and the fact that Ben hadn't cut those nails since the day they met. He pushed himself up so his chest was sticking out of the water, and dropped his feet in with a splash. Most of his body was still obscured by lavender-smelling foam.

"Anyway," she went on. "I have one semester to finish my thesis so it's kind of on my mind. So thanks for listening."

"I was listening."

"Right."

"A writer is like a weaver..." Ben prompted.

"You see, the writer is assumed to be male. But the weaver, according to Freud and history, remember? Is feminine."

"Oh." He picked up the blue shower puff she'd given him. "Puff me?"

What was wrong with her? The green cardigan buttoned over her T-shirt made her look bony around the shoulders, and obscured her breasts, which were actually pretty big. (Ben did not particularly like big breasts.) She made herself tiny and frail, like a bird. A furious bird. No: a fuzzy caterpillar. Ben laughed out loud.

"What?" Karen said.

"Puff me!"

Ben pushed himself up to standing. Bubble bath and water eased down his body. He could see himself in the mirror behind Karen's back, how his pubic hair was obscured behind a puff of white foam. He bared his teeth and growled. "Come here."

She didn't move.

"Come over here."

"Why?"

"Why? *Why?* You're my girlfriend. Why do you think? Get in the bath." He'd lure her into the soapy water and then, when she was least expecting it, lather up her hair and rinse out all the grease. "I want you," he said.

Karen glanced at the door, even slipped off the counter and reached for the doorknob. Without looking at Ben, she took off her cardigan and undid her pants. She pushed her jeans down to her ankles and struggled with her sock. Sat on the floor and removed each sock, and then the jeans. Opened the door, tossed the jeans, socks, and cardigan out, and then, in only a tight, ancient-looking burgundy T-shirt and lacy white panties, straddled the edge of the tub with one foot in the water and picked the dripping mauve puff out.

"Go on," she said. "Get back in."

As Karen soaped Ben's shoulders and back, and talked and talked about her research, he closed his eyes and fought the panic in his chest. He'd met Karen, a friend of a friend of a friend, at a bar, a week or so after Berry started dating the bearded freak —insect researcher — entomologist. He and Karen had talked about her masters thesis and he'd said, "Wow, weaving? I have this friend who works in a yarn store. I *love* yarn. Fabric is the oldest, most important technology of human civilization and now we're all completely alienated from it."

He was basically just repeating what Berry had said, but Karen's grey eyes got even rounder and she said, "I *know*."

The sturdiest, straightest yarns, Berry had told Ben, were tightly spun fibres like wool or cotton or flax, with two plies twisted around each other in the direction opposite to that in which they were spun. She'd demonstrated, peeling two Shetland plies apart. Some yarns had three or more plies; she showed him an orange wool, loosely spun, with a tight little line of red cotton through it. Berry's favourite yarn was recycled sari silk, thick, one-ply, chaotically coloured.

Ben and Karen went to Chinatown so they could keep talking over hot and sour soup, and at almost three Ben told her about the stolen cars, the whole story, about those guys he got mixed up with and how he ended up taking the fall, and the detention centre. He said he'd never told anyone those things before. She nodded, pale eyebrows drawn together, seduced. Said she'd posed for Internet porn one summer in high school, when she was on vacation with her parents, who were on the verge of a divorce. Said she'd never told anyone that before, either. Ben felt guilty as fuck. He'd told his sob story to how many people? Hundreds? A real tear slid down Karen's cheek. Her slightly fuzzy cheek, like girls with light hair sometimes have. So they were both crying. When she took off her skirt and blouse in his bedroom, as the sun came up, she revealed pink thong panties and a black bra on a slim, busty frame. She was obviously pleased with herself, and glad she'd worn the sexy underwear. Her whole body was fuzzy like her cheeks. In Ben's opinion, cuteness and sexiness could not coexist, and this chick was cute and hapless as a kitten. Two days later, she was wearing the black bra again, this time with matching panties. Ben could not help thinking the bra had probably been worn at least three times in a row without being washed. Karen lay there in his bed, eyes closed, expecting to be adored.

Now, she leaned over his shoulder to soap his chest. She rested her other hand on his back as she leaned lower and lower, trying not to get her shirt wet. She reached down almost to his naval with her little lathery circles. She said, "Have you ever noticed a cobweb looks like a cross section of an onion? Or, I mean, vice versa?"

Ben grabbed Karen's wrist and pulled her, in one swift motion, halfway over his shoulder and into the bath. He grabbed the back of her head with his other hand so she wouldn't bump it on the faucet. Her body was like a ragdoll. By the time she even had a chance to gasp and say, "Hey!" he was on top of her in the water, their legs tangled together, her panties and shirt soaked and soapy.

"Ha!" said Ben. "Now I've got you where I want you."

Instead of protesting, Karen watched his face, waiting to see what he'd do next.

He grabbed her breast and squeezed.

She pressed her pelvis up against his and closed her eyes, lifted her face, lips parted. He ground her hips down against the bottom of the tub, and she grunted in discomfort, but then smiled. Ben tugged her knees, sliding her until her head dunked under water. She came up sputtering, coughing with her mouth wide open like a little kid's in a swimming pool. He kept her arms pinned down so she had to hold her face above water with the strength of her neck, and she freaked out, wiggling like a fish. He released her arms.

"Let me out," she said, blowing her nose on her hand and then washing it off in the water.

"You know what your problem is?" said Ben. "Your mind is completely disconnected from your body. You're all brain."

Dripping all over the floor instead of standing on the bath mat, Karen took off her wet underwear, the tee-shirt and a purple bra, and rubbed herself all over with Ben's towel. She had little golden curls of pubic hair and the most protuberant labia Ben had ever seen. Skinny little body with enormous breasts and genitalia. Profoundly distasteful. She rubbed her hair dry. Some soap got rubbed into the towel. He had a dry fluffy one in his bedroom, but how would he get to it without tracking water through the apartment? Naked, Karen dropped the towel on the floor, on top of her wet clothes, before leaving the room.

"This really rots my socks," Ben yelled at the closed door.

"I definitely don't feel like this is working out," she called back.

"Damn!" said Ben. "You just need to chill out."

Karen did not speak again until she reappeared with her coat and toque on, holding the door wide open, letting out every little bit of heat. She'd put on the jeans and socks and sweater with nothing underneath. She was a walking disaster.

"You have sex with me like I'm a man," she said, grabbing her soggy garments from the floor. She was sweating, her face all shiny.

"*What*?"

"I'm telling you, you fuck like a gay guy. I'm sorry if no one's ever told you before, but it's something you should know."

"Maybe," Ben yelled, too late, "that's because you act like a man!" She hadn't heard him, had already slammed the front door — she always slammed doors; it didn't matter if she was angry or what — and was gone.

Ben ran wet to his bedroom to retrieve a clean towel, and sat, wrapped in it, in his green armchair. He played his guitar for a while, not a song, just the beginning of something new, or old. He phoned Karen's cell phone and broke up with her. Got back in the bath for an hour. Cut the nails on his right foot.

Called Berry.

"You still dating that insect guy?"

"Yeah."

"How's that going?"

"Not that great, I guess. He's doesn't really like to be around when Izzy's here...."

"Of course it's not going that great! He's not good enough for you. He's nothing compared to you. I mean, I dated someone, too. This *intellectual*. I miss you."

Berry didn't answer for a while. When she did, she just said, "Ben...."

Karen

Arachne, a mortal woman, declares herself the greatest weaver of heaven and earth; she even denies divine inspiration, boasting that she is self-taught. After Arachne has bragged for some time to anyone who'll listen, Athena, goddess of spinning and weaving, pays a visit disguised as an old woman, and warns the girl to beware insulting the gods. Arachne is not intimidated. So Athena sheds her disguise — and still, Arachne fails even to tremble; she knows she's the best, and she proposes a competition. Goddess and woman weave side by side, the goddess Envy as their judge. Athena's tapestry shows the gods in all their glory, committing great deeds and punishing mortals who dare cross them. But Arachne's tapestry depicts Zeus and several other male gods engaged in a series of raunchy sex acts with mortal women and nymphs. Zeus is disguised as a common man, a bull, a swan, a shower of gold. He is pure sex, and he doesn't wait for consent. Both tapestries are indisputably perfect, and Athena is enraged. She destroys Arachne's work and hits her on the head, filling the girl with a suicidal depression. Arachne hangs herself. But Athena brings the weaver-pornographer back to life: doomed to hang and weave forever, Arachne is transformed into a spider.

Karen was walking out of the Dundas West subway station when her phone rang. What Ben said was, "We're just not compatible physically. We should have just been friends. I'm sorry to lose you as a friend."

"I have plenty of friends already," Karen said.

"I'm sorry I have to break up with you," Ben said, pretending to cry.

"I guess I wasn't clear," Karen told him. "I was breaking up with you when I left your place, when I said things definitely weren't working out...."

Naomi K. Lewis

"I want you to know something I've never told anyone before. I owe you something I've never told anyone. So here it is: I never finished high school. I took this English class last year, my last credit? I failed it. I panicked and left the exam after ten minutes. I made out like I'd gotten my diploma in the mail. I hadn't."

"I don't get why you're telling me this," said Karen.

"How can you be so cold?" Ben snuffled. "After everything we've shared?"

Karen hung up. How dare he cry and call her cold, when she was the one whose heart was twisted into a knot, and he was the one who certainly didn't care, who was hollow as an empty bottle? She must have been crazy, anyway, getting into a relationship when she had so much work to do. Her master's thesis, *(World Wide) Web of Lust: Arachne and the Revelry of the Gods*, was due by spring, but the whole thing was crumbling, the whole edifice she'd been trying to build glaringly facile, obvious, and also too complicated to make any sense.

Evening, the sun beginning to set, Karen entered her apartment building on Howard Park Ave. Took the steps down to her basement unit. Her last roommate had left after a fight over the toilet paper situation — had been hoarding rolls in her bedroom because, she said, Karen habitually used too many squares, not the mention the piles of the dishes in the sink and the thick layer of clothing strewn across her bedroom floor, as if that were any of the roommate's business at all. Anyway, now Karen lived alone, and she couldn't afford it. She'd have to find a new roommate right away. Or later.

Karen shed her coat and hat and all her clothes in the middle of the living room floor, took her wet underwear and T-shirt from her bag and dropped them on top of the pile. Naked, she set up the TV she'd dragged into her room after the toilet-paper fascist left, and got in bed with her notebook and pen to watch the Japanese anime series she'd bought. For the character called Lady Arachne. Arachne in popular culture. Then she watched animated porn. Then she watched live-action porn. *The scene of heavenly guilt.* Those were Ovid's words. Maybe that should be her title, Karen thought. "Heavenly Guilt." But then she'd lose the parentheses and the Internet/web reference. "(World Wide) Web of Heavenly Guilt?" No, that didn't sound right at all. Web of Desire. Web of Revelry?

According to some interpretations, Athena is enraged by the tapestry's illicit content; according to others, she is simply envious of Arachne's skill. One thing, however, is far from clear. Was Arachne's intent really to showcase the flaws of the gods — to reprimand and expose? Or was she, rather, reveling in the images? After all, she bordered her work with ivy, a Dionysian symbol. If *The Story of O*, also a story told by a woman, could be heralded as an erotic classic rather than a mirror held up to the patriarchy, then surely Arachne's creation, exactly the same kind of decadent, masochistic fantasy (Karen argued), could be understood the same way.

But there: her point; it could be made in one short, concise paragraph. Instead she'd stretched it out into a twenty-page chapter one. And then came chapter two. In which, yes, the spider is doomed to weave without signifying, but her web doesn't just sit there doing nothing. It ensnares. Once you're in, you can't get out. You're wrapped up tighter and tighter; you lie there, waiting to be devoured. The Web. You allow yourself to become the pornograph, rather than the pornographer, and you are the fly, your insides dissolving into mush. You are dinner.

Chapter three: The semiotics of Internet porn, including women alone, waiting for men, but especially of the cum shot.

Chapter four: Arachnophobia. The French third-wave feminists.

Chapter five: Spiderman. Spiderman underwear, the little-boy kind, worn by women (a trend). Spiderwoman, also called Arachne, is blind.

Chapter six: Bullshit, bullshit, bullshit.

The point was, Arachne's depiction of the gods fucking the women was so orgiastic, so hot, it had to be destroyed. Zeus as bull, plowing through the sea with Europa on his back. And Leda, *supinely press'd, Whilst the soft snowy swan sate hov'ring o'er her breast.* Sate: that was the operative word. Arachne's tapestry was a series of cum shots. The faces of the gods in orgasm, the women trembling, supine, trying in vain to avoid *the briny tide all foaming hoar.* Web of Satiety? Or should that be Satiation? (She'd pointed out to Ben that when she'd posed for those photos herself, those horrible photos she'd found years later on the Web, under the fake name she had not, thank god, revealed to Ben — that when she'd posed in the velour Santa dress, there had been no ejaculation, no man involved at all. For this fact, she was immensely grateful, though she also thought maybe she would have been better off having had the whole experience, pushed to its limit, to truly know what it felt like to be obliterated as person by the male orgasm. Ben had told her to stop analyzing her own life like a series of symbols, and that it was life, not a movie. She and Ben had talked far too much about that long-ago photo shoot of hers, both kept bringing it up, a scab they couldn't stop picking. Good that they'd finally broken up. What had she been thinking? He repaired musical instruments for a living and hadn't even finished high school, though of course she hadn't know that part until now, because he was a liar. A pathological liar.)

   The WWW, Karen wrote in her notebook, *is a 4-D onion with an infinitely receding centre. In cross-section, the onion looks like a cobweb…*

missing
Feminine Origin
(The weaver/
pornographer)

Lifting the remote, Karen took aim, and depressed the pause button right on the money shot. The erect penis in the middle of the screen, white goo flying, *flying* (that had to be a special effect), out of it, toward a face momentarily off screen.

"Scholarship is not poetry, and poetry is not scholarship," her supervisor, a woman maybe ten years older than Karen, had said at their last meeting. Professor Lazarus was right, and Ben was right, too — that Karen failed, again and again, in her work and her personal life, to make any contact with the tangible, the nitty gritty, the real world. She had made such contact in her teens, thanks to the always willing Gavin, who had seemed so old at the time, and who had been some kind of sexual genius, with no other interests or talents she'd bothered to investigate. But then again, looking back, she suspected her bottomless craving had been at least in part a performance — a performance so convincing she'd convinced herself. One thing was for sure: she was ruining it all now. The harder she looked, the more she tried to picture Arachne's tapestry, the more revolting humans with their petty gods and their obsessive cravings and their slimy discharges became. She turned off the television and pulled the duvet over her face.

Larry

Larry typed *Berry* in the search field.

In everyday English, the first hit read, *a* berry *is a broad term for any small edible fruit. Most* berries *are juicy, round or semi-oblong, brightly coloured, sweet or sour…*

Halfway down the page was Halle Berry in her underwear, holding a gun.

He clicked through a few photos of the actress in skimpy outfits, but tiring of waiting for one of them, a big file, to load, he tried a new search.

Fucking bitch, he typed.

One of the last times he'd seen her, when things were getting really nasty, she'd said she wasn't really interested in having him sleep over if they weren't going to have sex. And she asked him not to answer her phone when she was in the shower or wherever, because it might be her parents, and what would they think.

"That you have a boyfriend?"

She didn't say anything.

Then they had a huge fight because of a novel she'd asked him to read. He said, "That woman sure hated men."

She said, "The writer or the character?"

"Well," he said. "I don't see how someone could write that, who didn't hate men."

"Is that all you got out of it?"

"What did you expect me to get?"

"I didn't know it would upset you," said Berry.

"How could you not?"

"How could I? I barely know you."

I barely know you, she said. When two nights earlier, she'd inserted her latex-gloved fingers, two of them, into his anus, and said, "Oh, you like that, don't you?" and stroked his massive erection, and said his name the way you say the name of someone you know. Someone you definitely *know*.

Then, only a few days after their breakup, he'd seen her at that show with Ben Bend. She'd told Larry she wasn't friends with Ben anymore. And there she was, probably sleeping with him, probably kissing him nightly in the abandoned way she'd kissed Larry a week before. Tall Ben Bend with his handsome vaguely European-looking face and no fat on his body and definitely not from a small town no one had ever heard of, where his father was a janitor at the same high school where his mother was a server in the cafeteria.

He typed, *Berry is a cunt.*

Larry clicked through a few random porn sites, pausing at a photo of one bright-eyed girl staring with delight and hint of fear at the huge cock about the penetrate her. He'd have to enter his credit card number to see the real action. He considered it, then changed his mind and went back to the search page.

This Canadian elf wants your cock for Christmas, one site promised. *Meet Berry*. Larry followed the link, entertaining himself with the fantasy that he'd find a picture of Berry herself. Such a discovery would kill him. He could practically feel his heart rip apart at the very thought of it. All those things Berry had done with him. Let him do to her. She hadn't known about those horrible nights of his childhood and adolescence, when he was so sure no would ever touch him. Sure no one would ever spread herself out under him and smile, and wait, and seem pleased. No: Berry hadn't known him. How could he have been so stupid? She hadn't known.

The girl on his screen was blonde. A teenager in a cheesy Santa dress. Something about the photo looked old. From the nineties, maybe. How did he know? Her hair? Something. In the first photo, she had the skirt hiked up and two fingers down the front of her scarlet panties. A childlike, mischievous smile lit her face. That was why she looked like the nineties. That girl from the old Aerosmith videos, not Steven Tyler's daughter, but the other one: she looked like that girl. She had a sweet, open face. Uncorrupted. Unlike the real Berry.

This Northern Berry needs her stocking stuffed.

Larry scrolled down to see the girl bent over. The panties were gone now, and the girl was spreading herself with her hands, smiling over her shoulder. He scrolled down again — but the girl was alone in all the pictures. He felt desperate to see something big and hard pushing into her little pink asshole. Some sites showed girls wincing or crying while they were being fucked. Sometimes that turned him on, but mostly Larry liked to see the girls really enjoy it. This girl would surely open her big eyes wide in surprise and delight.

He imagined holding that blond hair in one hand, and he pictured rubbing right up against her and hearing her moan as his semen filled her crack and dripped down her thighs.

He stood up and shot his load right onto the screen, onto the girl's face.

Then he carefully cleaned the screen with a moist monitor wipe before any fluid could drip down into the keyboard and fry its circuits. He'd cleaned his ejaculate from the computer screen hundreds of times before; that was what he'd bought the wipes for.

He'd even been nice to Berry's daughter, as if he needed that in his life, a child, and he'd never judged Berry, never said anything about her lack of education or the fact that she'd gotten pregnant in high school, at an age when Larry and the kind of girl he'd expected — hoped — to end up with had been virgins. He had never mentioned the wrinkles around her eyes, small but pretty pronounced for a twenty-five-year-old. And now she didn't even phone him to see how he was doing, or bother to hide the fact that she was spending time with someone else. Larry sat with his jeans still open and thought about Berry and cried for a while, because of the way they'd woken some mornings face to face and she'd pushed his hair off his face and smiled in an almost motherly way; that is, the way a mother does when you're young and sick, and she is checking to see if you have a fever and knows you even better than you know yourself and could never replace you, not with anyone.

ATTACHMENT

Subject: Bottle Rock-It Human Rocket Initiative

Bonnie Dey to me   show details   3:53 AM (5 hours ago)

Dear Mary Benjamin,
Please find my cover letter and resume attached.
Sincerely,
Bonnie Dey

_____

Bonnie Dey
Arctic Safety Expert
Staying Alive North Safety Services

Mary Benjamin, President
Bottle Rock-It Soda Pop Co.
Phoenix, Arizona, USA

October 15, 2020

Dear Ms. Benjamin,

I am writing to enter the Bottle Rock-It Soda Pop Corporation's much publicized contest to man the world's first self-contained extra-atmospheric rocket and skydiving device next summer, as advertised on your website and in the media at large.

I am uniquely qualified to operate this historic vessel, and thereby to become the spokesperson and mascot for your line of fine beverages. I have been skydiving since the age of six, have jumped as an adult over 2,000 times, and have worked as a skydiving instructor, personal trainer, and Arctic safety expert (with Staying Alive North Safety Services). I have been engaged in the progress of science since childhood, have performed many daring feats, and have surmounted staggering odds in my personal life. Having accomplished all this, I am still in the prime of my life (29 years old). Thanks to my ongoing commitment to a lifestyle healthy in all respects, including Bottle Rock-It Soda Pop as my beverage of choice, I suffer from no ailments or injuries.

I have been preoccupied with your posting since I first saw it, struck with its perfect match to my skill set, and thanks to certain recent revelatory events, I now feel strongly that manning — that being — the Bottle Rock-It Human Rocket is nothing short of my destiny.

I hope you will agree that my resume (enclosed) speaks for itself. I also append a few notes to clarify certain points. Please feel free to peruse these at your leisure.

I look forward to hearing from you, and am confident that I will be the world's first human rocket,

Bonnie Dey

BONNIE BATHURST DEY: RESUME

bonniedey@skyhigh.sky
2214, Tower 3, Clareview Lifestyle Villa
Edmonton, Alberta, Canada
Date of birth: November 21, 1991
Place of birth: Barrie, Ontario, Canada

EDUCATION

Arctic safety training diploma, levels 1, 2, and 3: Staying Alive North Safety College, Edmonton. *2015*

Personal training certificate (two-thirds completed): Central Ontario Technical College. *2014*

One year toward general arts degree: University of Ottawa. *2011*

High school diploma: Ottawa Centre High School, Ottawa. *2010*

OTHER CREDENTIALS

Class four, five, and six driver's licences

Canadian Sport Parachute Association (CSPA) ratings:
Coach 1; A,B,C licenses; Jumpmaster, Rigger A; Skydive school instructor

Total jumps: 2040

WORK EXPERIENCE

Arctic safety trainer: SAN North, Edmonton. *Sept. 2016–Aug. 2020*

Personal Trainer: Self Employed, Ottawa. *Dec. 2014–Aug. 2016*

Skydiving instructor and tandem master: Mega-Awesome Gravity Adventure Centre, Ottawa. *Aug. 2013-Aug. 2014*

Running workshop leader and cashier: The Running-Shoe Place, Ottawa. *Sept. 2010–Sept. 2013*

Cashier: Ripley's Repertory Theatre, Ottawa. *Summer, 2008*

AWARDS AND HONOURS

Honourary mention, Ottawa South elementary school science fair. *2002*

NOTES

A simple search of the word "resume" reveals its roots in the French *résumer*, "to summarize." So I have kept my resume itself short, nothing more than a summary of my qualities and achievements. However, I believe the most important feature of this application is not brevity, but to provide you, Ms. Benjamin, with all the relevant information, so that no doubt may be left in your mind that I am the best and only choice for the Bottle Rock-It Human Rocket. I implore you to give at least a cursory read through what I am about to relate. I believe you will be most grateful that you did.

I alluded in my cover letter to "certain recent events" that led me to write this application. Though these events are not entirely pleasant to recount, doing so will enlighten you and your hiring committee, and therefore I will do my best.

For the past six months, I have begun every day with a long bicycle ride through Edmonton, which is where I live, as part of my training for a triathlon. Every day I pushed myself further, until I was biking eight hours a day, down the river pathway through the whole city, past Devon and back again (map and route searchable online). My personal best in terms of both speed and stamina.

I would like to emphasize that my lifelong commitment to physical fitness will be one of my greatest assets as the Bottle Rock-It Human Rocket. I have never suffered from any serious health defect, nor any chronic complaints such as allergies, asthma, or migraines. I grew up with a sickly (headachy, allergic, asthmatic) brother, an obese mother, and a club-footed sister, so my own athleticism is the result of self determination. I do have my father's influence to thank, but only marginally, since he was an airline pilot and hobby skydiver, usually away, in midair, or sleeping.

Anyway. Two weeks ago, an hour into my bike ride, my progress was impeded by a waist-level length of yellow tape blocking my path, and a sign telling me to stop. According to this sign, the path was off limits due to "Dangerous Material's." Odd, considering that the scene looked the same as ever: picture a typical river bike path, emerging from a tree-lined valley to pass a block of concrete buildings that were once warehouses, then converted into restaurants, and then permanently abandoned. No particularly noxious smell: just the usual dusty prairie sinus ache, maybe a tinge of polluted North Saskatchewan River. Across a weedy expanse stands the former "Poppa-Jack's Crab Shack," with its sign and giant plaster crab still intact, both faded to brown. All the windows smashed. Six in the morning features a couple of construction-types in hardhats milling around over there, not really doing anything as far as I can see. Easily, I hoisted the bike (man's bike, slightly big for me, but I'd adjusted the seat) onto my shoulder, stepped over the yellow tape, rode a half-kilometre to an identical set-up, lifted the bike over that, too, and went on my way, back into the somewhat pathetic greenery of the river valley.

Six hours later, on my way home, I crossed the yellow-tape enclosed pathway again, in reverse. Noon now, and the construction goons on their lunch break. One of them, a man around my age, yelled after me, "Can't you read?"

This figure was to haunt my nightmares, and not only because, when confronted, he scrunched his face into something resembling an angry baby's. He also bore a disturbing resemblance to a boy I knew growing up, a Colin Ripley, who tormented me via various methods for my entire youth. Not to mention his relations with my brother and sister. Red hair; tanned, freckled skin that held the pungent odour of manly sweat — this guy was taller, thinner, with a squashed sort of face, as though someone had taken Colin and stretched his body, then squeezed his head in a vice. Unfortunate that the man's appearance brought back so many bad memories, because his behaviour was already bad enough. For reasons attributable only to the vagaries and complex logic of the human heart, this hard-hatted character became obsessed with me, declared war on me and my bike, and repeated the whole thing, yelling included, the next day and the next.

Naomi K. Lewis

The fourth day, I was confronted not with yellow tape, but with a fence. The kind on wheels. And a bigger, bolder sign, all caps this time:

CYCLISTS AND PEDESTRIANS DO NOT ENTER
DANGEROUS MATERIAL'S.

No one around. So, obviously, I wheeled the fence aside, walked my bike around it, forced perilously close to the river's rocky edge, rode the half-kilometre to the fence's twin, and moved that, too. On my way home, I met our friend in the hardhat. I was walking my bike around the fence when I spotted him on the former Crab Shack's roof with a couple of his sunburned coworkers, drinking what appeared to be beer (reminder: it was noon, and they were at work). As I casually pushed the fence aside, he yelled at me incoherently.

"It's my right to bike here," I called back, as calmly as I could. "I'm a citizen of this city, and this is a public pathway."

"Fuckin' retard!" (Excuse my language, Ms. Benjamin.)

His insult was empty, his battle already lost.

Until the next week, when I returned to find a permanent fence, for which they must have paid some ridiculous amount. Anchored deep; I dug for several minutes with the cap from my water bottle, but couldn't find the bottom. Just to keep me out.

I'll come back to this. I need to get out of these damp clothes.

Eight o'clock, Ms. Benjamin, and the sun is rising. The weather, now that I'm safely indoors, has grown post-tantrum calm, a guileless little breeze blowing a plastic bag across the compound below, as though nothing malevolent occurred in the day's early hours. You'd never guess that I woke at 4:30 this morning to little pellets drilling my windows, lifted my bedroom blind to frost, and rubbed my flannel sleeve (of the robe I just put back on) against the glass until I could see out. Seven storeys down to the shopping plaza, the LRT station across the street, and the towers of the business centre beyond that. The other condo towers on my side of the tracks were dark except for Christmas lights here and there, but many of the office windows glowed, and the plaza's parking lot was lit practically to daytime brightness. The icy air sparkled in the fluorescence. Protein shake, and I was on my way.

I want to clear something up, right now. You're thinking, no doubt, that eight-hour daily bike rides are not for the gainfully employed. You have observed on my resume that my three-year Arctic Safety Instructor job ended two months ago, and you require an explanation. First of all, three years is a long time, and the relevance of my experience with Arctic matters cannot be overstated, since the Bottle Rock-It Human Rocket will land on the North Pole, emphasizing the icy coldness of your refreshingly delectable and healthy sodas. I know more about Arctic survival than anyone else you could hope to find; not only that, but I planned to skydive in the Arctic on several occasions (unfortunately, these plans depended on promises broken by my former boss, the unreliable Mr. Bronski). These unusual facts are only the beginning of my uncannily ideal skill set for your needs.

But I am not trying to change the subject. Why I left Staying Alive North. Short answer: I resigned. No choice. You see, four years ago, I moved from my home town of Ottawa to Edmonton, to attend Staying Alive North Safety College, and in one year completed safety training diplomas for levels 1, 2, and 3 (see resume). I was paid half a normal salary for the training, and was required to sign a five-year contract. However, my contract was rendered null and void (I will hire a lawyer, if necessary) when SAN failed to fulfill their obligations stated therein — namely to send me to Sustainable Bay, on Baffin Island, for Safety Training Level 4 in actual helicopters and boats, in the actual Arctic Ocean. For three years, I lived in Clareview Lifestyle Tower 3, and worked at Clareview Business Complex, training facility 4, showing the same videos again and again. Every ten days, I'd complete another Arctic Survival 1 session. Day after day, I was strapped into a fake helicopter and submerged upside down into a frigid pool. After swimming to the surface, I taught a bunch of meat-heads to do same. Then we practised lowering each other from the ceiling to the water, and fishing each other out. I was also obliged to memorize several helicopter safety manuals. All this I did in good faith, never doubting I'd soon leave Clareview Lifestyle Tower 3 behind, to live in Sustainable Bay, as an integral part of the New Northern Energy Project.

But why wasn't I sent up north after 2.5 years, as promised in my contract, you ask? Dare I suggest sexism? Racism, even (I am part black, though raised by white parents)? Well, for reasons known only to my former boss, the square-headed Mr. Bronski, SAN became a dead end for me (sadly, I cannot recommend calling him as a reference). In any case, I can now see that the real reason I stuck to the job as long as I did was to train for my real destiny as the Bottle Rock-It Human Rocket.

Of course, I didn't know that two months ago, when I found myself unemployed, shocked into lethargy, and watching sickening amounts of television on my tiny computer screen (I don't have a TV; don't believe in it). Due to an unhealthy but understandable compulsion, the reasons for which I can't go into here, I watched episode after episode of the Emmy-award nominated *Earth Guard Y3K*, especially, and repeatedly, the infamous episode in which Blankity Veep floats outside the ship to fix the navigation device. I'd watch the whole thing and then go back and pause it at the moment when she looks up, clinging to the ship's fuselage with one hand, her body floating behind her. Her spacesuit helmet shimmers with the reflection of an approaching alien vessel, her face in perfect makeup behind it. It's the shot that, of course, appeared on the *Maxim* cover, though the photos inside featured no spacesuit, that's for sure (gold bikini; hasn't that been done?). Each time I watched the spacewalk scene, I felt worse, yet, as though slamming my own finger repeatedly in a door, was compelled to watch it again.

Two weeks of this, and I had to get out. I decided to train for a triathlon, as a personal challenge and something to reach for, because I am always striving for self improvement and extreme personal excellence. It so happened that Jon, the aforementioned Mr. Bronski, had left his bike at my apartment a few weeks earlier, having come over from Tower 1, that gated paradise for bosses, to discuss a student I'd failed — a crybaby type who scrambled out of the pool after the first cold-water immersion session, ran outside, locked himself in his car, and couldn't be coaxed out. The conversation led in misguided directions, until Mr. Bronski, too drunk to bike home, staggered off into the night. Anyway, after resigning, I felt no particular desire to return the bicycle, a navy-blue and red road-mountain hybrid, until he asked, which he hasn't, too nutless to contact me no doubt, so I took my opportunity. Now, unfortunately, the bike is toast.

I told you about the fence I found anchored to the ground. Six in the morning, and me kneeling on dead brown grass beside the path, digging with my water-bottle cap, realizing the fence was buried unnecessarily deep. Wishing I'd brought a flashlight. This was just a couple of weeks ago, so late September, dark at that hour, and not at all warm despite my sweatshirt. I was getting chilled, fast, sitting still like that, and I needed to get moving again. The fence spanned the whole path and beyond, joining with a pre-existing, perpendicular fence on the weed-field side, and stopping maybe two inches from the river on the other. Thanks to my upper-body strength, I was able to heave the bicycle up and launch it over. It crashed rather alarmingly on the other side. I must confess, I felt some satisfaction in treating Mr. Bronski's bike thusly. Then I quickly and effortlessly climbed the fence; found the bike a bit scratched but otherwise intact. Proceeded.

Of course, on my way back, at noon, sky bright blue, sun high, sweatshirt tied around my sweaty waist, I had no choice but to repeat the process with the construction crew looking on from their favourite lunch spot on the Crab Shack roof. I had steeled myself for this eventuality, and had little trouble tuning out their jeers. The red-headed one was clearly leading the juvenile war against me, a citizen with her bicycle, and this time he descended from his perch to run over and confront me. By the time I'd climbed the fence, he was standing there, waiting for me.

"What is your problem?" he said. "Can't you read?"

"This is my bike route," I said. "A public pathway."

"We're dealing with a toxic situation, here." A slick of sweat stood out on his forehead and the bridge of his nose. "Use your sense of knowledge."

Avoiding eye contact, I gracefully straddled the bike and starting pedaling, slowly, away.

"I don't give in to bullies," I called over my shoulder.

The last thing the Colin-look-alike said to me that day? "Just bike some other way — take a ten-minute detour!"

Now that the bike is lost, of course, part of me wishes I'd relented, but I've never been one to give in, to pedal away with my tail between my legs, thereby accepting and condoning an unjust situation.

Indeed, my attitude has always exemplified the kind of fearless individualism embodied by Bottle Rock-It's motto, *Rock-It Hard, Rock-It High*. I have had no choice but to rocket high by my own volition, since my family has never supported me. My parents were always sort of gelatinous, just acquiring children and then squidging into the background. Meanwhile, my poor brother has been dragged, credulously, nutlessly, into my sister's ongoing pathological attempts to hold me back at every step. I alluded to all this in my cover letter (i.e. "surmounted staggering odds in my personal life").

To be honest, my family is not showing much support, even now. Not for my triathlon training, not for my Human Rocket aspirations. My brother is still freezing me out because of an unfortunate chairlift incident last year that was not my fault, and what kind of parents insist on vacationing with their three adult children, anyway? My parents;

well, let's just say I'd take an upside-down plunge into an ice-cold swimming pool over a hysterical call from my mother (with my father sitting, perplex-faced, in the background), any day. She just doesn't get it. She didn't get my safety job, though I explained again and again that I was in no danger at all, that we used a simulated helicopter in a pool, and that I'd done it eight hundred times. Now she's convinced I'll drown in the triathlon (hello? I saved people from drowning for a living!). In fact, the swimming part is the least of my concerns — it's the running I haven't started training for, yet, but I'm not too worried since I used to lead workshops for the Running-Shoe Place. Just have to get back into it. Anyway, my mother says "the pop-bottle rocket thing" is "delusional and suicidal."

Finally, my sister, who must remain unnamed — I will refer to her by her childhood nickname, "Dumpling" — called me the other night from California, laughing hysterically: "Mom says you want to be shot through the air dressed as a bottle of cola!"

Rest assured, Ms. Benjamin: I see no indignity in shooting into space and orbiting our magnificent planet before skydiving back, dressed as a bottle of Rock-It OrangeMint Fizz™. Freefalling trailing green bubbles. What a breathtaking honour. I would also like to point out that my curvy yet fit body is the perfect shape for the Human Rocket vessel. This job seems tailor-made for a woman, since the soda pop bottle is clearly modeled after the feminine figure. My figure (five-foot-six; 130 pounds; waist: 23 inches; hips: 36 inches; bra size: 36DD) happens to be particularly feminine, which will certainly be a plus as my likeness is incorporated into your long-term product branding.

Before I return to the mc-vs.-hardhat-man saga, I'd like to insert a little personal history, here. You may be tempted to skip these pages, but I urge you to read every word. I worry you've been turned off by my negative remarks regarding my family of origin; of course, they are all lovely people whom I love with a vigorous and unconditional passion. I shudder to think you might misunderstand, and deem me unsuitable for Bottle Rock-It's fierce yet wholesome image. I have suffered at the hands of my siblings, yes; but I want you to understand the precise nature of that suffering, which has spawned my resilience and unique perspective.

Ms. Benjamin, my life was normal, even charmed, until I was six. I had been adopted while my mother was pregnant (one of those got-pregnant-as-soon-as-we-stopped-trying stories), so my brother Happy and I were best friends, basically twins, and our parents ecstatic, having finally managed to adopt the baby they'd dreamed of, and simultaneously gotten another, as a bonus. Adopting, as you may know, is not easy, and my parents had also applied to international agencies. Six years later, one of these applications came through: a binder showed up, full of photos of the club-footed four-year-old awaiting us in a Kolkata orphanage. I can't stress enough how cute these photos were. "Dumpling" had an almost demonic appeal — which is no less powerful now that's she's twenty-seven, but I can't go into that, for reasons I must not divulge.

Off we went. My mother, my brother and me. My father was a pilot, and couldn't take the time off work.

It takes twenty-two hours for a jumbo jet, beginning in Kolkata and heading for Ottawa, which is where I grew up, to get home. The whole way, my mother sat turned away from me, her attention on the aisle seat, on the newly-acquired Dumpling. Happy and I, six years old, lived for a day and night in the steady hum of the engines, our membranes drying out in the air-conditioning, our noses gradually tuning out the chicken, spices, perfume and sweat, and the faint hint of stomach acid. Mom forgot to rehydrate us, and forgot about adjusting our internal clocks with carefully regimented naps; she'd remembered two weeks earlier, flying the other way, but this time she even forgot about keeping us from under the attendants' feet. She was focused on Dumpling, noting that the kid didn't cry, even when she was sweating and flushed from overheating or shivering with cold, and that she stayed awake for eerily long periods, slowing as though battery-operated but not closing her eyes.

Happy and I, wearing pajamas, hair unbrushed — I had a knot at the back of my head that I couldn't even get my fingers through — played in the aisles with a boy whose Scottish accent was so strong, we couldn't understand a word he said. We played with him for hours, sitting in the aisles with his colouring books and pushing his toy cars on felted blue wool carpet. I couldn't have known that Happy was playing with me, giving his attention to *me*, for basically the last time. Unsuspectingly, I accompanied him to Dumpling's side, and we showed off our new, miraculously quiet sister to British and Indian and Canadian and American passengers, as proud as though we'd molded her from clay and infused her with life. They admired her cheeks, round by design though she was so thin. They cooed over her pouty bottom lip and those huge eyes, so light brown they're almost yellow. Poking out from under her toque was silky, short black hair with wisps falling over her forehead, and she wore one bright white new shoe on her right foot. On her left foot was only a yellow sock. The socks and the shoe and the hat, along with her green tracksuit, meant to protect her from the unfamiliar air conditioner, had been purchased in advance, at home in Ottawa.

The passengers looked at the foot, sometimes even touched it, and said,

"Lucky girl."

"Lucky me," Mom responded each time, in that husky voice that she thought was sexy, but actually arose from being fat. She hadn't bothered to apply mascara or eye shadow or lipstick, or to sweep her bangs over her forehead with mousse. It's easy to forget she was already forty-six that year. I realize now, looking at the old photos, that she looked younger. Until her late sixties, until quite recently, she had the kind of face that looked anywhere between twenty-five and forty, impossible to pin down. A face like a French actress's, Dad always said. She was technically big enough to be called obese, but it never occurred to her or to anyone to think of her weight as a problem. She almost always wore clothes of her own design, since she was, as she always said, her own walking advertisement. People complimented her dresses, and she handed over sybil-smart.com business cards. A lot of the compliments came from men, especially when she wore tops that tied in her trademark big floppy bows under her cleavage.

She'd learned that *lucky me* line long before, when she adopted me, since I am part black, and sometimes a target of racism (despite my sister's claims that I look "white as a porcelain ass," a typically nonsensical insult, and I'd like to see a white person with hair this dark and curly). Please note: my multicultural heritage will help pop-drinkers worldwide relate to me in my role as the Human Rocket.

Anyway, for my sister's adoption, Mom and Dad had prepared in a way they never did for mine (more about that, later), reading books and books and websites and websites. Not to mention the picture books about new toddlers in the family, and about India, for Happy and me. One of the international adoption sites advised Mom to bring her own water to India, and her own sanitary wipes, and boxes and boxes of granola bars. We'd been eating Indian food at home, to relate to Dumpling in advance, but — and Mom has denied this ever since — we lived almost entirely on granola bars for the two weeks we actually spent in Kolkata. We drank Canadian water until the bottles were empty, and then we resorted to Indian bottled water. That required Mom making a rare departure from the hotel room. She insists my six-year-old memory was faulty, and Happy says he remembers nothing, but I know what I know: my experience of India was the smell of gasoline and spices, one small room with two double beds, moisture-stained walls, a toilet that flushed with a chain when it flushed at all, and rain like I'd never seen drenching the windows. At mealtimes on the plane, we all had the Indian food options, to bond with Dumpling. It was the best food we'd eaten since leaving home.

One interesting thing about that flight, Ms. Benjamin, was the airline attendant with the perfect dark red lips, like Mom usually had, and a shiny brown bun at the back of her head. Who leaned over so I could see beige powder pressed into her face, shining a little on her forehead and said, "Griffin Junior and Bonnie? How would you two like to watch the landing up in the cockpit?"

Happy and I were led through the plane and up into the room occupied by two pilots, who said, "So you're Griff's kids," as we were strapped in behind them. Beyond the chaos of dials and gauges and disembodied voices giving indecipherable instructions, we watched England appear through the clouds, green and hilly, tiny and sweet. So, you see, I was already at the helm of the flying vessel, as though to signal my fated flight, twenty-four years later, as the Bottle Rock-It Human Rocket.

Our plane from Gatwick to Ottawa was delayed, so we spent that night in the shopping mall above the airport, trying to sleep on narrow wooden benches. Along with countless other passengers, some of whom had claimed the few comfortable-looking soft chairs, we tied shirts around our eyes to block out the fluorescent lights, left on all night, my mother said, out of sadism, and used luggage as pillows. Before I slept, I pulled the cotton sleeve from my face. The festive red bulbs of the candy store across from us seemed to grow and shrink as they blinked on and off. In the caramel-popcorn scented fluorescent night, I stared at my new sister, and she stared at me. Mom had warned us that Blythe wouldn't be toilet trained, wouldn't understand our accents, wouldn't know her new name at first, and would have a clubfoot. Dad had called her a "fixer upper" as a joke, but Mom hadn't found that funny, and he didn't say it again. Still — how can I explain? I'd thought I understood. Now I realized I hadn't.

"Try to sleep, Bonnie," said Mom, and I pulled the shirt back over my eyes.

It was impossible to know the time until early morning, when the store staff drifted in, and one thin girl with dyed black hair and pasty thick makeup stopped to watch Blythe, who was finally sleeping, fists clutching the duffel bag she lay on.

"She's an angel," the girl said, in an unrecognizable accent.

"Yes," said my mother.

"From India?"

"We're just bringing Blythe home."

"Lucky girl."

"Not lucky," Mom almost yelled, diverging from the script. "She's not lucky. She's my daughter. I'm sorry. I'm so tired. But it's not luck. It's destiny."

"All right," said the girl, nodding as though she understood everything now.

It was the end of August, and the day we arrived in Canada, we declared Blythe four years old. Her birthday was a mystery, but now she had a "plane day." And even back then, it was impossible to imagine her born the normal blood-and-guts way. Instead, she'd dropped neatly from the belly of a wide-body airliner, already in Mom's arms, Happy and me trailing behind through the arrivals gate. She arrived like a celebrity, to a crowd holding banners and cheering. *Welcome home, Blythe!* Dad's sign read, as though she'd gone away adventuring, fought through danger and obstacles, and returned triumphant.

Glancing back over these notes, as I eat a healthy ham and cheese sandwich and enjoy a refreshing Rock-It Fennelicious Green™ soda, I see that I forgot about the "Dumpling" thing and used my sister's name, Blythe. Rather than backtracking and deleting, I may as well come clean — though I must ask you to keep this information to yourself, and not to use my sister's identity to bolster my notoriety as your mascot. Nothing disturbs me more than the thought of you choosing me because of who my sister is.

Yes, she is Blythe Dey, otherwise known as Blankity Veep of the Emmy-nominated *Earth Guard Y3K*.

You would have figured it out, anyway — amber eyes, Indian, and the publicity over her "Human Bondage" marathon. Yes, she was born with a club foot; yes, it was corrected when she was four; yes, she just ran a marathon. And came in 80th out of 110, I might add, but whatever, no one cares, because she overcame her damn obstacles and raised money for the gimpy kids overseas. I mean, I have nothing against those *kids*. But, you'll just have to believe me: my sister, whom I love with an unrelenting fervor, will do anything for attention, and has a way of hiding her true motives from everyone except me.

You may be interested to know (I trust anything I write here is confidential) that our dad called her "dumpling" because, when she first came home to Canada, she ate like a fiend. She doubled in size, I'm not kidding, width- and height-wise within a year. She was chubby, our so-called lithe Blythe. Chubby. Anyway, here's the thing about Blythe. She was discovered. And I don't just mean the famous time, by that producer on the plane. She was discovered again and again, all her life. From the moment of her mysterious birth, she shone like a beacon, calling our parents across the ocean, commandeering their love, in the adoption-agency photos, long before they ever met her. We'd take family hikes in the Gatineau Hills near Ottawa, when autumn was still a thing, and even under that canopy of red and gold maple leaves and bright blue sky, even in her old jeans and windbreaker, Blythe was the brightest attraction. The attraction of all passersby. That was long before her flight-attendant days, when I'd meet her sometimes at the Edmonton airport. You should have seen her stride through the gate in her iLiner uniform, pulling that little black suitcase. Men, women and children stared at her shamelessly, discovering her like a personal revelation, like a glitter of gold in the mud. Was I jealous? No. I was proud to be the one waiting for her, the one to catch her in my arms. No one could have guessed we were sisters, and sometimes

I couldn't help but smile inside at the notion that we might look like best friends, maybe even a couple. Blythe and I always had so much fun those days, eating in the VIP lounge and laughing about all the characters we met in our travels.

The point is, when you're used to be being found, used to standing still and waiting for the next pair of hands to lift you and carry you and place you into your life — well, what I'm saying is, don't judge her too harshly, despite her undeniably atrocious impact on my life and our hapless brother's. Of course, I was adopted, too, and I never acted like she does; but as Mom and Dad relished pointing out throughout our youth, Blythe spent her first four years experiencing who knows what. According to my sister's therapist, apparently, she suffers from trauma or something to this day. Suffers! Blythe! But we mustn't laugh.

Now that I'm being completely honest, let me take you back to 1998 for another moment, to the year my family reconfigured itself to revolve around our pretty little ward. Please pay close attention: everything I am about to recount relates directly to my destiny as the Human Rocket. 1998. At first I was just as in love with her as the rest of them were. Her big amber eyes. Her silky black hair. Her insatiable need for affection, her silence, her left leg encased from toe-tips to upper thigh in plaster. Every few weeks, she was fitted with a new cast to push her upside-down foot a little closer to upside up. And though she claims now to have undergone a protracted and humiliating treatment, the truth is, she loved the attention. Happy and I, urged into action by the cast's stark whiteness, lined up our arsenal of markers and coloured pencils. We signed our names and wished her well; we played tic-tac-toe on her sole and up her shin. Even when I tried to lure him away, to play some other game, Happy was all about decorating the cast, and carrying the kid around like a doll. Dad drew an elaborate scene of clouds and rain, with a sun peering through the darkness and an airplane buzzing through to emerge above her knee. A pilot, presumably Dad himself, waved cheerfully from the cockpit.

"Sometimes," Mom said (though Blythe couldn't understand her yet), "God puts a baby far away from her family. Her true family. He dropped you, Blythe, into the world like a sweet falling star, and you landed all the way in India, in the midst of all those millions of people and whatnot, and I had to go there and find you."

Even Moses was adopted, she'd pointed out many times, and he was one of the most loved and successful people ever. And look at his first day — pretty bad — left in a basket, wrapped up snug and sent blindly into the world. Not really blindly, of course, because God or destiny or whatever was guiding that basket down the river, just as I was guided to distant-cousin Tiffany (more about this later), who knew Mom and Dad wanted to adopt, and just as Blythe was guided to the very curb where Mom would stand and know, just *know*, that this baby had been hers all along.

"Like a nugget in a swamp," my grandfather said, when he met Blythe. For years, I thought he meant a chicken nugget, and pictured it soggy and stinking, covered in grime. But Grandpa had grown up reading about gold prospectors, and that's what he was talking about. The glitter of something precious in endless, ankle-deep mud.

Blythe's casts were constructed to be light enough for a baby, and they didn't impede her (Happy really didn't need to carry her around the way he did!). She alternated between perfect stillness and breakneck speed, scrambling up stairs and inclines with her three good limbs, her left leg dragging alone behind, smashing with alarming violence against and past whatever stood in her way.

Early one evening, Mom ran out of her studio in the converted garage and called me in from the alley, where I was playing alone. Mom was wearing her denim overall dress with the patchwork pockets all stuck through with pins, the kind with big colourful bobbles on their non-sharp ends. We were forbidden to touch those pins, though Mom was allowed not only to touch them but to hold them in her teeth as she leaned over the sewing machine. At forty-six, she still dressed like a kid in her twenties, and had dyed her hair black with chunks of red. Now, I realize you are forty-five yourself, Ms. Benjamin, and favour jeans with crisp white blouses. At least on photo-day, your hair is clearly styled professionally, and very tastefully if I may say so. But I also know that your father was a truck driver and had "a stint as a professional balloon-animal twister" (Wikipedia), so you clearly know how weird people can be. So I feel comfortable telling you that my forty-six-year-old mother was a self-proclaimed textile artist, and her high ponytail was coming loose, wisps standing out as though she'd rubbed her head on a balloon. The alley and the yard were covered in red crab apples and yellow leaves, all in various stages of turning brown and mushy. Everything smelled like rotting apple pie.

Mom breathed hard.

"Where is Blythe? Help me find her. Help me find her."

She usually put Blythe in a playpen right behind her as she worked, but she'd turned around to find it empty.

"For God's sake," Mom said. "Help me look. It was the sewing machine. I didn't hear her over the sewing machine."

Happy had been watching Blythe, supposedly — I've always thought she must have convinced him, with a coy raising of her arms, to lift her out and set her free.

My mother's studio was all yellow and blue and blue-and-white-striped fabric rolls, and we stood facing the abandoned playpen as though the Daffy Ducks running around its sunny yellow rim might tell us what to do. The room was a shrine to chaos, and to Mom's love of fiddly little tools and machinery with grandmotherly names —pincushions and thimbles and bobbins and bobbles and treadles. Swaths of lace, and filmy and shiny fabrics, and huge spools of red and black ribbon. The air still smelled faintly of the sandalwood incense she had stopped using in case it made Blythe cough. A dress pattern lay on the floor, the tissue paper, flimsiest of flimsy materials, crumpled and torn.

"She must have crawled over that and outside," my mother said, already through the studio's door.

Mom was hollering Blythe's name down the alley when Happy noticed the screen door was open and we went inside. We found a kitchen chair pushed up against the fridge, and looked up to see a small face with its huge yellow-brown eyes peering down.

"Hi," Blythe said.

She was on her hands and knees, losing her balance as she leaned forward to reach for me. Her fingers grasped for something to support her weight, and she leaned her hand on the glass penny jar perched right on the fridge's edge.

The jar rocked; Blythe's face contorted.

"I'll catch you," Happy said. "I'll catch you."

He reached up, and the jar tipped so slowly, rocking, as though it might not happen after all. Coins rained down over his head, bouncing off his hair and his face. I reached up, too, but a penny hit me in the eye, and I doubled over. The jar smashed against the chair. Mom slammed through the door just as Blythe's weight sent Happy staggering backwards. He slammed into the counter, and then smashed to the floor, but didn't lose hold of Blythe, who ended up on his chest, unscathed.

"Catch," Blythe said.

"Catch!" gasped Happy, before the pain hit him. "She said *catch*!"

"And *hi*," I said.

Turned out Happy's tailbone was broken, but his affection for Blythe was unfractured, even as he spent the first month of first grade sitting on an inflatable rubber donut pillow, ensuring a whole year of bullying. If anything, he doted on her more than ever: the first sure sign of his blossoming nutlessness.

Anyway, after the fridge incident, Blythe was tethered to the playpen while Mom was working, by a long cord. That way, if she tried to escape, she'd drag the whole playpen with her, and there was no way Mom could fail to notice that. And it was a good thing, because Blythe had developed a taste for falling. Dad, citing the adoption books, strongly discouraged Mom from sleeping with Blythe in their bed, even when he was away. So I was stuck with her, night after night, as she sat on her twin bed in our shared room, waiting to catch my eye. A couple of times, she even managed to climb up on the dresser.

Then she'd say, "Bonnie. Catch." That meant she was about to tip off the edge.

"No!" I yelled every time, diving for her.

"I mean it," I said. "Next time, you're hitting the floor. Got it, Blythe?"

She snuggled closer, gazing up at me with those big eyes full of love and trust. No one had ever looked at me that way before, with eyes that beautiful. I hated it. I hated checking high places for her all the time, ready to throw myself under her weight. I dreaded waking during the night to her eyes glittering in the glow of the star-shaped night-light, fixed on my face.

"Bonnie," she'd whisper, as soon as she suspected I was awake. "Catch."

Then Mom moved Blythe into her own room for a night. And that's when it happened. Alone in the bedroom, I looked out the window at the poplar Dad had planted when I was born, and sat heavily on the floor, head spinning.

I was afraid of heights. (You can use this: the Human Rocket once feared the very thing she was destined to embody!)

Mom was prepared to let me see it through. She even placed a pile of phonebooks on the floor in front of my dinner chair so my legs wouldn't have to dangle. When Dad came home after five days, she had moved my mattress to the floor, and Blythe was sleeping downstairs until she got over the urge to throw herself off things.

"Maybe I should sleep in the basement for a while," I said, at dinner.

Happy groaned, shifting on his donut pillow.

Mom was cutting the gristle from Blythe's meat to form a small pile on her own plate. Blythe had become a pickier and pickier eater in the short time since her arrival.

"That's the rec room," said Happy. "She can't sleep down there."

"That's not generous," Mom said.

Dad held up his hand. "It's moot." He airplaned a piece of steak on the end of his fork, past his own face and high above his head. "Deys love heights. We're not afraid of them." He held the meat in front of Blythe's face. She opened her mouth, and he popped it in.

"Bonnie is," Mom said.

"We'll see."

My father took it upon himself to cure me. After dinner he lifted me into a standing position on the sofa, but I went limp against his superman arms, my face falling against his neck so the little hairs there tickled my nose. When he let go, I pushed myself flat, eyes shut, into the pillows. He lowered my thrashing body toward the dining room table, but hadn't removed the glassware first. I wanted to find courage in his touch, but the panic that came over me was like a monster that invaded my body.

I lay with my cheek pushed into the living room carpet and gazed along the floor, past the shattered glass to my father's sturdy moccasin slippers on the hardwood, the broom's black bristles pushing each faceted chunk and splinter into the dustpan. He straightened the rug, stepped back to check that it was perfectly parallel with the wall and the table, and gave it another adjustment.

"Baby steps," Dad said. "Baby steps."

"And *up*." He advanced on me next as I watched TV from my now perpetual stretched-out position on the floor, grabbed me under the arms and slung me over his shoulder, where I screamed threats of vomit until he left me cheek down, for half an hour this time, on the blue acrylic rug under the table. He eyed me with a dangerous, purposeful air for the rest of the week. Baby steps were not Dad's style.

Sunday morning, Dad woke me before sunrise, whispering so we wouldn't disturb Blythe. He was already dressed in jeans and his favourite black Roots sweatshirt, and had laid out a similar outfit for me, including warm socks and sneakers although it was still summer. I dressed myself and went downstairs, where he'd prepared bacon and egg sandwiches, just for the two of us. He said, "Wait till you see the surprise I have for you."

He filled his travel mug with coffee and mine with juice, and we took our breakfasts out to the car. He opened the garage door to the dim dawn light.

"Rising early is a sign of good character," said Dad, as we pulled into the alley.

He held his napkin-wrapped sandwich in one hand, driving beside the canal toward downtown. I was usually asleep when he left for the airport.

"It's the best time of day," he said through his sandwich. "You get to hear the birds waking up. The sunrise. Everything coming to life. And most of the world would rather stay in bed, in a dumb slumber."

"Dumb slumber," I repeated.

"All the better for us, because we get it to ourselves, right? Eat your sandwich. You like it? You're starting first grade next week. That's a big deal. The beginning of your education. Oh yeah, kindergarten, sure. But that's kid's stuff. Now you'll be there all day, learning information. And you know what? It's scary. But Deys look fear in the face. And you know what other emotion feels most like fear? Think about it. Excitement. The way you've been feeling lately — all wound up. Maybe you're *excited*. It would feel almost the same, right?"

"I don't know...."

"It's all in how you look at the thing, Bonnie. Same physiological response, different points of view. That's the key."

I nodded as though I understood the words he'd used. We crossed the Ottawa River and drove along streets with French names, out past the neighbourhoods and into the trees. Two or three cars passed us the other way. The sun's rim appeared over the horizon's edge in front of us. That meant we were heading east. My eyes tried to close a few times, but I shook myself awake.

"All *right*." Dad pulled into a parking lot with fields around it, and a few buildings that looked like barns. To our left was a wide road that stopped and started without going anywhere. A runway. A white and red plane sat at its end, looking small as a fly. I'd been to this tiny airport before. I began to sense what Dad was up to, and I screamed. Dad drank his coffee, gazing calmly through the windshield until I exhausted my voice to a whimper.

"I want you to think about what I said. Blow your nose." He handed me a tissue, and I blew. "You're about to have the best experience of your life. An experience most people never have. And you're only six. But you're not most people, are you? You're Bonnie Dey. Destined for something out of this world." (As though he knew something, right, Ms. Benjamin?)

I nodded, shrugged, shook my head.

"This is going to be a secret, though. Not from Sybil and Junior and Blythe, you understand. But from everyone else. Agreed?"

"Why?"

"What do you say we get out of the car."

I asked him again as we walked hand in hand toward one of the barn-like buildings. "Why is it a secret?"

"Because, Bonnie. We happen to live in a country whose half-baked government wants to control every aspect of our lives." (I know — remarkably similar to your stance when you ran for city government in 2012, Ms. B. Those are the values I was raised with, too.)

"Why?"

"Because the people in charge think they know what's best for us and our children better than we know our own minds."

"That's stupid."

"It sure is. Do you remember what this building is called?"

"It's a —"

"Hangar."

"— hangar."

"Exactly."

Inside, Uncle Rick was waiting for us. He wasn't really our uncle, but used to bring us ginger beer, which I loved and Happy hated because of how it sparkled up our noses, and foreign coins — as though it hadn't occurred to him that Dad was a pilot, too, and would have provided us with those all our lives. Anyway, I felt better when I saw Uncle Rick, waving at me and smiling, creasing up his handsome face.

"Some fine morning, eh, Bonnie? You are one lucky lady."

I nodded, hoping my face wasn't too blotchy from crying.

From a rack on the wall, Dad took a big flight suit and a little one. He got into his first, and then he had me lie on the concrete floor so he could dress me snowsuit style. Then he asked if I needed to pee. I did. I stayed in the bathroom for a while, wondering if I could escape through the window, like in the movies. It occurred to me that if I did make it through the day, Happy would probably kill me. He had been begging for months to go flying with Dad, but the rule was, he had to perform a successful flight over Quebec first, with the flight simulator. So Happy spent most of his evenings at the computer under Dad's print of the Wright Brothers photo. Their first flight. Not, in fact, humanity's flight, as the common misperception would have it, since hot air and helium balloon had been around for ages. It was in fact the first controlled, powered, and sustained heavier-than-air human flight. Anyway, the point was, if the Wrights could be a family of the skies, so could the Deys.

Mom didn't like the idea of us flying at all, and was especially nervous about the implication that Happy, at the age of six, was supposed to be capable of taking over command. But he was determined to go up, and Dad was determined for him to earn it. I had often sat in the armchair — they needed a passenger — while they played this dead-serious game, Dad commanding in a calm quick voice. "Yaw left, Junior. Lift your nose. Pull back." Oddly enough, Happy could fly a lot better when Dad wasn't around, but when it counted, his digital Ottawa River swung from side to side. "Initiate water-landing sequence," Dad said. "Emergency. Initiate water-landing sequence."

I acted my part realistically, lurching left and right and finally hurling myself to the floor as the river's white digital rapids grew to fill the screen. I lay twisted in a gruesome, bone-broken death on the rough carpet.

"The driver's seat of any vehicle," Dad said, "carries the most immediate of responsibilities. You have people's lives in your hands. People who *trust* you."

"But it's not real," said Happy.

"It's real enough," Dad said. "Real enough to make or break a career. And character, Junior. This is about character."

I know it seems unfair. Happy wanted to go flying so badly. Why hadn't Dad taken him? But I deserved a break, Ms. Benjamin. I hope you see that I did.

"Bonnie? You need me?" Dad knocked on the bathroom door, his voice all cheerful, so I wiped and flushed and washed my hands.

Over the flight suit, he made me step into a harness that fit around my legs and shoulders, and he pulled all the straps tight. He put on my soft helmet with ear flaps and goggles, and took me back to the bathroom so I could look in the mirror. My hair puffed out under the helmet like an animal trying to escape.

"Pretty cool, huh?" he said. I couldn't deny it.

Outside, Dad spoke loudly, over the plane's engine. "This is a Cessna 182. Stripped down. No seats or insulation. This baby's been around since 1957."

Refusing to acknowledge that I was now shaking all over, my bacon and egg sandwich dangerously close to resurfacing, Dad and

Uncle Rick walked around the plane checking things. Dad bounced from wing flaps to engine, talking a mile a minute and explaining everything in words I didn't recognize.

"All right," he said, at last. "Your mother's probably on the road right about now. Let's go. We'll ascend for about twenty, twenty-five minutes." The plane, as he'd said, had no seats. Dad lifted me through the door and sat me between his legs on the floor. I had to turn around to see Uncle Rick in the tiny cockpit. He turned around with a grin and big thumbs up. I tried to feel my nausea and urge to run as evidence that I was excited as well. The instruments up there looked different from the ones I'd seen in the plane back from India, when we picked up Blythe. There were fewer of them. I looked for the one that showed our position against the horizon — Dad's simulator on our home computer had it, too. For now, the line was perfectly horizontal. But not for long.

Dad turned me around, and steadied me with his legs on either side of me. He was talking, but I couldn't hear what he was saying over the engine and through my helmet. He leaned over me to kiss my forehead. The plane braced itself, and as we gathered speed, fear left me. I prepared myself for death. Dad gripped my arms as we made the seamless lift from ground to air, bodies vibrating with the flimsy metal frame. I tried to memorize the sensation so I could describe it to Happy. A wave of dizziness made me close my eyes and curl into a ball, forehead on my knees. But when I opened them again, the ground looked so far away, and so much like the flight simulator, that it didn't seem real, and my stomach unclenched a little before clenching up again. The computer wasn't loud, didn't hum through your chest, didn't shake the room and tip you as it turned. That was the ground down there. Trees, roads, buildings, the real thing.

"See the river!" he said close to my ear. "See Ottawa? Over there? That's Ottawa!" The Ottawa River was shrinking surprisingly quickly to the size of a snake. I held tightly to Dad's hand. He'd always told

Happy that a pilot should trust his instruments, not his intuition. "Your gut's a liar," he always said. Uncle Rick knew what he was doing; he would ignore his gut. We were safe in the hands of science, technology and expertise.

My mother has always told the story to horrified dinner guests (so much for the secret): "I found Griff's note in the fridge, taped to the milk," she starts. "He'd drawn a map to some field in Gatineau Park, and instructions for me to drive the kids there right away. He'd written, *Bonnie and I will meet you here.* There was an X. *We'll have a surprise for you.*" Dad wasn't answering his cell phone, so Mom put Blythe in a car seat — Happy was just big enough to sit beside her in the front — and she placed the hand-drawn map on the dashboard.

What Mom's story leaves out is the moment I became fearless. Maybe it's hard to believe that I became who I am from one second to the next, but I did. Dad wriggled me closer, and pulled my harness tight, securing me to him at the shoulders and hips. I was nauseous, yes, but the point is, I suddenly knew all dangers were surmountable. Just then, Mom was driving through the park, looking for the wide open space Dad had indicated. I like to think she pulled over and then walked, struggling through a track field with binoculars around her neck as instructed and a cast-legged four-year-old clutched to her chest, just as I dangled out a doorway ten thousand feet up, strapped like a baby to Dad at the hips and shoulders. He sat in the plane's open hatch, bracing himself with one hand and pushing at my hands with the other, making me cross my arms across my chest.

"Daddy, Daddy," I yelled, my voice torn away by a wind so powerful it carried my legs sideways. Far past my own feet and Dad's were the patchwork fields and those dark swaths I knew, from the flight simulator, to be forest. The sun was above the horizon, now, painting the world in vivid greens and blues. If it hadn't felt real before, it felt real now.

"I'm cured," I yelled, my voice blowing away before I could even hear it. "I'm cured!"

Naomi K. Lewis

Dad's voice was right in my ear but still faint. "Breathe through your nose. Keep your eyes open!" He pushed my head back against his ribcage.

And we're sitting, solid metal holding us up, but the next second, Dad's whole weight leaned forward onto my back and tipped me forward, and we were falling. The wind ripped through me, and the whole world flipped. The plane, a cardboard cut-out, flashed through my line of vision, above me, already so far away, and then blue and the sunrise sky below that, red and orange, and then Ontario and Quebec spread out like a chaotically patterned rug.

Dad grabbed my hands to spread my arms, and the wind pushed them back and up. It pushed my feet up between Dad's legs, and I was flying. Dad's hand appeared in front of my face, thumb up.

Happy would tell me, once he forgave me, how Mom struggled out of her jacket and placed Blythe on top of it in the grass.

"Don't get your cast wet," she said, and took up the binoculars to survey. She turned in a slow circle. Of course, there was nothing to see but the road and the trees and more fields. She chased Blythe and put her back on the jacket, then surveyed again.

"There's Daddy," said Happy.

Mom followed his gaze upward, and squinted at the tiny speck in the sky. "Good eye," she said. "That probably is a plane." She adjusted her binoculars to take a better look. "But not all planes are your —"

Then, Happy would tell me, Mom screamed.

"Griff!" she hollered. "Griff!"

She lowered her binoculars to stare naked eyed at the second ant-sized dot moving across the sky.

"Let me," Happy said. But Mom was immobile, staring at the sky. "Let me see." Happy leaned against Mom's hip and grabbed at the binoculars.

At first he couldn't see anything because the sun was in his eyes, but Mom moved him until the glare was at his back. He would claim later he could see the grin on my face, and saw me open my mouth in a howl of pure joy. Of course, it's impossible that he saw any such thing from that far away. But he was right about the joy. A lot of people talk about skydiving as though it's some kind of out-of-body, otherworldly experience. But it's the opposite. The world becomes solid when you see it spread out like that; and gravity is real for the first time as it whips you toward the Earth's centre, the atmosphere a tangible substance pushing you back up with a force that has your limbs flapping above you like rubber.

The roar stopped suddenly, and, with a jolt, I was no longer flying but hanging feet-down, the weight of my body pushing against my harness's leg loops.

My lungs expanded. I laughed. I looked down past my sneakers to Dad's still so far above the world. I laughed and laughed, perhaps filled, though I couldn't have known it, with the sublime satisfaction of having taken the first step onto the road of my destiny as the world's first person to orbit the Earth and then skydive from space.

"What do you think?" said Dad.

"What are we hanging from?"

"What are we hanging from? A parachute! We're still falling twenty feet a second." He held his wrist, with its altimeter, in front of my face so I could see the numbers changing.

I leaned my head back. I could only see the parachute's white outer edge, and couldn't see Dad's face at all.

"I have toggles here, that I'm using to steer us." He turned us in a slow circle. "See the river over there? See the Parliament buildings? That green spot? Some way to watch a sunrise, eh? Now, let's be quiet for a while. That's the best part."

I wouldn't skydive again until I was legal, on my eighteenth birthday, would still be another year before I finally went alone, then started going every weekend, sometimes every day. But I got to hear the silence that first time, because Dad knew being alone was the whole point. It was a windless day. I could feel him there, solid at my back, but he let me have that time to myself, a full five minutes, just to breathe.

When he spoke again, it was quietly. "We're going to land down there. See that field? Between the trees? If there happen to be any strangers — there probably won't be — don't say anything to them. Got it? We'll just get in the car and drive away." It didn't occur to me to ask what car.

"See our shadow on the ground?" said Dad. "It's stretched out like that because the sun's so low. See how it's getting closer to us? When it's directly below us, that's when we land. Go limp, okay? I'm going to sit down so we land on our bums, got it?"

I saw that we were falling fast after all, and I braced myself. Dad maneuvered us over the trees, zeroing in on the very field where Mom and Happy and Blythe were small specks, then doll-sized. Happy was darting around mouse-like, and Blythe's hair caught the sun like black plastic. Mom was wearing her navy tracksuit, the same one she'd worn on the trip back from India with Blythe, and a pink hat of her own design, which I knew was printed with little cherries. She stood like a helpless blob. Even from above, she looked helpless.

"Go limp," Dad said, and I closed my eyes, opened my eyes, and Dad's feet hit. We sat down hard, the ground knocking the breath out of me. Dad detached my harness from his, and I sprang free, leaving him to deal with the parachute. Mom was running through the damp grass as best she could, holding Blythe, who was repeating my name and pointing at the sky.

Happy sped past them, yelling, "It's not fair!"

Mom caught me with her free arm, and Blythe grabbed my shirt. Seconds later, Dad collided with Happy, laughing and promising they'd go flying the next weekend.

"And parachute?" said Happy.

"Sorry," said Dad. "Not until you're eighteen."

"*What?*"

"Bonnie's not going again until she's eighteen, either. This was an emergency. Be a man about it." (In fact, my brother never did skydive or fly a plane; completely lost interest; became a nutless wonder, founded our high school's poetry journal and never even played an intramural sport.)

So that's how I came to skydive for the first time at the age of six, and though the jump was technically illegal, I think you'll agree, Ms. Benjamin, that it prepared me uniquely for the task at hand. I'm sure you noticed my email address (bonniedey@skyhigh.sky), and perhaps suspected that I registered it for your benefit. Now you will understand that I have been using it, or something nearly identical, since I got my own email address, at the age of ten. Because I had been allowed a fleeting joy, had flown clear of the attention-sucking vortex that was and is my sister, and that experience, a gift from my otherwise absent or sleeping father, I held dear; it defined my life.

For those brief, epiphanic, moments, however, I have been punished relentlessly ever since.

If you think I'm exaggerating, please take as evidence the so-called "vertical puddle incident" — so called by my brother, laughing so hard he has trouble getting the words out, whenever he finds someone new to tell. Need I add that my sister laughs too, sitting incestuously close to him and grabbing his arm to prevent herself from falling on the floor to roll around with mirth?

Spring, the spring I was seven, the snow melting. Puddles everywhere. Puddles in the park as big as rivers. I was walking home alone, taking my time to splash, two-footed, in every one, to make the most of my new red rubber boots. Happy and I were supposed to walk together, of course, but he'd run home ahead of me; Blythe was not in school yet that year, still wore the shoes connected by a long bar at night, and had a funny accent, so Mom and Dad were waiting until the next year, when she'd be more normal, to introduce her to society.

Naomi K. Lewis

Anyway, I turn the corner into our back alley, and there are Happy and Blythe, poking with long sticks at a perfectly circular puddle — an abandoned telephone-pole hole. They were both wearing boots just like mine. Happy's blue, Blythe's yellow. She was sitting cross-legged on the damp asphalt, staring at the water without blinking, those giant eyes, fixated. She was wearing her little grey parka with the fur, darling as the devil.

I stopped beside them, and Happy said, "Blythe wants to know how deep it is."

He leaned forward, poking his stick in further.

"Stand back," I said.

As I bent my knees, Happy protested, "*I* want to do it," so I shoved at his chest and jumped.

Both my feet hit the puddle.

And I sank. Straight down. Down down down, water over my head, water in my nose, water pitch black and cold as death, and walls close on either side, pinning my arms straight up; I'd instinctively lifted them over my head. Death, Ms. Benjamin; I say it again. This was death. The Earth was swallowing me whole. Bending my head back, I could see a circle of light above me, and kicked as hard as I could. Finally, I saw a hand, an arm. I reached up. Happy. I dragged myself up his body, hand over hand (he was too weak to actually pull me). Air. Air. I gasped and coughed, and dragged myself out, bit, by bit, onto the clammy ground.

In Happy's version, he poked around with a stick for several minutes until he felt my weight tug it down, like a sturgeon on a line. At which point, he hoisted me to safety. Trust me: our Happy has never hoisted anything anywhere.

"And then she goes staggering off down the street," Happy says, if he's not laughing too hard to speak by now. "Little bossy Bonnie, dumbfounded for once in her life, and with every step she takes, more water squishes out of the tops of those rubber boots. Squish. Squish."

What I remember is Happy bawling like a useless baby, and Blythe just staring from the hole to me and back again like there was nothing inside her head but fluff.

After relating the story to whatever new friends we've just made (for instance, to that family we met in Banff during last winter's ill-fated ski-vacation), my brother and sister invariably start in with the, "Oh, come on, Bonnie! We're all adults now. You know it's funny!" And so on.

At which point I am forced to save face by smiling and saying, "We were crazy kids, that's for sure."

And meanwhile my parents smile and shrug, and say things about vivid imaginations, claiming the whole thing is a fiction.

I have long claimed to recall nothing of the incident, either. Many times, I've said, "No telephone-hole pole is deeper than the height of a seven-year-old child!" But between you and me, I have relived every second a thousand times, and that hole was a passage to the world's centre, a passage straight to hell.

And yes, we were children, mere children, but incidents like the vertical puddle continued throughout my childhood and adolescence, and continue to plague my life on a regular basis. Probably explains why I'm so strong and stubborn. I've spent the last two years being submerged upside-down into cold water *voluntarily*. And I won't be bullied. And there are bullies everywhere — people like that Colin-Ripley look-alike. Colin Ripley, the boy who bullied me all through elementary school, and whom I spoke about at home so often that my parents and siblings clearly knew the truth — that my rivalry with Colin had given way, sometime near the beginning of high school, to an all-consuming crush. And yes, Ms. Benjamin: my first job, cashier at Ripley's Repertory Cinema? Same Ripleys.

While we're on the subject of my resume, I want to explain, while I'm thinking of them, a few more items. First of all, why my second- and third-last jobs ended (I need not stress how they helped prepare me for the human rocket).

So, the skydiving job — I had enough jumps, and thought instructing would be a dream come true. Jumping every day, getting paid for it, *was* fun. I definitely had a lot more money than ever before, too, and living with Mom and Dad, I saved most of it. The thing was, the clientele. Ninety percent of them only came once, and though they'd talk about the experience afterwards in exultant terms, it was basically just a cheap thrill, a means to get some adrenalin flowing. A couple of times, one passed out, and I'd have this floppy, unconscious body strapped to my chest; occasionally, someone puked all over both of us, the chunky spray whipping into my face. Some of them screamed for the whole freefall, and the noise always seemed the loudest just as I pulled the ripcord, as though the world and my passenger's brain were going to fly apart, just before that jolt when the roar stops. The passenger always stopped screaming then, too, like a mute button had been pushed. They got to pretend they were alone, then, but I didn't have that privilege; each time, I was a mother with an infant. One Japanese girl sang "I'm Like a Bird" in its entirety.

So, I left Ottawa's Mega-Awesome Gravity Adventure Centre, and became a personal trainer. That didn't pan out. Partly because I didn't have time to complete the official certification, but mostly because the damn people drove me crazy. You know who hires personal trainers? Well, in my experience, it's a bunch of rich middle-aged slobs who want to look like they do manual labour. Not even that — they want to look like actors who play people who do manual labour. And the complaining! You know who has a personal trainer? Blythe does. She works out every day so she can walk around in tank tops in her fake space station. So she can throw fake punches at her fake enemies, never smudging her mascara. Meanwhile, she never even accepted my offer to take her skydiving, back when I could have gotten her a discount. She made her living in the skies then, too, but her job was to dress in pencil skirts and walk up and down with a cart. She had to learn first aid. She was always pointing that out, was preoccupied with it. Because she was, you see, waiting for her chance.

If you've done any supplementary reading about my sister (which, of course, you have; who wouldn't), you will have noted that in 2015, the same year I moved here and studied for my Arctic safety certification, Blythe delivered that baby over the Atlantic, appeared on every news site known to humanity, and got scooped up by the *Earth Guard* people. By the time I'd moved to Edmonton to train for SAN, my sister was muscle-bound and aboard the *Y3K* space station, defending Earth against hostile aliens from 9:00 to 10:00 on Wednesday nights. The woman had no training as an actor beyond high school drama and that arts camp she went to, and one community play! What a joke.

But back to my resume. A couple more eccentricities beg explaining, namely my place of birth (Barrie, Ontario), and my middle name (Bathurst). Both of these involve an unsavoury element of my life that I am definitely not particularly interested in: my birth mother. Yet another obstacle I have overcome, and that will make me an inspiring role model for foster kids and hoodlums and sketchy people like that, because they, like me, can drink Bottle Rock-It Soda Pop and overcome the odds. I can only assume that you've surmounted certain odds yourself, Ms. Benjamin, since your parents don't even have Wikipedia pages. I mean, they're probably very nice people, but let's face it, they never really accomplished anything. (Balloon animals? That really says it all, doesn't it?) And neither has your sister, your only sibling, I believe, and look at you. I know you know what I'm getting at — that some of us are not satisfied with anonymous mediocrity, and that's not a judgment on anyone else.

However, I don't believe you're adopted, so you may not understand why, as a kid, I couldn't get enough of my adoption story, and insisted my parents impart the sordid facts nightly. Pathetic. The whole Mom and Dad giving up on the adoption agency, and then the phone call from

Dad's distant cousin Tiffany five months into Mom's miracle pregnancy. Dad had met Terrin, Tiffany's niece, at a family reunion years earlier, when she was a chubby little girl with chipped purple nail polish and a hank of hair missing where she'd chewed gum into it. He'd watched her push food around her plate and then slide down, down in her chair until she slipped under the table. She was under there all through the main course and part of dessert before her mother noticed.

"Would you have ever believed that girl's fate and whatnot, and yours, were so intimately entwined?" Mom said, as they sat by my bed telling the story for the millionth time.

"Not on your life," said Dad.

My mother, pregnant with Happy, flew with Dad to Toronto and drove to Barrie in a rental car. Tiffany hugged them at the door, and they had to stand there chatting for a minute, which was torture, because all they wanted was to see me.

"She was wearing a sweatshirt with a picture of a unicorn on it," Dad said.

"And she told us to come in and see you. You were sleeping, wrapped in a pink blanket," said Mom.

"With a unicorn on it."

Mom held me first, and she knew as soon as she touched me that I was her child. She'd held other babies before, and she'd found them sweet and all that, but they didn't give her that special feeling. That feeling of being a mother.

"I felt it, too," Dad added. "We both said afterwards, about what you were wearing and everything — we felt like someone had stolen you from us and put you in someone else's clothes. Strange, but...."

"Yeah," said Mom.

If only the story had ended there, with its high notes leading into a speedy get-away drive to the airport. But there was more. Tiffany said they should go meet Terrin.

"She's not coming here?" said Mom.

"She'd rather meet us at the diner."

Mom walked the three blocks wearing the sling on her chest, her palm against my tiny warm head. They waited. Dad wanted to hold me next, there at the table, and when he did, it was all he could do to keep sitting there instead of running to his car.

"It wasn't exactly a diner," Dad put in here. "It was more like a resto-bar. Wooden table, walk-up bar, jukebox. Guys sitting around in the middle of day, drinking beer. Not exactly the kind of place you'd normally think of taking a baby."

"Anyway," Mom said. "Dad's holding you in his arms, I'm watching you, stroking your little black fuzz of hair and whatnot, and the music is playing...."

"I'll never forget that goofy song. Like fate."

"*You were made for me...* And in walks Terrin. I knew it was her right away. She walked over and I stood to hug her. Then I took you from Griff and he hugged her."

Mom and Dad quizzed Terrin about my biological father, who Terrin had known for approximately twelve hours, and thought was probably part black, maybe part Middle Eastern —"of course we were curious about your ethnicity, and medical history," Mom told me, but Terrin just didn't know. They explained to Terrin how they didn't judge her, how they loved her and would always love her. Terrin's Coke arrived around then, and Dad took out his ancient Polaroid camera to snap a shot of her, elbows on the table, drinking straw in front of her face threatening to enter her nostril.

Mom said, "We were both secretly afraid Terrin would want you back. On the plane ride home, Griff told me his heart would break and never heal if that happened. He didn't sleep for a week when we got home. Literally. He'd sit with you. Like, guarding you." Sometimes Dad's eyes actually filled with tears at this part of the story.

Though they were scared, sitting in that diner, Mom had offered Terrin a chance to say goodbye to me. "I went to put you in her arms, but she went stiff. She wasn't interested in anything that might make her feel like a mother."

Those are my humble, so humble, beginnings, and I am not ashamed of them. But why couldn't my parents have walked away, then, forever? Forgotten my birth mother's name, thrown out the Polaroid, and erased Tiffany's number from the list of important contacts by the phone? Instead, my mother, out of guilt or masochism or true goodness, didn't stop trying to put me in Terrin's arms, and Terrin didn't stop going stiff. Mom even put the awful Coke-drinking photo in my baby scrapbook, along with the pictures of me coming home. For years, Mom phoned Terrin every year on my birthday and insisted we speak; sometimes she did the same on Mother's Day.

Every now and then, Terrin even phoned our house of her own volition to tell Mom about some personal crisis and get a lecture about being "better than all that." Mom would say, "You're family, and I have complete faith in you," and things along those lines. Each time, Terrin was forced to speak with me, and to pretend that's what she called for. That's Mom, convinced everything can be okay, no need for banishments, no need for hurt feelings. Terrin's Christmas cards, sent each and every year only, I was sure, at Mom's prompting, were the blank drugstore kind, and always wished me a "festive holiday season." She signed them with her first name. No *love*, no *xo*, no *the woman who carried you in her womb*.

Terrin even showed up at our house once, the winter when I was eleven. She was between jobs or something, and needed a place to stay. I avoided her for most of the week she was there, but one afternoon after school, I found her in the living room, sleeping on the good, green sofa in a patch of sunlight. No one had ever opened those curtains or stretched out on that sofa, not since they'd been installed. I took a long look at her. Her hair was no longer black, as in the infamous resto-bar photo, but light brown, past her shoulders, with bangs that fell over her eyes. Her nose turned up slightly at the end. Like mine. It was a lot easier to look at her with those eyes closed, hiding that eerily pale shade of blue. Aside from the nose, she didn't resemble me in any way. Her skin was pale and looked as though it should be freckled, but wasn't. Her face, formerly rounded, was pinched, almost skeletal. I took in her hips and breasts — still big, or curvy, as Dad would say, despite the weight loss. That's the way I was going. I could already tell. Curvy. The really creepy part was that I came *out* of her. My hand hovered over her belly, almost touching. I wanted to know what she'd been doing, thinking, while I was in there, the foods she ate and the drinks she drank that had coursed through my developing organs.

My mother had said this visit was our, my, chance to get to know Terrin. What she was into, what she hoped and desired. I leaned close and sniffed her hair. She had the sour bean-fart smell of a vegetarian. (I, like you, enjoy a good steak. I have never actually hunted, but would be certainly be willing, if you ever wanted to take me on some kind of Bottle Rock-It company getaway.)

Terrin's eyes popped open, and her pupils shrank to dots in the marble-like blue. There was a little crust in the corner of her left eye.

"Hi," she said.

"Oh," I said. "Oh, no. Sorry."

"Listen," she said. "Do you ever go to Toronto?"

"Not really...." I had never set foot there.

"Well, I can't tell you much about your father, but if you're ever in Toronto, go to the Bathurst subway station and find the far-left pillar by the streetcar stop, okay?"

"Okay...."

"I was in town for a show. This band, Disorder Attachment. I knew the bass player; I mean, they were okay. And that's where this guy and I first made out after the show. Up against that pillar. Right in front of everybody and everything. That's how hot the guy was. I didn't even care. That's what a great kisser he was. If he hadn't kissed so great against that pillar, I doubt I would've taken the streetcar for over forty-five minutes to get to his place, and you wouldn't even exist. That's why I gave you that middle name. Bathurst. Hey." She propped herself up on one elbow, letting her hair fall into her face, a strand sticking to her lips. "You look like him, too. He had dreads. You could have dreads so easily. Green eyes. Same lips." She looked at my lips in a way that meant she was remembering making out with them, on that guy. My biological father. I sucked them in.

"Okay?" she said, as though I'd asked for the sick story she'd just forced on me.

"Okay," I whispered.

What Terrin was into, it turned out, was being messy and playing Mom's old video games from the last century, which she found while snooping through the rec room cupboards. I avoided her, staying upstairs to work on my telegraph machine project and learn Morse code while Blythe was at gymnastics. Happy jumped right on the video-game playing bandwagon.

When Dad woke up in mid afternoon, before his red-eye to Hawaii, I followed him downstairs to see how he'd react to Terrin lying on the floor beside Happy, ColecoVision games spread out around them and all over the black leather furniture, along with a few of Dad's spy novels. She had pulled an entire wardrobe of drapey black clothes from her suitcase and dumped them on the black leather sofa. I didn't know why Mom and Dad had her sleeping downstairs instead of in the guestroom across the hall from their bedroom. A glass of cranberry juice stood beside her on the carpet, where she lay on her stomach, playing Cabbage Patch Kids. I stepped into the room behind Dad. When she turned to see us watching her, a low-flying bird hit her Kid on the head, knocking it upside down and dead.

Happy groaned. "She was about to do the *lily pad*." They both contorted with hilarity.

"Aw, man, Griff," Terrin said. "You made me die."

"These are so completely *anc*ient," said Happy, with Terrin's intonation.

"We don't drink beverages in this room," Dad said. "Junior, you know that."

"These are so old school," Terrin said. "I bet you could get a fortune for this crap on eBay."

"Young lady," said Dad. "We don't use that kind of language in this house."

"What kind of language?" said Terrin.

"Thank you very much," said Dad. He picked up Terrin's glass and left. He was following his own advice: he'd told me, if I ever encountered someone too thick to engage with, to remember that arguing was futile. Just say, *Thank you very much*, and walk away. I'd never seen him actually do it before.

"She's a user," Dad said in Mom's white Honda, then new, as we drove him to the airport. Usually Mom left us at home, or he took a cab, but this time we'd all squeezed in, since it was the only way to get away from Terrin and talk about her. Blythe was still in her blue gymnastics outfit, her favourite white sweatband around her forehead and her hair in a high ponytail. Gymnastics was one physical activity her weak ankle could basically handle.

"User," Dad said. "The kind of person that lies on your sofa spilling chip crumbs between the cushions — crumbs from the movie-watching chips they took from *your* cupboard — and not even bothering to flush the godforsaken toilet after a wee-wee."

"Terrin says, *If it's yellow, let it mellow*," Happy said.

"Dot," I said. "Dot-dash-dash."

"Okay, Bonnie," said Mom.

"That means, *Ew*, in Morse code." (I was building a telegraph machine for the annual science fair, in which I received an honourable mention. As I stated in my cover letter, I have always been fascinated by the progress of human knowledge and technology and felt I'd eventually become part of it.)

Blythe stretched her hands toward the ceiling. She was no longer dumpling-like, but, as her tabloid-bestowed nickname puts it, *lithe*.

"For environmental reasons and whatnot?" said Mom. "That's valid."

Dad took a swig of protein shake from his travel mug. "It's not valid when you're staying in someone else's house to leave your effing yellow wee-wee unflushed."

"No," said Mom. "Clearly not."

"Why?" said Blythe.

"There's the environment," said Dad, "and then there's common decency."

"But let's remember," Mom said. "Please, let's not forget that this isn't some stranger we're talking about. Let's remember the miracle Terrin has given us; she's *family*."

Blythe obsessed over Terrin during that visit. She didn't get it at all.

"No," I told her again and again, when she sat on the end of my bed at night. "I don't feel like she's my mother, okay?"

"You grew in her stomach."

"*Gross*."

"You look like her." Blythe held her fingertips against her face.

"No, I don't."

Blythe's eyes glowed so amber they were almost yellow. Sometimes I wished she'd just cry, like a normal kid.

I tried to set her straight. "You think you want Terrin? She's a loser. Have you seen her? I hate her; do you get it? You are so lucky, and you don't even know it." Blythe didn't look like anyone but herself. She'd walked into our lives whole, like Aphrodite from the sea. An arrival with no baggage, no birth parents, no photograph of Terrin, with her acne-marked face and her hair dyed black, trying and failing to smile over a wooden resto-bar table. No subway-station encounter between two people with no more intelligence or ambition than the pillar they made out against — and no funky DNA lying in wait to turn Blythe stupid and destroy her dreams.

Anyway, I haven't seen Terrin since, and haven't even heard from her for ten years, and I certainly don't care enough to give her any thought whatsoever, ever.

No, my thoughts are occupied by much more important matters; are focused like a laser on the Bottle Rock-It Human Rocket Initiative. Ms. Benjamin, I've said the urgency of manning the Human Rocket came to me today, but please understand, I have been dreaming and daydreaming for weeks of those jet-engines strapped to my sides, the power at my hips, lifting me straight through the sky and out, where I will orbit the Earth before skydiving back and landing on the North Pole. So elegant and perfect, the ultimate acrobatic routine.

I've also taken the liberty of acquainting myself with your personal journey to president of the Bottle Rock-It Soda Pop Co., if only to assure myself (which I have) that you understand how great innovators must live beyond the confines of the ordinary in order to impact the world. How else could you have conceived a healthy soft drink, indeed, single-handedly reinvented soda pop, bringing it into the 21st century? And now you outdo your own ingenuity, attaching your product's name to the world's first self-contained one-person space shuttle and skydiving device — a technology that promises to transform the nature of travel, and the extremity of extreme sports, forever. The individual transported by this revolutionary vehicle will, as the world watches, take her place in history with the Wright Brothers, Chuck Yeager, Neil Armstrong — maybe Christopher Columbus is more along the lines I mean. Anyway, I say "her" because *she* will be *me*. I must be the one.

Please assure yourself: I am not concerned about your current legal issues, and am undeterred by guilt- and fear-mongering phrases such as "unconscionably expensive" and "technologically impossible." Trust lawyers and journalists, those human obstacles to progress. Ms. Benjamin, I wish to keep nothing from you, so, full disclosure: my poor brother is a reporter, my poor spineless brother, no pun intended (he broke his back ribs last winter, fell from a chairlift, Blythe's fault, full recovery imminent), and he was the one who wrote last month, in his characteristic sapless style, that the Human Rocket was "sure to combust re-entering the atmosphere, if by some miracle, it makes it that far." Surely you saw the column; he uses his "real" name, Griffin Dey, Junior. Then again, no one pays attention to bylines, and I'm sure you haven't noticed it. Hardly anyone even reads news, anymore; I mean, his job was basically redundant ten years ago. Poor Happy. He is just a trampled soul with a congenitally weak body, doing his best.

That is the kind of person I refuse to be, which is why, when I found the fence across my bike path topped with a single strand of barbed wire last week, I summoned all my strength to throw the bicycle clear over top, and then swung myself around the fence's edge, my body suspended above the river like Spiderman's. Ignored the taunts of my nemesis. Prepared for whatever obstacle he might set up next. Colin. All I could think when I saw that construction guy, with his angry squashed face, his chapped bright lips flapping with contemptuous bile, was Colin Ripley. Why did this guy, this bully, have to look so much like the one person who reminds me, more than anyone else, of my sister's single-minded malevolence?

You've probably been wondering if there were early signs of Blythe's true nature, beyond what I've already related. There were. In fact, when Blythe first came, our parents thought everything was a sign of something sinister at work beneath the angelic face. They looked up her every action and reaction in their older-children international adoption guides. Eating: she was filling a void in her soul. Not crying: she was repressing her grief. Bouts of giddiness: grief bubbling up the only way it could. Falling: testing us. And competing mercilessly with her sister? Allegedly, this resulted from feeling unlovable and compelled to overcompensate, constantly to prove her worth (i.e. psychobabble). I was supposed to "be the bigger person," which meant letting her get away with everything. Like, for instance, she had this uncanny ability to disappear at chore time, all through high school.

One time, at table-setting time, I caught her sitting on the toilet's closed lid, languidly brushing her hair. She threw the brush at me, and the hard side smacked the middle of my forehead. I started to protest, and she hollered, terrifyingly loud but without hysteria, "Get out!"

And all my mother said, as I stepped back, hand over my burgeoning bruise, was, "Listen to the lungs on her. No wonder she picked tuba."

Like I hadn't been rejected in my earliest days, too. Maybe I have these "issues" Blythe and her therapist are so fond of, myself; did anyone ever think of that?

Anyway, there were always signs of sinister sisterly intent, but things took a sharp turn for the worse the summer Blythe turned thirteen, when Happy and I were fifteen. That was the summer our mother, as part of her ongoing Indian education attempt, bought Blythe some henna to colour her hair and got her hooked for life. The brown powder mixed with water to make a muddy goop, which was full of grains Blythe said stuck in her butt crack when she washed out the henna in the shower. Afterwards, her hair was even blacker and shinier, with a red sheen that hovered a millimetre above her head.

So it's a steamy hot afternoon, and Happy and I have been watching Blythe play soccer. The game's over, and the kids are cooling down in the sprinkler park; Blythe, Happy and I are on a bench together, watching, his "I Was Abducted" T-shirt clinging to his skeletal frame, unwashed hair adhering greasily to his bloodless head. Shora Ripley was there, leaping through the sprinklers, each in turn. Even if I hadn't known her from school and Blythe's gymnastics classes and the Rip, I would have recognized her as Colin's sister. She was a tiny, wiry replica of him with her reddish hair and freckles sparkling with water and sunshine and no problems. Blythe had lost all signs of her limp, but still wore a tensor bandage on her left ankle for sports, which was why she lamented she'd never make it onto the high school soccer team.

"Don't look," I whispered to my siblings, "but Colin Ripley's coming."

He was swaggering like a drunken cowboy through the grass from the direction of the skateboard park by the river, his board under his arm. His hair flopped into his face. Happy stared at his feet, in supplication to our grade's alpha male. Blythe hadn't seen Colin in two years, since he was scrawny and chasing her down the street from the 7-Eleven, calling her a terrorist and telling her to go back to where she came from. I waited for her reaction; he was almost seventeen now, and tall and broad as a man. He reached the concrete trail that led up the hill toward us; I heard his board hit the ground, then the scuffling of its wheels. In my peripheral vision, he glided through the soccer kids, towering over them. He nudged his board into the grass.

"Hey, Bonnie," he said.

"Hey." I picked at the wood under my thigh, uncomfortably aware, all of a sudden, of how much I spoke about him at home.

"Colin," said Shora. "Watch this." She cartwheeled through a sprinkler, her freckled legs swinging a perfect, glittering arc. He completely ignored her. I watched with dread as Colin approached me and my siblings. Shora pirouetted closer, and stopped in front of our bench.

"What's eating you?" Colin said.

I glanced up at him and he held his hands out to me. "C'mon."

I shook my head, tempted to take his hand, but not tempted enough to touch him in front of Happy and Blythe.

"How come your brother's a pasty freak, and your sister's an Indian? And they're both so *weird*?" Colin touched the bench beside Blythe with his foot.

"Hey," said Shora, shivering just behind him, her lips bluish pale. "Blythe's my friend. What's wrong with you?"

"Sorry," said Colin. "I just want to know what the deal is. I was just wondering — why are you just sitting here, Deys?"

None of us answered.

"Come on," he tried me again, holding out a big, summer-freckled hand, and I backed away. "You," he tried Blythe. "Girl. Shora's friend. Don't you want to get wet?"

"I don't like water," Blythe said. I inched closer to her.

"Sure you do." Colin grabbed Blythe by the wrists, and I took hold of her upper arm.

"No. I don't," she said.

As Colin pulled her up to her feet, I lost my grip, pinching her skin in the process. I could see the red spot. The tensor bandage tight on her ankle made her look fragile, as he dragged her, struggling, over to the closest sprinkler.

Happy and I both stood, and he yelled incoherently as Colin swung Blythe around and into the water. Her ponytail whipped around her head, and she screeched, arching her body as the frigid water hit the small of her back. Bent at the waist, she wrenched one arm free, but Colin managed to keep her swinging around until the sprinkler jet hit her full-force in the chest. Blythe leapt away, her arm outstretched, Colin still holding her wrist. She gasped, like her lungs didn't want to work.

"Oh my God," said a male voice, one of Blythe's teammates, somewhere behind me.

Blythe's eyes widened, her lips bluish. Then her expression hardened into rage. Colin's arm fell to his side. He almost seemed ashamed. Every eye was on Blythe's now see-through white shorts and navy team shirt, but Blythe didn't meet any of those gazes. She ran.

Happy and I stood side by side in the sprinkler haze, helpless as she sprinted through the middle of the concrete, green and white striped panties clearly visible. She needed new underwear — it was too small to even cover her jet-black pubic hair, which I hadn't realized she'd grown. She needed a better sports bra, too.

Blythe ran right past us and kept going, down the hill toward the sidewalk. Happy took off after her, fell on the concrete, got back up, and ran even faster down the hill, blood dripping from his knee. "Idiot!" I yelled. A second later, I realized everyone thought I'd meant Colin. I decided to go with it.

"Fuckwad!" I was amazed by the strength of my voice, how it seemed to hover in the air, shocking the whole crowd, freezing the soccer kids and skater kids into place.

Usually he would have called me a twat, and I would have told him, good luck living with no brain, but this time he said, kind of quietly, "It was an accident." I could see that he meant it, and I wanted, strangely, to cry. I wanted it to have been me whose hand he grabbed. I wanted to punch him in the stomach. Unnerved by the raw, un-Colin-like regret in his expression, and the water droplets sparkling in his eyebrows and lashes like tears, I ran.

I was panting by the time I caught up with Blythe and Happy.

"I'll walk in front of her," said Happy. "You walk behind."

So we created a fortress around our sister, dodging to protect her from the gaze of anyone walking or driving by. Blythe didn't say a word. She walked quickly and evenly, looking straight ahead. I couldn't help but take in her new body. Happy kept his back to us and didn't glance her way at all. When Blythe was little, she had always been cold and covered in layers. Then she warmed up, but became private, dressing in the bathroom or her closet to avoid being nude in our shared room. But whatever her closed doors and baggy clothes had managed to hide, the secret was out, now. Blythe was a woman among pre-pubescent Shora Ripleys, and her soaked white shorts would go down in history. The boys who'd witnessed them would tell the story again and again, and those who'd missed it would stare at our sister's legendary midsection with longing, imagining ways they might spray her down again.

Blythe had always been cute, then pretty, and then beautiful, and now puberty had washed over her like a bucket of bad luck dumped from above. After the sprinkler incident, men started yelling at her out of car windows; sometimes it was a whistle, sometimes an incoherent yell from the gut. Once that summer, I was walking with Blythe down Bronson Ave. when a truckful of boys slowed so one could bellow, "One fuck, one fuck. Then I could die."

"Losers," I yelled.

One of them hollered back, his voice distorted into a drawn-out jeer, and I turned to Blythe, shaking my head. But she didn't look at them or at the car speeding away; she just stood up straighter, pulled her shoulders back and swung her hips a little more. It's funny, when I watch her on TV now, or see her picture in a magazine, sometimes it really bothers me that she's exposed to a world of assholes, and that I'm not there to give any of them the finger. Almost as much as it bothers me that she insists on keeping us a secret, never even mentioning our names in interviews, and certainly never mentioning that her sister was adopted, too. Anyway, until that year, no one would have yelled at her from a car window. No one would have described her as sexy or hot. No more than they could have described the Mona Lisa or an angel in those terms. But personally, I think as soon as that water hit her, her destiny was fixed (like mine is now), everything laid out like a map. The whole world looked at her, saw how it was.

Anyway, we went back to school shortly after that, and I don't think I really spoke to Colin much — I don't remember exactly, of course; I was only sixteen — until one Saturday, when I was walking home holding a Coke Slurpee, and wishing I wasn't. I didn't have mittens, and the cold cardboard cup was freezing my hand. The sidewalk was covered in bright, brown, and decaying leaves, and everything was lit heartbreakingly, in that way it gets right before the sun becomes a sliver, and the sky turns red, and then it starts to gets dark. I hadn't even realized I was walking past the Ripleys' house. Not my usual route home; I'd gone a different way all fall just to avoid this very scenario. Colin, wide shoulders swathed in faded blue sweatshirt, sitting on the porch holding a mug of something hot and steaming, his eyebrows just slightly raised. A rake and a box of garbage bags sat beside him, and red leaves lay all over the lawn. I hesitated. He didn't seem poised to get up and chase me.

"Hey, Bonnie. Stop a minute. Come here. Talk to me."

I stopped, but stayed on the sidewalk.

"What's up?" he said.

"Just going home...."

"Hey," said Colin. "I just wanted to tell you, you look really good this year. I like what you're wearing. You like that vintage look, right? The sweatshirts with the *Flashdance* thing. And those big belts?"

"Well, yeah. I guess." It was true. I'd become uncharacteristically interested in fashion that year.

"We played *Flashdance* and *Footloose* the other night. I was working the door. The shirts and the curly hair. I thought of you."

I took an involuntary step backwards.

"I like it. Hey, Bonnie, remember when you stormed the guys' locker room in grade five and tried to strangle that Adam kid? And he was, like, naked? That was hilarious, I mean, awesome...."

I looked around, and couldn't see any signs of a trap. I held out the almost full Slurpee cup. "I don't really want to drink this," I said. "Could you throw it out for me?"

"Sure. Come on." He stood and motioned for me to follow. I stepped onto the unraked Ripley lawn, then stepped again.

I followed Colin through an indoor porch with a dusty-looking patio swing, and through another door into a big kitchen with a wooden table big enough for the whole Ripley clan, and a yellow patterned vinyl-tile floor. Someone had scattered cornflakes across and under the table, and a few of the cupboard doors were slightly open. It looked like at least twenty people had eaten their breakfast there, many hours earlier, then fled. Colin led me to the sink, into which I poured the rest of my Slurpee. I turned on the tap to rinse away the remnants along with a pre-existing scattering of crumbs.

"My father hates crumbs," I said.

"Really?"

"Yeah. He sees a crumb and it's over."

"That's funny." Colin stood close to me, just stood there like a mountain of masculinity. Partly to avoid eye contact, I looked around for a garbage can, and spotted a full one in the corner. I started toward it, but he took the cardboard cup out of my hand and put it on the counter with the other dirty dishes.

"Where's your family?" I said.

"Out. At the Rep. Here, there." It was funny that everyone called Ripley's Repertory *the Rip*, except for the Ripleys themselves. It was even stranger that I was inside Colin's house, talking as though we weren't sworn enemies, as if I weren't in love with him, as if he hadn't dragged my bodacious sister through a sprinkler.

"Well, thanks," I said.

Colin held out his hand. "Friends?"

"What?"

"I was just thinking that I'm glad you walked by. I've been meaning to say sorry about that whole thing with your sister and the sprinkler, back in the summer. That wasn't cool."

"Oh — really?"

"It's just that you were ignoring me, and I — And when I said was she an Indian, I was joking, like joking about that time when we were kids when I called her a terrorist —"

"Okay...."

"— yeah, and how dumb I was back then. But it wasn't a good joke. I mean, your sister's a good kid. I didn't mean her any harm."

I stepped back a safe distance from him before looking at his face. His eyebrows and eyelashes were closer to brown than red.

"I'm laying it out here, Bonnie. Come on. Friends?" He held out his hand again.

"You mean as in a truce?"

"I mean like friends. As in, being friends."

"Well…" I wanted to ask exactly what I was agreeing to, since I didn't have a lot of time for friendship in my schedule, but Colin's face started to look like he was going to make fun of me. His hand was surprisingly soft, and his shake was pretty firm, a sign of moral integrity.

That night, I sat at Blythe's desk while she lay in bed in her trademark black turtleneck and skintight black jeans, making disgusting noises with her tuba mouthpiece — she'd been banned from playing after eight, and the instrument was too heavy to carry home, anyway, except on days when Mom arranged to pick her up.

"Isn't that weird?" I said, about Colin.

"Uh, yeah. Listen to this." Blythe inhaled deeply and spit one long note through the mouthpiece. The sound went on, unwavering, for about ten hours before she finally ran out of breath.

"Great. But yeah — he said to tell you he was really sorry about the summer."

"Whatever."

"Cool. So, do you think I should've said no to being friends with Colin?"

"I thought you hated Colin Ripley. I thought he was the one person in the world you truly despised. I thought you said he was a walking scrotum."

"Whatever."

"What do you mean, whatever? Shora says he's an idiot."

"Well, I guess he is, kind of. But it's important to give people a chance, if they're committed to self improvement."

"Right. He did it with Wendy Bennett in his basement, and Shora found the evidence when she went down to get apples."

"That's ridiculous." I quoted Dad: "Forgiveness is a sign of good character."

"*In* the apple box. Plus, she says he leaves pubes all over the soap in their shower, and she bought her own body wash that she keeps in her room because of it." I didn't respond to that, so Blythe blew into her mouthpiece for a while and then said, "So, are you going to be hanging out with him?"

"I don't think so. Nothing like that."

But on Saturday afternoon, I was doing my homework, and the doorbell rang.

And there, at the front door, was Colin.

"Whatcha doing?" he said.

"Just homework."

"Oh. Well. I thought maybe I'd drop by and, you know, apologize to your sister in person. Is she here?"

"No. She does a lot of extracurricular activities. You should call first, if you want to see her." I stepped back into the house, but he put his hand on the door to stop me from closing it.

"Hold on. I was wondering if you wanted to go for a walk. To the arboretum?"

"I thought you were here to see Blythe." He got that look again, like he wanted to give me a hard time, so I added, "Isn't it cold?" He was just wearing the faded blue sweatshirt and black toque with baggy jeans. No jacket.

"I've got the car. We'll drive there, then walk a bit." That was one plus about failing kindergarten — he was the first person in our grade that could drive. Seems funny now that I was so impressed, considering that I now have my class four, five, and six licences, a testament to my natural ability to man any vehicle, such as the Human Rocket.

I put on slouch boots and my pea coat instead of the usual hiking boots and fleece, even considered and dismissed wearing Blythe's navy faux fur jacket instead, and told Mom through the sewing-studio intercom that I was heading out. Before she had a chance to ask any questions, I was in Colin's car.

At the arboretum on the other side of the university, most of the orange and red leaves were on the ground, over a thick layer of brown rot, and the trees were already nearly naked. I was glad I'd worn boots; Colin's suede sneakers were already soaked through with mud as we left the path to walk under the trees, but he didn't seem to mind.

"Check out the foilage," he said, holding out his arms like he'd put the leaves there, just for me.

"I think it's pronounced foliage."

"Naw. *Foilage*. I like how it sounds." He bent and touched a tree trunk, then picked a withered blade of grass, brought it to his nose, bit it with his front teeth and tossed it away. "Man, I was such a jerk before, right? I mean, the stuff I said to people? Ignorant. I guess I was just trying to get attention, because of being the second oldest kid. Birth order screws with your personality."

"I think I've heard that before...."

"What about you? You and your brother are twins, right?"

"I'm five months older. I'm adopted. He isn't."

"*Oh*."

I guess he hadn't noticed I was black.

"So do I have the personality of an oldest child, or of a twin?" I said.

"Huh, well. You have a personality, that's for sure. You and your personality. Bonnie Dey."

We wandered further into the muck, Colin looking around at the trees like he was in love with them.

"Do you know Wendy Bennett?" I said. "I mean — are you — friends?"

He pushed his hands into the pocket at the front of his sweatshirt and rounded his shoulders, kicked at the leaves underfoot, and pushed his toe right into the mud. "I thought we were."

"What do you mean?"

"I thought we were tight, but she won't even talk to me anymore."

"Oh...."

"After giving me her virginity and everything." Colin laughed a little, sadly, as though Wendy had used him and flung him aside. "Can you believe it?"

I shook my head, trying not to look shocked.

Colin put his hands on my upper arms and gripped, pushing down a little like he was planting me into the earth. His eyes weren't brown as I'd always thought, but a deep green, and the sun was shining right into them, shrinking his pupils to specks. "You're fucking crazy," he said. "I mean, Bonnie, you are completely fucking insane."

"I don't really care what people think." I tried to step away, but he was holding on pretty tight.

"I know! That's what makes you so hot."

"I don't —"

"Do you know you're hot?"

I shook my head.

"Well, I'm not the only one that thinks so. But I do think so." He leaned down, and the second his lips touched mine, I turned my head. His tongue brushed my cheek, and I knew it had been intended for the inside of my mouth. My face felt like it was on fire.

He released my arms. I thought for a second he was angry, but then he said, "Let's go. I want to show you something."

Grateful for the change in tone, I followed him back to his car. Colin turned some guitar-heavy music up loud, but then turned it down to tell me how his brother had grown out his hair and made dreadlocks using bees' wax and rags. "He didn't wash his hair for sixth months, right, and he gets this weird itch, and his girlfriend says his head smells rank. So it turns out he has a fungal growth on his scalp, and now he has to use this prescription shampoo."

We pulled up at Colin's house, and the lawn was cleared of leaves, a row of bulging garbage bags at the back of the driveway. He must have done it that morning; he had that dusty autumn smell all over him.

"I'd better go home," I said.

"Definitely. I'm going to drive you. Just please, I want to show you something. You'll be stoked, I swear."

I pictured myself stepping out of that car and running towards home, but I knew something important was going to happen, and I had to step into it, with the kind of giving-way of tipping out the hatch of an airborne plane.

Colin's mother was in the kitchen now, sitting at the shiny clean table and cutting up an entire bag of carrots. I'd seen her before at the Rip, and she was definitely where Colin and Shora and that older brother got their looks. She was really pretty, in a hippie kind of way, and was wearing sandals with socks. Someone was playing drums in the basement, shaking the house.

"Hi, kids," she said, speaking above the drum solo downstairs, as though Colin and I hung out every day. "Have you done your homework?"

Machine guns fired upstairs. Videogame.

"Yup," said Colin. "Bonnie and I are just going to hang out for a bit."

"Do your homework, guys."

I didn't even have a bag with me.

Upstairs, Colin and I passed the room full of videogame bleeps and boys' voices, and then Shora's room, which had her name painted on the door in huge rainbow letters.

"Is she here?"

"Who cares?"

He led me into his own tiny bedroom and told me to wait. I assumed he was getting whatever he wanted to show me, but he came back a few minutes later empty handed, shut the door, and sat on his twin bed. There was nowhere else to sit, so I stood by the dresser. He plugged his iPod into a pair of speakers.

"You like oldies?" he said. "Nirvana? Or Neil Young, Unplugged?" I nodded, and he pressed play, turned Neil Young — I knew it wasn't

Nirvana because Happy played them all the time in his room — up loud.

I had to project my voice for him to hear me. "What is this?" I picked up a small, metal hairclip from his closed laptop, and held it out.

He patted the bed beside him and I squeezed on, careful not to touch him.

"What did you want to show me?" I said.

He grabbed me around the waist and pulled me down so I was lying flat, then rolled on top of me, keeping most of his weight on his knees so he didn't actually crush me.

"I wanted to show you that I like you." He pushed my lips apart with his tongue, kissed me for a while, then lay on his side, pressed against me. "So, what do you think?" Machinegun fire, again.

"I think... you smell like leaves." The videogame players hollered.

"Yeah? You like it?"

"It's nice."

"You have to make the next move."

I guess I admitted to myself around then that this was exactly what I'd been hoping would happen. I rolled on top of him, and he reached over to turn Neil Young up even louder. We kissed for a while, and then Colin got up and stood at the foot of the bed. I propped myself up on my elbows to watch, and he took off his shirt. He had strong-looking arms and a flat belly, and a line of red hair led down from his belly button. Without taking his eyes off mine, he took off his socks and tossed them aside. He undid his belt and pants, and let them drop to the floor. His boxers were yellow and worn out. He stuck his thumbs inside the frayed waistband, and for a second I thought he was joking, but he then pulled those down, too, stepped out of his pants and underwear, and kicked them away. He stood there, and I stared. I'd never guessed that boys had so much pubic hair. And his was bright orange. His penis was like a beige baseball bat pointing right at me. You know what I mean; you've been married twice and have that daughter, Ms. Benjamin, so you are certainly no stranger to erect penises. The rest of him, sturdy and freckled, looked almost slight and soft in comparison.

"Your turn," he said.

I shook my head.

"Your turn, Bonnie Dey. I've wanted to see you naked for so long. Haven't you wanted to see me?"

"I…" I focused on his belly button, which had a little ball of lint in it. "I can't."

"Okay. I'll help you." And here I implore you to imagine the music swelling (if you have it, I'd listen to the song in question while reading this), as the seminal encounter of my young life moved inexorably toward its climax. Colin climbed back on top of me and pulled my shirt over my head. Then he started kissing me like crazy again, stopping only to tell me that *I* was like a hurricane. Soon I was completely naked, and he'd maneuvered me on top of him. All over, it was skin against skin. Warm, smooth, blood-pumping amazing. I licked his neck, I smelled his face, I filled my hands with the red hair of my childhood tormentor. I pulled back and looked at myself, and at him. The expression on his face was so intense, I had to laugh.

"You're amazing," he said. "You're amazing, you're so so… amazing…."

Neil Young sang about dreamers and dreams. The simulated machine-gun fire from down the hall had stopped. Colin was waiting for me to do something. I took the lint out of his belly button and placed it on his chest. He still didn't crack a smile, just put his hands on my breasts, which I'd just grown that summer.

"You're a goddess," he said.

I shook my head.

"Your body…" He eased me onto my back. "I worship your boobs."

I was finally getting over the shock and getting turned on. It had something to do with the music; the organ part triggered the part of my brain that signaled when something real, sexy and bittersweet was happening. A part of my brain that had never been triggered before, except when thinking about that famous teenaged vampire late at night. When Colin finally got tired of my breasts, he kissed my belly, tickling and making me shiver, and kept going all the way down to my pubic hair, which I wished I didn't have so much of.

"What are you doing?"

"It's okay. No one's ever done this for you, have they?" he said.

I wasn't about to tell him no one had even kissed me before that day. Just as the song ended, in a wave of applause, I felt his tongue for a split second, right where it counted, and I gasped.

Something collided with the outside of his door, hard. A deep voice: "Colin!"

He jumped up. "Shit! My Dad."

The doorknob rattled, and I covered myself with my arms, breathing so hard I thought I would hyperventilate.

"Don't worry," Colin whispered. "The door's locked."

"Would you turn that down?" Lyle banged on the door again. "Dinnertime."

"Okay, Dad." Colin turned off the stereo completely. "Just a minute."

Thea yelled something from downstairs, and Lyle said, "Does your friend want dinner?"

"Yeah," said Colin, but I shook my head violently, and he said, "Oh, I guess she can't."

Downstairs, I said goodbye to the Ripley parents quickly — Shora wasn't in the room to see me, I noted, gratefully — and practically ran home. I didn't even do my homework, just lay on my bed and stared at the wall until our dinner, at least an hour later. It wasn't until late that I finally got my mental faculties back and pulled my math textbook out of my bag. I'd barely started factoring polynomials when the phone rang.

"Hi," said Colin.

"Hi...."

"Bonnie?"

"Yes."

"It's Colin."

"Yeah. Hi."

"Sorry about earlier."

"You are?"

"I mean that I didn't get to drive you home. My dad...."

"I'm just doing my homework with my sister."

"You mean your sister's right there, so you can't really talk?"

"Yes." I glanced toward Blythe's side of the room. Sometimes I wished I could see what she was doing over there behind the three Marilyn Monroe panels we'd set up.

"Okay," said Colin. "I'll talk, and you just say yes or no. I just wanted to say I really liked today. Did you?"

"Yes, I think so."

"I was sorry I didn't get to finish what I was doing. Aren't you?"

"Um...."

"And that you didn't get to have a turn."

It took me a second to realize what he meant.

"I hope I can see you next Saturday. Wear black panties?"

"Oh. okay. Yes. Definitely." I'd never really thought of my underwear as *panties*.

"Bye for now, Bonnie. It'll be beautiful." He hung up.

After school on Monday, I went downtown and bought the laciest, blackest bra-and-panty set I could find at the Bay. That night, I thought about Colin. In school the next day, I thought about Colin, and my approaching "turn," which I'd begun preparing for with online research.

I don't want to go into too much detail, but let's just say a month went by. A secret, delicious month. Strange how it all seemed so luscious at the time, how full body contact brought me as close to ecstasy as I could get while stuck on the ground. Though, objectively speaking, I was always afraid one of his many family members would appear. Sometimes we avoided that scenario by making out in the train tunnel on campus, which was cold and moldy. I was always afraid a train would come, and my back was sore as he pushed me back against the damp concrete wall, his crotch against my thigh, whispering in my ear that he was going to come in his pants.

"Seriously?"

"Oh, god. Yeah, yeah, do you mind?"

Well, it didn't matter if I minded or not, at that point, because he backed me hard against the wall, grinding my lower back into the cement, opened his mouth and groaned, his teeth against the side of my head. As we hurried home, I eyed his jeans, looking for a wet spot. "Isn't your underwear full of — uh…"

"No worries," said Colin. "It'll dry."

Though we'd wandered there together talking about everything — about Terrin, for instance, and how annoying Mom was — we booted it back, practically running, without saying much. The feeling of Colin's lips and tongue, hands and everything, lingered like a sticky but protective film. Walking through the back door into the kitchen, I felt strengthened by my secret. It was good, knowing I had something invisible, a whole side to me that none of my family suspected.

But why only a month, you ask? Because after a month, I walked past his house after school and saw him kissing another girl on the lawn. A girl with metal clips in her hair. And that was that. No, my perceptive Ms. Benjamin, of course that wasn't *that* (break-up songs in my earphones late into the night), but that was that, if you know what I mean.

The winter passed, and we find ourselves, now, at the very beginning of my employment history. That spring, Dad got Happy this job carting rocks at the garden centre and told Blythe and me to get jobs, too, and the next thing you know, Blythe's telling me she got us in at the Rip. It's kind of a relief to tell someone, because I couldn't tell anyone back then just how horrified I was.

"There's no way I'm working with Colin Ripley," I said.

"Oh, come on now," said Mom. "It'll be fun, Bon. A summer job. Every teenager wants a summer job. You'll make *friends*." (My mother has a long history of wanting me to make *friends*.)

"Colin's mean to us," I said. "He used to bully Happy."

Happy shrugged. "Whatever."

"He apologized to me," said Blythe. "When I was over at Shora's. He said he was sorry for all the stuff he said to all of us. He really wants to be our friend." *When she was over at Shora's.* I should have picked up on that. When had she ever spent time at the Ripley's house?

"Right," I said.

"Seriously. He feels really bad. I can call their house right now and get him to tell you, if you want."

What could I do?

"It's nine fifty an hour," said Blythe.

"There are so many places we could work…"

"I'm interested in film, okay? Very interested in film."

"*Film?*" I said. "You mean, like, *movies?*"

The next thing you know, I'm spending my summer in the ticket booth while Blythe's selling popcorn.

Just picture how I felt when I heard Blythe laughing in the confection nook, crossed the hall to visit her, and found her standing by the sink with a bag of popcorn in her hand, flicking kernels at Colin, who was leaning over the counter with his mouth open. Bending his knees and moving so each piece of popcorn fell into his mouth. A kernel hit him in the middle of the forehead, and Blythe laughed, low and sultry — no girly giggles for her.

"Hit me, baby," said Colin.

She grabbed a fistful and threw it all. Most of it landed on the counter and floor, only one kernel grazing Colin's hair and then falling off.

"Foul," he said. "Ten minutes in the penalty box."

"Uh oh," said Blythe.

"Sweep that up, would you, woman?"

"Screw you."

They smiled at each other as though they'd just heard a dirty joke, happy and a little shocked.

"I'll sweep it up," I said. I grabbed the broom from behind the door and started on the floor. I kept my eyes on the bristles.

"Ha," said Blythe, at last.

"Okay, ladies," Colin said. "I'd better get back upstairs. I left Shora in the projection booth. Math homework. She's probably strangling herself by now. How's it going out there?" he asked me, stopping before he passed. "You feel comfortable with everything?"

"Yeah, it's fine."

"Good." He squeezed my upper arm for a second, like a dad.

I stopped sweeping, and Blythe ate a popcorn kernel before dropping the bag in the sink.

And within a week she's lying on her bed at night playing "Like a Hurricane" on her old recorder.

I know what you're thinking: what did I ever do to Blythe, to deserve all this? The constant one-upmanship, aimed at exclusively at me, that has taken over her entire life and shows no sign of fading, even now that we're adults. I have asked myself that same question many times. How did I ever wrong her? You want a catalogue? Well, once, the first year she was with us, Blythe was acting like a psycho, clinging to the sofa at bedtime and using her cast as a weapon if anyone got close, and I said, "How can she act like this? Isn't she *grateful*?" Mom just about kicked me out of the family for that one. But Blythe hadn't started speaking decipherable English yet, and couldn't have understood me.

And frankly, *isn't* she grateful? As far back as I can remember, and surely further than that, Mom and Dad were getting their names on lists, filling out paperwork, subjecting themselves to home studies. And as far back as I can remember, Happy and I looked forward to the arrival of our little sister from India. Even when we were three, we knew she was coming. That summer (which I do remember, despite what anyone says), Mom inherited an old collection of Victorian children's books, and Happy — then "Junior" — and I loved flipping through them. My favourite drawing showed a little blond girl with ruddy, round cheeks, a frilly dress, and a bonnet, arms out at her sides, skipping through daisies. The nursery rhyme on that page assigned a trait to children born on each day of the week. *The child that is born on the Sabbath Day*, read the last line, *is bonny and blithe and happy all day*. When Mom read that line aloud, I thought it was about me and two other Dey children. My brother could be Happy, I decided, and the little blond girl in the daisies was our imaginary sister, Blithe.

"Come on, Blithe," I'd say, before crossing the street. I insisted we walk in a line, Mom holding my hand, Dad holding Happy's, and Blithe in the middle. Happy and I each held out a free hand for one of hers. Imaginary Blithe never just walked. She skipped, and my hand jolted up and down accordingly.

I'm not saying I wanted a white sister rather than an Indian one. In fact, I clearly remember thinking an Indian one would be ideal, because she'd relate to my non-whiteness. But Blythe, I could tell immediately, would never relate to me at all. Her perfect little face. Her smooth, if sparse, hair. I pushed a hand into my own tangled mayhem and tugged at the knots, heard strands rip. Sometimes, in those early days, it was hard to ignore that the real Blythe couldn't even take a bath without her cast wrapped in a plastic bag and a lot of help. She was still learning to use a toilet, and sometimes she smelled like one. And Happy and I were supposed to be twins. Now, thanks to this strange creature, we didn't even share a room. My new sister's shortcomings,

I felt, were vaguely connected to Mom's misspelling of her name, with a *y* instead of the *i* I'd always pictured. When I complained, Mom said it was too late. The paperwork was done. So, from the beginning, I felt in my gut that Blythe wasn't quite right.

The other thing I felt guilty about for ages happened shortly after Terrin's visit when I was eleven, I crossed over to Blythe's side of our bedroom when she was out, breaking the rule that we stay in our own territory except with express permission. Her yellow skipping rope was hanging over the back of her desk chair, and I picked it up and stepped into the space between her bed and the wall. I made it over the rope once before it slapped me in the shins. You were never one of those girls that skipped at recess, were you, Ms. Benjamin? You're probably like I was — trying in vain to organize some airheads into an astronomy or chess or Monopoly club, and then retreating to a private corner with a science textbook. Anyway, I shook the kinks out of the rope the way I'd seen Blythe do, and tried again. I made it over the rope five times, and was already out of breath — despite my basketball-star status — when one of the handles flew out of my hand, and the thing whipped over her dresser, sending her elephant statue, which she used as a headband holder, flying.

The elephant was one of many Indian knickknacks Mom had bought over the years to help Blythe get in touch with her other culture, but the only such object not stuffed onto the closet shelf behind Blythe's sweaters. I picked it up; it was chipped on one foot. Crawling under Blythe's bed, I found the chip, and then I fixed it with crazy glue and put everything back the way it had been: headbands in place, skipping rope over desk chair. I felt guilty about that for a long time, though fittingly enough, she ended up much later throwing that same elephant across the room at me, to miss my head and bounce off poor Happy's cadaverous, acne-picked face. Cheekbone. And break on the floor. Blythe had just heard the rumour, from one of her black-clad drama friends, that I'd performed a certain sex act with a certain

Demian Carter, her so-called boyfriend at the time. Typically, everyone blamed me. But I beg you to recall Blythe lying on her bed playing "Like a Hurricane," a red pubic hair stuck to her thigh — I checked while she was sleeping.

I begged *her* to recall just that, quite recently, like last week — had to, because she's still obsessed like you wouldn't believe with these matters from our adolescence. She was in town for the Comic-Convention at the West Edmonton Mall, and I went over to her hotel, the Fairmont downtown, after. She was still dressed up as Blankity Veep when I got there, which was kind of surreal. I watched what she went through to get all that makeup off. The gold stuff they put around her eyes? Has to be toxic. The next thing you know, we're chugging champagne and eating room service burgers and dancing to music from our childhood that we never would have listened to at the time, Britney Spears and crap, and I picked Blythe up fireman style and swung around until she almost had to puke. It was so funny — you would have laughed so hard, Ms. Benjamin. We woke up with an empty self-service fridge and bed full of chip crumbs and melted Smarties. It reminded me of her flight-attendant days, when her purse was always full of those little liquor bottles. The time we chugged three each in the airport bathroom, spent two hours giggling over magazines in the gift store.

Anyway, that was a weird night. Really weird. One second we're stretched out on the bed watching *Labyrinth* on pay-TV (she was all in love with David Bowie the pervy goblin king as a kid) and the next second, Blythe's all serious, and all, "Bonnie, are you going to stay in Edmonton? Don't you think you should be looking for a new job?"

And I'm like, "I'm applying for jobs. And I told you, I have money saved. I'm training for a triathlon."

"Right…" she says, as if she totally doesn't take me seriously. Then she's all, "I want to ask you something. Why'd you do that shit with Demian Carter?"

"Like back in *high school*?"

"Right."

"Why'd *you* do that shit with Colin Ripley?" I said.

And she says — HA — she says, "I didn't do *shit* with Colin Ripley. Ugh." And she goes, you won't believe this, she goes, all serious, "I want to tell you something. That summer, I was fooling around with Shora. Like, making out and stuff." And then she goes on for a while about how her therapist says it's normal to experiment at that age, and how Shora's a real lesbian now (according to her online profile), so there's really nothing to be ashamed of.

Anyways, then she says she was *in love* with Demian Carter.

"I have to pee." I started sitting up, but Blythe swung her leg over me, and pushed me back down, sitting on my chest.

"I need you to *listen*," she said. "I dated him for two years. I *loved* him."

"Barf," I said.

"Why do you hate me? You were the popular sporty one — you could have had any guy. *Why him*?"

"You're wasted, Blythe."

I was starting to sweat under her, but when I tried to shift, she put more weight on me, and I couldn't move.

"We're adults now," she said, "and I forgive you. For everything. I know Happy wants to forgive you, too. But I just need to understand. My therapist says there's no point, but I definitely need to understand. Because it was such a painful experience for me, having my first love and my sister betray me like that. Bonnie, my therapist says you're pathologically competitive... your own worst enemy...."

I pushed her off me — she let me this time — and ran into the bathroom.

When I returned to the bed, she was curled into fetal position. I thought she was asleep, but as soon as I closed my eyes, she said, "I told you not to sleep with your boss."

Then she did fall asleep, and I lay there watching her, the way her mouth hung open and her eyelashes lay on her cheeks like centipede legs. Her breath smelled like a burning ashtray soaked in liquor. Why does she have a therapist? I guess celebrities get them automatically. I mean, she says she still struggles with "issues" related to the first few years of her life, and with having to adjust to Canadian life, a new name, and a new language. The club foot and fixing thereof. She says there are lasting effects. Which of course I sympathize with completely, but also find a little bit difficult to believe.

Every few minutes, Blythe snored a little and moaned and moved her head around. I tried to wake her by singing the song of her guilt, my voice cracking because I *did* want to love her but was deterred by her hurricane-like tendencies. I got all tearful, as though the song were about me and Blythe all along. I wanted to follow her lead and open everything up, the vertical puddle incident, and all the other crap she's done to me.

Then again, I was drunk out of my tree.

Anyway, I'd missed my chance; her sleep was a locked box, and in the morning Blythe was her usual dramatic self, with the silent searching looks, and didn't mention any of that stuff again.

Seriously, though — was she kidding? *She* forgives *me* for everything? And Shora? Love? Betrayal? *What*? Demian Carter wasn't even cool, all tall and gangly and in the brass band and Scrabble club. They practised trumpet and tuba together, romantic, right? And he wore this striped yellow and black scarf, like a bee, on the outside of his coat, hanging down. Didn't even wrap it around his neck. That drove me crazy. Anyway, she took everything from me, from day one. She took Happy. She even took being adopted; I mean, her adoption was clearly *better*. Where I had Terrin and the resto-bar, Blythe had all the glamour of orphanhood, with her mysterious first four years and her "plane day" instead of a normal old birthday. So my dad gives me one thing of my own, my skydive, *my* plane day, and what does Blythe do? She tries to drown me. I like a boy; she steals him. I get a job jumping out of planes; she gets a job flying around in them. I decide to save people for a living; she delivers a baby and gets to be on the news for it. I dedicate my life to athletic prowess; she grows muscles and parades them around on TV, and then makes herself look like a saint by going on about her club-foot surgery and raising money for other babies to get it, and running a marathon despite her ankle problems! I wonder if she's told her precious therapist about all *that*.

So I'm *so sorry* I sixty-nined with Blythe's high school boyfriend, who was just about rupturing, she'd held out for so long. Big deal, and I was the one everyone thought was a bitch after that, because he told all his lame friends about it, and she told all her lame friends, and no one except me has ever been able to see what a psycho she really is. I mean, I would *love* to do this whole let's forgive each other thing, but we both have to be honest first, you know? Like, she could start by admitting she goaded Happy off that chairlift, after he lifted the safety bar, threatening to jump if we didn't stop arguing! But oh, no — they both claim she was just trying to give me some helpful advice about my personal life, and that I turned it into a fight, and that Happy was just being dramatic about jumping, and that I made him fall when I tried to grab Blythe's friggen phone, like who keeps texting their boyfriend in California from a chairlift in Banff, anyway? So that is the official story, and according to my parents and siblings, I am this unemployed misfit, squatting in an apartment I should have left after I was fired from or quit, or whatever you want to call it, the job I ruined by screwing Jon Bronski and his stupid square head, who made her brother fall off a chairlift.

I mean, you see, right? You see how it is? And when I try to turn the tables —when I try to raise her marathon with a triathlon, some idiot construction crew decides to thwart me.

Well, not this time. Not this time.

Naomi K. Lewis

Here I am. I just took a little break to take some deep breaths, and prepare and eat a wholesome balanced meal complimented by one of the many flavours of Bottle Rock-It soda I keep stocked in my fridge.

Shit. I don't know how to convince you. I mean, what more can I tell you? I just know that I'm supposed to be that rocket and skydiver. I just have to be.

Whenever I hear someone in the hallway — someone's stomping around out there, now — I cringe, sure it's finally happening. They're here to expel me. I'm homeless. But, no, it stopped now, just some heavy-footed neighbour. Mr. Bronski's fear of lawsuit and/or personal humiliation (he wasn't drunk enough to black out his memory of humping away at my thigh and asking me to, well, let's just say insert my finger somewhere fingers aren't meant to go, before puking all over my couch) — his shame should hold out a little bit longer, though now I guess I really do need to get out of here before he finds out about the bike. The fate of which I'm getting to, I'm getting to.

You'd probably find my apartment depressing. I don't have a lot of furniture or dishes or anything like that. I don't have Christmas lights, unlike those bozos across the compound (it's October!), as if we need light pollution when we're trying to sleep, and I don't have a television, either. My mother doesn't seem capable of absorbing this information. She's always asking if I saw the last *Earth Guard* episode, but I don't believe in television, and if I really need to watch something, I can see it online (yes, mother, the computer screen *is* a bit small). The only thing mounted on my bedroom wall is the LCD map of the Arctic Circle, which SAN never asked me to return. I just spent ten minutes lying on my bed and zooming in on the North Pole, visualizing my triumphant descent. My mother always said we should visualize our goals. Oh, my mother, and her life-success tips!

What's that smell? Some neighbour's dinner. Something fried, and fishy.

There's not much point decorating now, anyway, since I probably won't be living here much longer. Technically, the towers are for

Clareview Business Centre employees. As my helpful mother keeps pointing out, I should leave before the bureaucracy notices I'm still here, and kicks me out. Yes, mother, that *would* be demoralizing. ·

As if I'm not demoralized enough, already.

Ms. Benjamin, I may be a star when it comes to stepping casually into ten thousand foot drops and ice cold salt water pools, but put me in a square, white-walled condo halfway up a high-rise, a situation vaguely resembling normal life, and I have no idea what I'm doing. If I had a guest, he'd have to sleep with me, because I don't even own a blow-up mattress or an extra set of sheets. I don't have a dresser; my clothes are on an old, pressboard bookshelf. I did have a pull-up bar secured in my bedroom doorway until a misguided attempt at certain sexual acrobatics with a certain boss brought the whole thing down in an explosion of drywall and wood. I did my best to clean it up, but who has a vacuum cleaner? And believe me, I could afford the best vacuum cleaner. And I could afford real wood, antique or new or whatever I wanted, thanks to my financially responsible behaviour that no one ever gives me any credit for.

Yes, I've been biking from five until one every day, but what about my afternoons? Sure, I get a lot of reading done. Lots of science books, especially, and books about the history of soda pop, and product branding, due to my lifelong interest in such things. Often, just to get out of the condo, I take a book on the LRT and ride up and down the line for hours. But aside from that, between warding off family members who call to dump a pile of shit on me, and cooking wholesome meals, I get pretty much desperate for something satisfying to happen. Which I'm sure explains Mario. He was serious and pleasant enough, taking me to see his friends play in bands, gorgeous, sweet as hell, but some of the things he said reminded me of that silliness Mom was into when we were kids — the crystals and dream catchers over the doors. And worse, that Jonathan guy; there were some nice dinners with him in the beginning, sure, but sexually it got out of control really fast. I mean, there's dirty talk and there's dirty talk, and I was through when I discovered his long-standing tough-girl fetish. That pile of crusty bodybuilder magazines under his bed. And even when I was employed. Mr. Bronski. Mr. Bronski staggering to the elevator at 3 am, his dignity and mine in shreds.

Maybe I'm being too hard on myself. It's a sign of good character to leave a situation that's below oneself, after all, and SAN was starting to hold me back. All I want to say is, I do get discouraged sometimes, but then I remind myself I could be, will be part of something great. Until recently, I thought there was no chance of history remembering me, Ms. Benjamin. History remembers the glitzy people — people like Blythe. I like to think about Dad's Wright Brothers' print when those thoughts keep me up at night. How Orville and Wilbur took turns attempting to fly the plane, and how chance alone had Orville in the cockpit the day it finally worked. I ask myself: which is preferable — to sit at the controls, out of view, at the moment of truth, or to be the one immortalized in the photograph? That's the key question. The question of what kind of person I really want to be.

This is getting a bit too deep for me. I'm probably tired. I have been writing for almost twelve hours, now. Twelve hours we've been on this journey together, Ms. Benjamin, and I can only hope I've expressed myself clearly, have said what I've meant to say. Listen. Maybe it seems weird that my family gets me down so much, but I mean, it's hard to take. It really is. I mean, I called my brother yesterday, and he's all, "you are so deluded," like so condescending, and "it's time someone told you to get a grip," etc. I'd called to take issue with his column about the Human Rocket, because he *knew* I was thinking of applying for it. The next thing you know, he's demanding an apology for the chairlift incident, claiming that Blythe has thrown herself at his mercy, but that I — I, who am in fact at fault — remain stubbornly silent, and he's saying, "and my name's not Happy. It's Fin. Or Griffin. Or even Junior. You are such a control freak, naming me and Blythe in your own image...."

I was six years old! I don't think anyone should be held accountable for anything they did before the age of eighteen, maybe twenty-one.

And for his information, I do care that he fell and broke his ribs! I hated the chairlift incident and replay it in my mind all the time! I mean, one second I'm trying to get that stupid phone out of Blythe's hand — was going to throw it, I admit — and Blythe reaches around Happy to grab me by the coat, and the next second, I don't know what happened, we're swinging forward, and Mom and Dad are yelling incoherently from the seat behind us, and then Happy kind of yelps, and he's in the air, twisting around. Next second, he's lying on the snow down below, on his back, his skis skiing down the mountain without him, and he's silent. I mean, and we're still moving, and Mom is hysterical behind us, and for all any of us knows, Happy is *dead*. For ten full minutes, we didn't know. Blythe was clinging onto me, hyperventilating, and shaking, and I'll admit it, I was clinging back, tears freezing my eyelashes together. It wasn't until the helicopter had come and scooped my brother off the hill (ironically, a task I am trained for, but never actually got to do) and we knew he was okay that Dad started asking what happened, i.e. whose fault it was, and I realized Blythe was going to try to pin it on me.

And for Happy's information, I *do* realize he's a columnist at the country's biggest newspaper and I *am* proud of him.

But that doesn't change the fact that he's a bit on the milquetoast side. If you could see him. His arms are like sticks. His skin's the colour of paper, and doesn't tan, just turns red. I wonder if he's ever gotten laid.

And if you think *that's* bad, try talking to my parents. I told them what Happy said yesterday, and they kind of glanced at each other. Did they forget the camera was on? That I could see them? Dad's hair is all grey, now. He was wearing his running outfit — he has one of those old-man-runner bodies, the muscles firm under loosening skin. Mom was in some bulky wool sweater, and I could see that crystal around her neck, the one the fortune-teller gave her right before she got pregnant with Happy and adopted me. I wondered how Dad puts up with her crystals and whale music and recycled sari silk, never uttering one cruel word to her face or even behind her back.

Mom said, "Bonnie, maybe you *should* think about getting a job. I mean, this triathlon thing. Do you think it's realistic? Just because Blythe ran that marathon doesn't mean you have to…" and she said I should just forget about the Human Rocket, and she said I should apologize to Happy, and she said I should go back to Ottawa and buy a condo and get my life together, i.e. find a husband and a normal job, and all the while she's nagging me and Dad's nodding in agreement, I'm forced to look at the giant image of Blythe on the wall behind their heads. Of course they're proud of her success and blah blah blah, but I find it creepy, weird and gross how they enlarged that *Maxim* cover into a poster, complete with "Blythe Dey, the girl we'd like to blankity-veep" printed across their darling's fake spacesuit, framed it like a piece of art, and hung it on their living room wall between the waterfall painting and fake-Aboriginal whale print. I must mention here the ridiculous rumour spread by that very magazine article, that the scene in question was filmed in orbit. Blythe told me, that night in the hotel, that she was instructed to spread that story, to hint at it without outright lying. If anyone considered for one minute what it would take to get an entire television crew into space — the logistics — I mean, the lighting alone! And it's so obvious that Blythe's spacesuit isn't real. But, sadly, most people lack the logical faculties you and I enjoy.

Anyway, my parents will soon be able to replace that poster, or at least complement it, with one of their elder daughter in *real* space.

As stated so boldly in my cover letter, I am confident that I am your ideal choice for the job. I have said the Human Rocket is my destiny. I say it again. To ensure that your confidence in this matter matches my own, I will now fill you in on the concluding chapter of the bicycle saga, which occurred this morning — or, technically, yesterday, since I sat down to write this application in the morning, and finish only now, significantly after midnight.

So, this morning. Five o'clock. Long pants, sweatshirt and jacket. Icy air sparkling in the fluorescent-lit Lifestyle Village. Took the bike down in the elevator, crossed the concrete complex, headed out into the city, toward the river bike path. I was equipped with a flashlight this time, and when I reached the fence at 5:50 (my time is improving), I was ready. At least, I thought I was. They had raised the stakes again — by four more rows of barbed wire atop the fence. Not only that, but they had extended the fence several feet *into* the river.

I assessed the situation. Two possible approaches. I could throw the bike, or I could attempt swimming with it around the fence. Swimming was clearly my only option for getting myself around the thing. Yes, the water would be beyond cold and dirty. But consider: this is what I spent two years training for. I knew I'd warm up afterwards if I biked fast enough. And I could shower when I got home. I am not a quitter.

I did admit to myself, however, that I might not be able to throw the bike that high.

I removed my clothes except for my padded sports underpants and bra, bundled them together, and strapped the bundle to my upper back with my fanny pack. With any luck, I thought, I'd be able to stay dry above the waist — except of course for the icy rain still hovering in the air. I barely felt it. Walked my bike to the edge of the water, and then, with no hesitation, stepped in. One hand on the fence, the other holding the bike frame. The frigid water took my breath away, but I soldiered on. Up to my shins, up to my knees. Then, suddenly, I was underwater. My whole body under, my whole head, and the current trying to pull me away from the fence. Luckily, as though by fate, SAN, not to mention the vertical puddle incident, had trained me for this very situation, and I did not panic. I did not let go of the bike or the fence, but calmly pulled myself back, back, and out. I was no further ahead; I was drenched and freezing. But nothing was lost. Yet.

First I emptied my shoes of water and wrung out my clothes to minimize their weight. I took my time, calming my mind. I no longer felt the cold. Adrenalin. I readied myself and my bike at the correct distance from the fence. Breathed in through my nose and out through my mouth. I checked my stance. Bent my knees, holding the frame near the front and back wheels. Breathed. Checked my stance. Practised my follow-through twice. And threw the bicycle as high and far as I could.

Failure.

Failure.

That's when I heard the laughter. The shrieking, malicious laughter. And I was drenched in light.

Blinded.

What was this?

Didn't panic.

The Colin-look-alike and his lackeys had been waiting for me across the field, up on their beloved roof, with some kind of spotlight. Their voices seemed to come from everywhere.

"Crazy bitch!"

"Holy shit!"

"Holy *shit*!"

Ms. Benjamin, I'm sure you'll agree that we all have our weak moments, and that oddly, the deeper we plunge into indignity (as though into a rain-filled telephone-pole hole), the more sublime the epiphanies that follow. Yesterday morning, I stood in my underwear, in the icy rain, blinded by floodlight, drenched and dripping muddy water — mud that has now flaked in large part onto the floor around my desk chair — to see Jon Bronski the anally fixated premature ejaculator's bent bicycle dangling by one shredded tire from the fence's barbs. I thought, so much for my triathlon, so much for making something of myself, why not just lie down and die. The men on the Crab Shack roof raised their voices and presumably their middle fingers, and the Colin one yelled, "Stupid bitch, that ground is full of asbestos. What's wrong with you?"

For a moment, I felt like a bug under a lens, chastised and impotent as my brother the nutless wonder, my arms flailing, my voice hollering. Did I really scream, "Do you know who my sister is?"

The light switched off. The world switched back on around me. My attention skimmed past the grunting silhouetted simians on the roof to settle on the wide, murky black sky. Their laughter shrank into a little blob somewhere far away, and I was filled with certainty and optimism, with the enormity of my life's purpose. The sky. Into which I shall shoot like an arrow, like a needle into the infinite starstack. I (recorded by cameras on numerous satellites) will circle the world, see everything, just me in that perfect cold and silence. Then penetrate back into the waiting blue world, and fall and fall, fierce as a blizzard, toward the Earth's white cap. With a jolt, I'll be floating, the Arctic spread out below me. The sun smudged and bleeding against the bottom of the sky. My shadow will stretch out below, the only visible mark on all that snow and ice until I'm close enough to see the waiting public, the upturned faces. And when my Rock-It suit boots touch the snow, the shining clean world — oh, Ms. Benjamin — the people will be waiting, and they will say, *There she is, there she is*, and *Bonnie, welcome back, what was it like, tell us everything*, and Bottle Rock-It soda pop will flow like blood, like tears, like scrumptious, healthful rivers, like, oh fuck it, just choose me, choose me, it has to be me, Ms. Benjamin. Please. Please. Blast me off.

Naomi K. Lewis

Acknowledgments

Versions of the following stories have appeared previously in the following publications: "Warp" in *Dandelion*; "Swear It" in *Menda City Review*; and "Seesaw" in *Freefall* magazine. An excerpt from "Attachment" appeared in *Freshwater Pearls* (Recliner Books) with the title, "We Will be Airborne." Nix and Six owe a debt to Myrna Kostash's *No Kidding: Inside the Life of Teenage Girls*. My heartfelt thanks to the many people who helped ease these stories from nothingness into being – especially Rona Altrows, Mark Anthony Jarman, Nomi Claire Lazar, Chloe Lewis, Jason Markusoff, Elaine Morin, Terry Rogers, Barbara Romanik, Mari Sasano, Philip Sword, and Calgary's Kensington Writers Group, who helped shape pieces and parts; Theanna Bischoff, Catherine Bush, Greg Hollingshead, and John Metcalf, for invaluable writing advice; Deborah Maw, Michele Meijer, and Beth Schuld, who talked candidly about adoption; Barbara Dacks, Tracy Hamon, Mar'ce Merrell, Robert Pogue, Sila Senlen and Sarah Steele for all manner of wise and surprising insights; Hazel Mousley, who seriously considered digging a hole with me (thanks for the line); Kimberley Howard, who described survival training; Peter Walpole, who shared his aviation expertise; Dave Withrow, who pushed me out of the plane, opened the parachute, and later answered my questions; Maurice Mierau, Catharina de Bakker, and all the fine staff at Enfield & Wizenty, for taking this book on and being so good to it; the Alberta Foundation for the Arts, the Banff Centre for the Arts, the Calgary Public Library (particularly Marje Wing), the Canada Council for the Arts, the Saskachewan Writers' Guild, and the monks of St. Peter's Abbey, for time and space to write; and my families, Lewis and Markusoff and all the offshoots, for their love and support.